MICHIGAN MOORCROFT

R.I.P.

MARTIN CHATTERTON

■SCHOLASTIC

To Dave Bearfield,

who died doing something he loved.

We miss you.

Scholastic Children's Books,
Commonwealth House, 1-19 New Oxford Street,
London, WC1A 1NU, UK
a division of Scholastic Ltd
London ~ New York ~ Toronto ~ Sydney ~ Auckland
Mexico City ~ New Delhi ~ Hong Kong

First published in the UK by Scholastic Ltd, 2003

ISBN 0 439 97853 X

Printed and bound by Nørhaven Paperback A/S, Denmark

10 9 8 7 6 5 4 3 2 1

The right of Martin Chatterton to be identified as the author of this work
has been asserted by him in accordance with the
Copyright, Designs and Patents Act, 1988.

MICHIGAN MOORCROFT

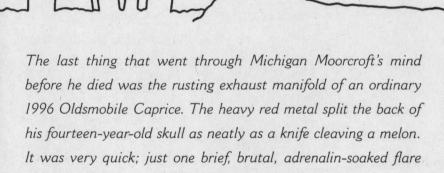

The last thing that went through Michigan Moorcroft's mind before he died was the rusting exhaust manifold of an ordinary 1996 Oldsmobile Caprice. The heavy red metal split the back of his fourteen-year-old skull as neatly as a knife cleaving a melon. It was very quick; just one brief, brutal, adrenalin-soaked flare of white light and the certainty that something had gone Very Wrong Indeed...

Look out for more books by Martin Chatterton:

Bad Dog and all that Hollywood HooHah
Bad Dog and those Crazee Martians!
Bad Dog and the Curse of the President's Knee
Bad Dog Rockin' up a Phat One in Da House

PART ONE
DEAD

The last thing that went through Michigan Moorcroft's mind before he died was the rusting exhaust manifold of an ordinary 1996 Oldsmobile Caprice. The heavy red metal split the back of his fourteen-year-old skull as neatly as a knife cleaving a melon. It was very quick; just one brief, brutal, adrenalin-soaked flare of white light and the certainty that something had gone Very Wrong Indeed.

It didn't hurt. Not exactly anyway. The pain was so intense, so alien, that Michigan had difficulty identifying it as pain at all, let alone anything connected to himself. It was, in Michigan's words, extreme. He barely had time to realize this (it was nothing short of a miracle that he was able to realize anything given the fact that a large lump of metal was occupying the space usually reserved for his brain) when, with a white-hot electro-static crackle, the reassuring perspectives of his life shifted for ever and all the noise and ice and sensation filled up his eyes and ears and nose in one final blinding rush.

Michigan Freebird Moorcroft was dead as a nail. He just didn't know it yet.

Finding out he was dead came later. Much later.

CHAPTER 1

Susie Stephens, 36, considered to be America's top expert in pedestrian safety, was run over and killed by a bus while attending a conference in road safety in St Louis, Missouri.

Ananova, 22 March 2002

"DIE!DIE!DIE!DIE!DIE!
GONNA DIE!DIE!DIE!DIE!DIE!DIE!DIE!DIE!DIE!DIE!DIE!DIE!
DIE!DIE!DIIIIEEEEEEEE!
GONNA GO TO HELL!
BABY I THINK YOU SMELL!
I DON'T FEEL WELL!"

Michigan Moorcroft took off his headphones as the last crashing guitar chords of "Armageddon Meltdown Baby" by the kings of thrash metal, Alien Death Factory, faded in his ears. It was Wednesday afternoon, Christmas Eve, and

Michigan, clad entirely in black as was his custom, slumped morosely in the back seat of the family ride, a big battered Chevy Traveller with 97,000 miles on the clock and a heater given to periodic bouts of inactivity.

He coughed as a small cloud of smoke drifted back from the front of the car where his mother, Urma, was multitasking: simultaneously talking on a cellphone, smoking her seventeeth cigarette of the day and giving driving instruction to her husband (and Michigan's father) Michael, who sat silently, resigned, behind the wheel.

"Just comin' up to some place called Morton," yelled Mrs Moorcroft into the cellphone. "Morton! M-O-R-T-O-N! Oh, forget it. Look, we'll be there in a coupla hours WATCH OUT FOR THAT TRUCK! No, not you, Mom. . ."

Michigan effortlessly tuned her out. It was a skill he had achieved almost complete mastery of. Despite Urma Moorcroft's bulk (she came in at a shade under two hundred pounds) and her having a voice like a bucket of rusty nails, Michigan had managed to avoid listening to a single word she had said since he'd turned nine.

Behind his parents sat Michigan's elder sister, Dakota, and his younger brother, Alaska. Several years ago Mr and Mrs Moorcroft had gone through a (thankfully, now abandoned) flirtation with New Age jiggery-pokery. It had left only two lasting effects: Urma Moorcroft's taste in ugly, multicoloured crystal jewellery and, more disastrously for Michigan and his siblings, the naming of their children after those states of the union which held some meaning for his parents. Alaska narrowly avoided being called Maryland. Only Mr Moorcroft's uncharacteristically stubborn opposition had prevented this disaster.

Michigan thought there should be a law against giving stupid names to your children.

Looking round for a distraction, he expertly flicked a peanut so that it bounced off Dakota's nose. It was a half-hearted effort, almost beneath his dignity, but he was so bored he couldn't help himself.

"Creep," said Dakota.

"Loser," replied Michigan, but the exchange was formulaic, passionless. Over the years their spats had taken on the flavour of ritual, like Sumo wrestling without the actual bodily contact (or the large semi-nude Japanese guys wearing diapers for that matter).

Despite the lack of heat in their argument it acted on Mrs Moorcroft like petrol on a barbecue. She had a short fuse.

"Will you two just knock it off!" she yelled, raising the cell-phone like a grenade. "I'm *trying* to talk!"

"God!" said Dakota. "It was *him*."

"Relax, Mom," said Michigan. "Take a chill pill. You need to work on your anger management."

"I'll anger management you, smartmouth!"

"He started it!"

Perhaps feeling left out, Alaska asked the question he had been asking at regular intervals since they left home.

"Are we there yet?"

Alaska, at ten, knew he was too old for this kind of thing, but he just couldn't help himself – it was what he was supposed to do.

Michigan and Dakota gave their younger brother the briefest of hostile glances before returning to their exchange.

"Did not."

"Did too."

"Do I have to climb back in there and start banging heads?"

This, then, was the Moorcroft family. They were eighty miles from their destination, they were nearing Morton, New Jersey, a town of 4,326 inhabitants. They were moody and irritable, as they usually were on these kind of expeditions. They were on their way to spend the Christmas holidays with Gamma and Gamps Slubb in Silvertown, a prospect so appalling that, given a choice between it and having his eyes poked with sharp objects, Michigan would certainly consider his options carefully before arriving at a decision.

Last Christmas had been typical. No cable. No warmth. Weird food. For lunch he had been given something that sounded like "vukla". It had looked and tasted like fried rat.

 6

The Moorcrofts were almost there.

They were four and a half minutes from catastrophe.

Had Michigan known he had less than five minutes to live he might have paid more attention to his surroundings. Not that they were particularly inspiring. He looked out of the grime-encrusted window at the passing landscape. Heavy grey-white clouds squatted low in the bleak sky, reducing the thin light to a watery, apologetic murk which dulled the senses, coating everything in a mean varnish of misery. It was the middle of the afternoon, but looked and felt much later. Wet snow lay on either side of the road, blackened and soiled close to the passing traffic.

It was a horrible day. And now Michigan was on his way to three days with that most feared of species: Old People.

The truth was that Michigan Moorcroft, although not particularly nasty or selfish by nature, didn't like being around old people, even those he happened to be related to.

It wasn't that he had anything actively against them, in *theory*.

It was just that in the flesh (and what wrinkled, creased and mottled flesh it was) coffin-dodgers were a rude physical reminder of the Big Important Thing that had begun to occupy almost all his waking hours over the past couple of years: Death.

7

It wasn't death in general Michigan Moorcroft was worried about. He found he could cope pretty well when hearing of heavy death tolls in far-off foreign countries due to earthquake, flood or famine. News of air crashes, train smashes, mudslides, sinking boats, fire, lightning strikes, gunshots, shark attacks, hurricanes, heart attacks, cancer – all the various deadly ways in which death appeared – failed to register as more than a blip on Mich's radar as long as they didn't directly involve *him*.

It was specifically his *own* death; the mind-numbing, gutchurning, inescapable, inevitable, totally outrageous and unacceptable *certainty* that he, Michigan Moorcroft, would one day get old and die, that struck Michigan as unacceptable.

It didn't bear thinking about. Except, these days, he found that he couldn't think of anything else.

Another, less-than-helpful factor was that as a fully-paid-up, black-clad, Nu-Metal skate-punk-live-fast-die-young-streetfreak, Michigan knew he should view death pretty favourably, perhaps similiar to some sort of extreme snowboarding accident, only permanent.

There was only one problem with this theory: it didn't work. The reality was that the merest thought of there *not* being a Michigan Moorcroft walking around the planet scared him in a deep, standing-on-the-edge-of-a-big-cliff kind of way that made him want to whimper "Mummy"

in a small voice and go hide under the bedclothes.

The only positive thing about worrying about death was that it wasn't boring.

Michigan found almost everything boring, apart from death, girls and thrash metal music (and, if he was honest with himself, he only liked the more melodic thrash tracks. A secret he would take to his grave was his guilty fondness for the music of Jennifer Lopez. But anyone wanting to know this information would have to tear it from him under extreme torture).

Michigan was also troubled by (in no particular order):

1. His inability to grow any convincing facial hair.

2. His total failure so far in getting a date with Veronica Whitelake.

3. A statistic he'd gleaned from a TV show; that there were an estimated 200 billion galaxies in the universe. He didn't like how small this information made him feel.

4. Living in Communion, New Hampshire.

Michigan thought that, on the whole, he'd probably prefer life in an urban high-crime area. There was local crime, of a sort, in Communion but nothing with the authentic glamour and metallic tang of the big-city urban wastelands that Michigan Moorcroft longed for with a desire that people usually reserved for Caribbean islands or ritzy Alpine ski resorts.

He watched the crime reports on the TV news every night

like a fan; war correspondent messages delivered by trenchcoat-wearing reporters from far-flung foreign battle-fields like Boston or New York or Baltimore.

He frequently imagined life in the worst parts of these places; it was in point of fact his favourite daydream. He pictured himself skating through a wrecked and dysfunctional cityscape, his 'phones clamped down over his knit cap as he weaved around the broken bottles and discarded trash piles; sirens and gunfire providing a satisfyingly edgy backdrop.

The crackle of automatic weapons came from high up on one of the ramshackle warehouses, black as nightshade and twice as deadly, but Razor Moorcroft, the kingpin of the East Side Bloods and lead guitarist in the chart-topping thrash metal outfit "Rancid Green" didn't bat an eyelid as he skated effortlessly past the burnt-out cars en route for a meet with his homies at the crib. Gunfire was the norm, danger his constant companion, on these mean streets which he called home when he wasn't in his Malibu beach house or in the eighteen-bedroom penthouse in Manhattan. He checked the time on his diamond-encrusted Rolex and flipped open his cellphone to call one of his ladies—

"Michigan!" said his mother. "Turn that godawful noise down; I can hear it from here!"

Mich opened his eyes and with excruciating slowness, as if the effort of turning the switch was more than an ordinary mortal could bear, lowered the decibel level a microscopic notch.

 10

Michigan gave his mother his recently perfected scowl. He had adopted this scowl believing that it gave the impression that he was *just* on the verge of kicking some serious ass. He hadn't actually ever kicked any ass, serious or otherwise, outside of a PlayStation game. In fact, if there was any ass-kicking activity going on within ten metres of Michigan Moorcroft it was usually his ass getting the kicking, mainly from Brandon Gruner and the other happy members of the East Communion High football team. In any case he was mistaken about his scowl. It made him look constipated.

His mother rolled her eyes and dragged deeply on her eighteenth cigarette of the day (the last one of her life, as things turned out) and Michigan tried to get back inside his urban dream. It was no good. It had gone.

Two minutes, forty-three seconds to go.

He slumped back in his seat and picked at a loose patch of blue vinyl peeling from the car upholstery. A stray fragment caught underneath his chipped thumbnail and he inspected it closely, as if examining a particularly unusual and exquisite diamond he'd unearthed.

I am so bored, he thought.

To cheer himself up Michigan looked down at his new T-shirt.

He'd bought it a couple of weeks back at The Record Shack in the mall. It was all black, like ninety-three point six per cent of his clothes. The Alien Death Factory logo, a pig-like skull set above a pair of crossed bones, peered out aggressively from Michigan's chest.

"Gonna die, die, die, die. . ." Michigan Moorcroft hummed.

Thank God for Alien Death Factory. He didn't know how he'd survive this trip without his headphones.

He stroked his chin thoughtfully.

Despite his dedication over the past three weeks, the hair-growth treatment he had surreptitiously acquired and had secretly been applying had had zero effect. If anything his face seemed to be getting smoother. It was as unblemished as a cheerleader's. To make things worse, Theo Van Sant, who was in his grade at school, already had completely valid boss sidechops coming down the lines of his (admittedly spotty) jaw. Theo, annoyingly, was a couple of months younger than Michigan.

He spotted Dakota eyeing him and stopped scratching his chin. Maybe she knew something; certainly she *looked* like she knew something. He'd have to review his security measures, upgrade them. As things stood, Michigan's security measures regarding his secret facial-hair treatments were at least as stringent as those required by the Israeli Secret Service.

He contented himself with giving Dakota The Scowl, but she didn't seem to notice.

Michigan had a relationship with his siblings of the sort Mafia godfathers had with rat-fink stool pigeons, and he would be happy never to see them again his entire life.

He, of course, had no way of knowing that his entire life had less than a minute to run: disaster loomed.

A shiver ran up Michigan's spine as a draught blew in from a gap in the door. He screwed his face up against the icy wind and gingerly touched the raw scab on his nose, still sore where the new silver stud in the shape of a grinning skull had pierced his nostril. His parents had gone predictably ape when they saw it, but had been too distracted by the Everest-expedition preparations deemed necessary for any trip to Gamma's to dish out any meaningful punishment. Mrs Moorcroft had contented herself with a five-minute rant on the stupidity of her offspring which had washed over Michigan like spring rain off a new tile roof.

Michigan tuned out his family and looked out of the window. There was plenty of wet snow lying in the fields, but nothing that promised any excitement – like getting stuck in a drift and having to survive by eating one another, for instance. The roads had been clear coming down from Communion, which wasn't always the case. Sometimes it took several dismal centuries of slow driving to get down to Gamma's.

Despite the snow, Mich noticed a cow staring back at him from a field. As the cow faded from view, a row of spectacularly boring telephone poles streamed past. Then another cow, nibbling idly at some feeble shoots of long grass poking pathetically through the snow.

Mich sighed. This was worse than last year's trip.

Just then, Mr Moorcroft, sitting bolt upright in the driver's seat and holding the steering wheel of the Chevy Traveller, bumped past Michigan's window, a surprised expression on his face. *Strange*, thought Michigan. *Shouldn't Dad be driving the car?*

In the time it took for that thought to register, Michigan Moorcroft became conscious of a great number of things happening all at once:

1. Mr Moorcroft was definitely *not* driving the car.
2. There was another car, or big chunks of it, occupying the space where Mr Moorcroft had been sitting.
3. Mrs Moorcroft was screaming.
4. There was a lot of oil and glass and metal and rubber and snow and bits of car all over the place.
5. Alaska had stopped picking his nose while Dakota's mouth was formed into a perfect "o" of astonishment.
6. The cow in the field was upside down.
7. No, correction: Michigan was upside down, not the cow.
8. This was a car crash.
9. He wasn't bored any more.
10. They were all doomed.

Everything happened in an eerie bubble of total silence, or so it seemed. Even Alien Death Factory had fallen strangely quiet, and, though his eyes registered that all around him metal was tearing apart like wet paper, Michigan's ears heard nothing. He felt like he had time to absorb everything, look at everything.

He felt completely, absurdly, relaxed. He almost laughed.

A red truck, almost impossibly close to their own car, drifted past in super-slow motion. It was close enough for Michigan to make out the tattoo on the driver's knuckles, which were clamped meatily around a leopardskin-covered steering wheel. A crucifix dangling from a line of beads wrapped around the rear-view mirror danced crazily.

The driver had tattoos, Michigan noticed enviously. *LIFE* was spelled out on his right hand, *SUCKS* on the left. To fit the word *SUCKS* on four knuckles, the last two letters had been crowded together on one knuckle, giving the impression that the tattoo had not been planned out too well in advance.

The driver, a big, heavy-set, hard-looking guy, wearing jeans and a checked shirt and bearing a passing resemblance to the actor James Gandolfino, looked Michigan straight in the eye as he coasted past and winked lazily at him, like all this was just a bit of a hiccup in an otherwise perfectly fine day, and, if it hadn't been for the god-almighty car wreck that they were having, he would like nothing better than to shoot the breeze over a nice cup of coffee. The driver flipped the wheel and peeled away from the Traveller, clean and free.

Michigan didn't have time to think about the strange, smiling driver, he was too busy crashing.

With a smash of metal and screech of tyres and wail of screaming noise, the kind that Alien Death Factory could only dream about, all the sound came back on full volume completely filling Michigan's head.

He opened his mouth to suck in a great big gulp of air (his last), and prepared to join in the screaming, when the exhaust manifold from the Oldsmobile caroomed through the side window and beamed him smack on the back of his head.

As it did, in the nanosecond of time before he pegged out, Michigan Moorcroft's life flashed before him.

It didn't take long.

Potty-training, first day at kindergarten, new skateboard, bags of candy, WWF on the tube, skating, late with his homework, Spud Murphy stiffing him out of his lunch money, pimples. Pretty pathetic really. *But then I am only fourteen*, thought Michigan, feeling very sorry for himself and not at all like a fearless punk-skate-freak-street-warrior.

Everything turned black.

"It's horrible. Just horrible," sobbed Patrolman Flint into the radio mike as he stared down the freeway run-off to where the

 16

Moorcroft family car lay on its back, its blackened carcass a spiky black inkblot stark against the snow. There was blood and oil, plenty of both.

Flint wiped his eyes, hitched his pants over his colossal paunch and blew his nose. The siren of the ambulance gave an answering bleat as it arrived. Flint was looking at the rear fender of a powder-blue Oldsmobile, which was lying ten metres from the rest of the car, and had been bent into a pretzel shape. A narrow scrape of bright red paint ran for sixty centimetres along the side pointing at the sky. There was something wrong about the fender, thought Flint; he just couldn't put his finger on it presently. *Give me time*, he thought, *and it'll come to me*. Flint took out a small bar of chocolate and unwrapped it. He found he ate lots more of these things when he was stressed. As he chewed, he forgot all about the stripe of red paint on the blue fender.

"OK, boys," he signalled to the paramedics with his handful of candy. "Bag 'em and tag 'em."

From his comfortable position upside down in the back seat, with part of an exhaust system jutting out of the side of his head at a jaunty angle, Michigan saw and heard everything, or at least he thought he did. It seemed to be happening to somebody else. There was no pain.

He closed his eyes. *Perhaps I'll just have a little nap.*

* * *

17

It had been a million to one deal. The lottery in reverse.

Just as Michigan turned to look out of the window, the car hit a small bump in the road, jolting Mrs Moorcroft's cigarette. A red-hot sliver of ash fell into Mr Moorcroft's lap, causing Mr Moorcroft to jerk suddenly away from the pain (and proving in the process that smoking was indeed very bad for your health). Unfortunately, Mr Moorcroft had not closed his door properly, or put on his seat belt as required by New Hampshire state law, and almost fell out of the car. As he struggled to clamber back in, the car slewed across the median strip and into the path of an oncoming Oldsmobile also coming across the divide, driven by Mrs Dorothy Kismet of 3432 Marilyn Gardens, Chatsworth, Ohio.

Fortunately for Mrs Kismet, but fatally for the Moorcrofts, she was stone dead well before the crash. In fact she had passed away peacefully a full nine and a half minutes previously, while dreaming of a holiday in St Pete's she'd taken in 1955 with her late husband, Ossie.

With the Oldsmobile on cruise control, and the highway running in a perfectly straight line, Mrs Kismet was driving better dead than she had ever done alive. If it hadn't been for the red truck giving the Olds a nudge, Mrs Kismet would have breezed by the Moorcrofts without a hitch. As it was, the little tap from behind her nearside back wheel slewed the car right into the Chevy as it left the grass strip in a flurry of mud and icy water.

When the impact came, at a combined speed of 144 miles per hour, Mr Moorcroft, together with seat and steering wheel, popped out on to the freeway like a cork from a bottle. Mrs Kismet's Olds then spun 360 degrees before slamming into the Moorcrofts' car for a second time.

There were only two survivors found in the wreckage, one of whom was Mrs Kismet's pet poodle, Buttons, who had been strapped in safely on the rear seat and slept through the whole thing. He eventually found another home with a retired dental technician from Idaho and lived a long and happy life.

Of the third car, the red truck driven by the guy in the check shirt, the one who'd given the fatal tap to Mrs Kismet's car, there wasn't a sign. Unless you included the black rubber tyre marks striping the freeway and leading off into the distance.

CHAPTER 2

Felipe Ortiz, 48, of Colombia was killed when the baited hook he was fishing with blew back and lodged in his mouth. Efforts to resuscitate him failed.

Daily Mail, 17 March 1998

"Michigan!"

"*Michigan!*"

He opened his eyes and blinked at the ceiling. Where the hell was he?

"Wake up, Michigan, for God's sake!" Mrs Moorcroft bellowed from the foot of the stairs. She sounded like a wounded Cape buffalo. "There are people here to see us."

Mich looked around.

He was in bed, in his bedroom, in what seemed, at first glance, to be his house.

He rubbed the side of his head where he'd dreamt the exhaust manifold had hit him. It was certainly sore, but nothing like the damage he would expect to find had he really been almost decapitated by a large machine part during a major automobile accident. Maybe he'd just slept funny.

Mich slid out of bed and opened his curtains. Everything in Communion seemed precisely as it should be. Mich rubbed his eyes and yawned so hard his jaw spasmed and he had to close his mouth quickly. He felt like he had been asleep for several decades.

Man, that had been some dream.

He shook his head and took another look out of the window and this time noticed something: there were one or two things Definitely Not Quite Right.

The sky was divided cleanly in two precise segments, an angry crimson red on one side and a flawless azure blue on the other.

On the red side, at some distance from the Moorcroft house, flaming black rocks trailing fiery debris streaked through the air before smashing savagely into the ground and sending showers of smoke, fire and pulverized earth high into the skies. A rock the size of a truck slammed into what looked like a well-manicured golf course. There was a muffled scream followed by a blackened and smoking golf cart drifting slowly skywards, pausing for a moment at the top of its arc before falling back to earth with a soft thud.

On the blue side, Mich's side, little fluffy clouds bobbed peacefully across the bluest of perfect blue skies.

"Holy f–" Mich began as the paper delivery boy pulled round the corner on his bike and hurled a bulky newspaper on to the lawn. He was at least thirty-eight years old and, apart from the new-looking pair of Nikes where his sandals should have been, was convincingly dressed as a Roman centurion, right down to the ochre dust on his bare legs. He waved cheerily to Mich and cycled down the road, weaving lazily out of the path of the trash wagon heading in the opposite direction and exchanging a couple of words with the driver.

Almost as soon as he came into view, Mich could see there was something familiar about the trash truck's driver. He was a thickset, olive-skinned man wearing shades and sporting jaunty mutton chop sideburns. His jet-black hair sat high and proud on his head in a precisely casual quiff and his white suit, studded with an abundance of rhinestones and gold spangles, glinted in the morning sun as he thrummed his fingers on the side of the truck. He was singing softly to himself, "Well, since mah baby leff me, ah found a new place to dwell. . ."

Mich scratched his chin. He'd seen that guy many times on the cover of the *National Enquirer*, his mother's favourite tabloid. The last time was just a couple of weeks back when the paper had found him on the moon, marshalling an alien attack force to help him reclaim his rightful position as the Emperor of Earth. Seemed unlikely but, as Mrs Moorcroft always said, you could never tell.

"Mornin', pardner," yelled Elvis, looking up at Mich's window and waving a lazy, ring-heavy hand in greeting. "Welcome to the neighbourhood!"

Mich waved absently back. His mind seemed to have stopped working.

"Input data not computing," he murmured, watching Elvis hoist the garbage into the back of the truck. This could not be happening.

Elvis was driving the garbage truck.

He wondered if anyone else had seen the King collecting the trash, and headed for the stairs.

Scraps of mumbled conversation drifted up the stairwell. Mich paused to listen but could pick up nothing. He noticed, with some surprise, that he was already dressed. He didn't remember it, but somehow there he was in his usual black skate pants, T-shirt and bulky, scuffed sneakers.

On his way downstairs Mich stopped by to wake Alaska up. If Mich was awake he didn't see why the little squit should get a lie-in. Besides he wanted to get some back-up confirmation before he went blathering downstairs about Elvis. The last thing Mich needed right now with a headache like this was another lecture on the evils of drugs.

"Get up, cheese-breath!" he yelled, giving his brother a playful dig in the eye.

There was no response. Mich pinched Alaska's arm. It was cold to the touch and had the flabby resilience of a deflated football.

"Quit foolin', Alaska. You're scaring me."

There was silence.

Mich looked at his younger brother for a moment, then turned and raced downstairs, taking the steps two at a time. He loped gracelessly into the family room, all thoughts of staying cool gone in an instant.

"Mom! Mom! There's something wrong with Alaska. He –" Mich stopped.

Apart from the rest of the Moorcrofts, the room contained two people Mich hadn't seen before, a man and a woman seated side by side on the rattan couch. They were quite a sight.

The man was huge, and for a moment Mich had the disorientating feeling that he was almost too big for the room, that should he get up the walls would buckle against his size. But there he was sitting on the furniture so how could that be? He wore an expensive-looking jet-black suit, perfectly tailored to his bulk, and made from some weird, softly shifting, silky material. As Mich looked, the cloth shivered across its surface like wind blowing on a field of wheat. When the cloth moved

Mich heard the faintest of noises somewhere at the very edge of his hearing, like a vast crowd screaming in the distance mixed with an undercurrent of electro-static. The man's hair was slicked back and he sported a tiny glittering silver skull in his ear. As the guy shifted on his gigantic buttocks, Mich caught a glimpse of tiny, stubby horns sprouting from the top of his head. The big man brushed his hair back with a disconcertingly graceful gesture and the horns (if they had ever been there to begin with; Mich couldn't be sure) disappeared. A sharp pointed little beard sat coiled on his chin like a pet sewer rat.

It was impossible to guess at his age. He could have been about thirty, but when the morning light hit him a certain way he suddenly looked very, very old; old in the way that mummified corpses look in horror movies. His eyes flickered red and yellow, as if a fire was burning out of control some-where deep inside his head. A small black crocodile-skin briefcase sat on the floor next to him and, as Mich looked at it, he was almost sure it twitched.

The big guy held up his hand in a rocker's greeting, making a fist with the little finger and index finger raised. "Dude!" he said to Mich, winking. Mich gave him a blank look and the man nodded as if something he had been mulling over had been confirmed.

Squashed alongside the big man on the couch was a mousy-haired old lady. She was much smaller, hardly noticeable when set against the flamboyance of the man next to her. She wore a wrinkled cardigan the colour of oatmeal over a faded blue dress which had been carefully patched in places. Her thin legs tapered down to a pair of scuffed Reebok running shoes. Her thin face was pale, with red cheeks. Large round spectacles perched above a rather sharp nose. Her hair stuck out at odd angles and Mich spotted stray bits of toast tangled up in it. A vast bag sat on her lap, a ball of wool jutting from the top.

Mich shook his head and remembered why he'd raced down the stairs.

"Alaska," he said. "Alaska won't wake up, Mom!"

Mrs Moorcroft wasn't listening. She leaned against the mantelpiece sucking on a cigarette and watching TV.

Everyone was looking at the TV. The programme was one of those hospital dramas: a group of surgeons were bent intently over a small figure on the operating table – a matter of life and death, very dramatic. It looked very realistic. Mich looked more closely at the screen and realized with a sudden jolt that the small figure was Alaska.

"That's Alaska!" said Mich.

"We know," said his mother sourly, dragging heavily on her cigarette and turning away from the set. She looked at the cigarette and laughed a nasty bitter little laugh.

"These things are bad for your health, you know that, don't you, Michigan?"

 26

Then she laughed again and looked at Mich, an odd expression on her face.

"You tell him," she said to Mr Moorcroft.

"Do we have to go through all this again?" said Dakota, sitting with her knees tucked underneath her on an armchair. His sister, barely sixteen, looked haggard. Dark circles ringed her eyes. She knew something, thought Mich and he suddenly felt breathless, as if he was standing at a great altitude, or the air in the room was running out. Something bad had happened, of that he was in no doubt, and he wasn't at all sure he was ready for it.

Mr Moorcroft sat on the edge of his armchair fiddling with a bundle of papers.

"Er, we've got some bad news, son," he began.

Mich knew it. It was Alaska. Much as he didn't like the little septic germ, he wasn't at all sure he wanted him to be actually, you know, *dead*. He was regretting even thinking it.

"It's about Alaska," said Mr Moorcroft. "I, erm, we, that is your mother and I, we have to tell you that, that he is. . ."

"Alive," said the big guy on the sofa brightly. "Just about. Although it is only early days so plenty of time yet." He gave Mich a wink and smiled broadly, reassuringly. His smile seemed to skate loosely around his lips as though it wasn't sure it was allowed on there. There was a brief flash of pointed white teeth and a sharp little tongue before the smile settled down into focus. Mich caught a whiff of expensive cologne together with an unpleasant, underlying smell of decay, like meat left in the fridge too long.

"Nice shirt, kid," said the man, pointing at Mich's Alien Death Factory T-shirt. "I dig those guys. In fact we started them out in the biz. Kind of a Robert Johnson deal," he smiled again and narrowed his eyes. "You could say they owe us."

He stuck out his hand. "The name's Barry. Barry Rheingold. Most people call me Baz. I'm your Resettlement Consultant."

There was a small cough behind him and Baz rolled his eyes theatrically, giving Mich a "what-can-you-do?" sort of look.

"OK. OK. I'm *one* of your Resettlement Consultants."

Mich shook Baz's outstretched hand and recoiled as though he had been burnt. Baz's hand was hot. Real hot, and clammy, like someone running a temperature of, say, 2000 degrees.

"F –, ouch," said Mich. He looked at his family. "Can someone tell me what's going on? If Alaska is OK, what's the bad news? It's not as though anyone's dead or anything."

"Ah," said Baz, looking up at Mich from under his coal-black eyebrows. "That's not strictly true."

Mr Moorcroft shifted in his chair and suddenly found something very interesting to look at on the living-room carpet. Mrs Moorcroft sucked deeply on her cigarette. Neither of them said a word.

"It's you, Michigan Freebird Moorcroft," said the little

 28

woman on the couch, briskly. "You and Dakota and Mr and Mrs Moorcroft."

She paused and looked up at Mich.

"You're all dead, I'm afraid."

She picked up her knitting and began to clack away.

"Oh," said Mich. He didn't know what to say. "Er, OK."

He looked at his mother and raised his eyebrows. She looked back at him, drew deeply on her cigarette and gave a quick shake of her head.

"Glad you feel so calm about it, Mich," said the little old lady still intent on the bundle of wool on her lap. "Most people usually wail a little, even rend their garments, although I think rending has become a little 'old-hat' recently. Maybe it's all the man-made fibres."

"I'm sorry," replied Mich, "but, like, who *are* you, exactly?"

The woman produced a small book from her handbag and handed it to Mich. "Holy Bible" was picked out in delicate gold letters on the cover.

"Oh, I've got all sorts of names. 'The Lord of Lords', 'Host of Hosts', 'The Most Mighty and Highest and Wrathful Creator of the Universe', 'The One', 'The Holy of Holies', even 'Eric Clapton' at one time."

She nodded at the book. "It's all in the manual."

She smiled at Mich who gazed at her blankly.

"You can call Me God," She said.

CHAPTER 3

A German man in the town of Montabaur died in April 1999 when he lit a cigarette while sitting on a campsite toilet. The toilet exploded.

Reuters, 13 April 1998

"Whoa, whoa, whoa, time out," said Mich, looking at his parents and making a T-shape with his hands. "Let me get this straight. I get up this morning and find out that we're not back home in Communion; that in fact *I'm* dead, *you're* dead, Alaska's not quite dead but could be soon, Elvis is our garbage man, and this small librarian-type lady in a grey cardigan is *God*?"

They all nodded, happy that Michigan had, at last, got the situation clear. Baz made a gun with his finger and pointed it at Mich.

"Like, du-*uh*," said Dakota. "Finally, he gets it."

"Strictly speaking, I'm just one tiny part of God's Holy Magnificence," said God. "But I'm afraid that your brains are just too small to cope with the sight of Us in the raw, so to speak. If you saw Me as We really are, your mind would liquefy and run out your ears just before your body crumbled to dust, and that wouldn't do at all. That's why I appear to you like this." She opened her arms and raised her palms. "Most folks call Us The Organization."

Baz muttered something under his breath to Dakota. She sniggered and God made a small note in a tiny notebook She'd produced from Her bag. Dakota stopped sniggering and looked at her hands.

"Let Me explain what's happening," said God, briskly. She rummaged in her handbag and produced a ball of light from within. She blew on the ball and it instantly expanded into an electric-blue three-dimensional map which bobbed gently in the middle of the room. Radiating map lines whirled and spun in a dazzling display of technology.

Mich could see his house right in the middle. He had no trouble picking it out because a big red arrow saying "You Are Here" hovered helpfully above it. Suddenly the map shifted and Mich's house shrank in size until it disappeared into the confusion and jumble of a big city. Around the edge of the city ran a glowing river. Beyond the river on one side was another city. This one pulsed with neon lights and bristled with sky-scrapers. A red glow hung over it like smog. On the other side was yet another city, this one much smaller and tidier. Beyond this city, far in the distance, stretching into infinity, there were many, many other cities.

"Nice map," said Mich, nodding appreciatively.

"Amazing," said Mr Moorcroft. "Top class workmanship, Your Maj – er, Your Highne – erm Mrs . . . er, God."

"Hrrmph," snorted Baz, pointedly examining his nails. "Party tricks."

"This is Purgatory," said God, ignoring Baz Rheingold and waving her hand towards the map. "Or at least that's what you lot down there call it. It's real name is –" She lifted her head, threw back her throat and made a sound like a constipated dolphin swallowing an accordion. A mirror on the wall cracked and Mich could hear ringing in his ears.

"You can see why We let you call it Purgatory. It's kind of like a big waiting room."

"A waiting room?" said Mich. "I thought that when you died you went to Heaven?" He looked at Dakota. "Or Hell."

"A common mistake," said God. "And all those old earth names are very inaccurate. Things are actually a lot more complex than that . . . aren't they always? But your explanation and names will do for now. 'Purgatory', which is where you are now, is like a big machine. A machine for processing

 32

people and making an assessment of, well, of what sort of person you are. More importantly, We are looking at the type of person you have *been*, if you catch my drift. When We built the machine it was designed to cope with a much smaller number, but you people are breeding like rabbits; and, of course, dying in pretty large numbers too. If things were perfect you'd probably have been processed by now and be busy making plans for all eternity. But it's not perfect. . ."

"You said it, sister," muttered Baz, getting a guilty snigger from Dakota.

"As I say," said God, shooting a nasty look at Baz Rheingold. "It's *not* perfect but it's all We've got. Besides, We like to take our time making the decision by taking a closer look at you here under laboratory conditions before helping decide on your Final Destination. That's the easy explanation, obviously; the reality is a great deal more complicated. It's a big project, believe you me. Especially when some people I could mention don't even lift a finger."

She eyed Baz Rheingold meaningfully.

"It took two billion years to build and it's starting to creak at the seams, what with the population growth and so on and so forth." She took a piece of candy from the pocket of Her cardigan, inspected it closely through Her spectacles, flicked a couple of pieces of lint off it and popped it into Her mouth.

"Plus, of course, ours is only one of several 'Purgatory

Machines'. Each religious group has their own. There's even one for those Jedi Knight idiots."

She pointed to an area of the map far out on the other side of the room and it came into close-up. It showed a series of large spacecraft orbiting a planet with two moons. The surface of the planet bore a disturbing resemblance to the film director George Lucas. God sighed.

"Anyway, with your particular background you've ended up here. The Organization does its best to keep things running smoothly but you'll find that it may take some getting used to. And, of course, it's not *all* assessed up here. Your coursework will be taken into account when you are marked." She looked around the room and Dakota gave a nervous little laugh.

"'Coursework'?" said Mrs Moorcroft.

"Your life on earth, dear, everything you did before you arrived here," said God, picking up Her knitting. "That was your Afterlife Preparatory Certificate Grade 1. Didn't anyone tell you? I thought We'd been quite specific in the manual. You know: 'Thou shalt not. . .', 'Do unto others. . .' and all that stuff."

"Oh," said Mrs Moorcroft, looking a little thoughtful. There was a general pause as everyone digested this nugget of information.

"Don't worry," said God. "You all passed." She looked at Mich. "Just."

God adjusted the knitting on Her lap and continued. "Of

 34

course if you fail Our assessment you get fast tracked straight to 'Hell'."

" 'Sweetwater Canyons', you mean," said Baz.

"Whatever," said God.

Mich looked at the map again and pointed to something he had spotted lying at the outer edges.

"What's that?"

God made another slight movement with one of Her knitting needles and the map zoomed in again, revealing two giant-size gates covered in silver fur.

"What are they?" said Mich.

"Those are the Furry Gates," said God. "That's one of the entrances to Paradise."

"I thought they were the Pearly Gates."

"Spelling error in the manual," said God briskly. "We never bothered to correct it. There's always something more important to get on with."

"Can we see what it's like inside?" said Mich.

"All in good time, Michigan Moorcroft," replied God. "You'll find out more at school."

"School! We're dead and we have to go to *school*?"

He sat down. This was turning out to be a very bad day.

"Hey, hey, lighten up, Momma," said Baz Rheingold to God, holding his hands up towards her, palms out. He turned to the

Moorcrofts, a beaming smile plastered across his face.

"It ain't all doom and gloom up here, you know. Let me give you the good news, folks. Being dead does *not* mean you can't have fun!" He punctuated his words by pointing a surprisingly dainty finger at them.

"Let me guess," said Mich. "You must be the Devil, right?"

"Actually, no," said Baz, flashing Mich a fierce grin. "He's the managing director of the company."

Baz put his hand lightly on his chest and closed his eyes in an expression of modesty.

"I, on the other hand, am just the humble Regional Sales Manager for this part of the netherworld. And, to be honest, we've sort of ditched that hokey old 'Devil' and 'Hell' stuff. Too old-fashioned. So 'yesterday'. Lemme show you guys what I mean."

He snapped open his briefcase and took out a sheaf of thick, expensive-looking glossy brochures that smelt strongly of quality printing. Baz lifted one off the pile, handed it to Mich and passed the others around. The cover depicted a laughing family, showing lots of clean white teeth, looking out at the viewer. They were all dressed in pristine white tennis clothes and seemed ecstatic. "Welcome to Sweetwater Canyons," read the lettering on the cover, "Heaven Can Wait!" Mich squinted at some tiny print at the foot of the page.

 36

"Looks dandy, don't it?" said Baz, as he slipped a matt black disc into his black laptop. With a practised flourish that reminded Mich of a conjuror he turned the display to face the Moorcrofts.

"Apologies for the low-tech presentation, folks," Baz said pointing at his laptop and grinning maniacally. "Us working stiffs at Sweetwater don't get the same promo budget as Her High Holiness over there. We got all the best tunes, though."

God made no sign that She had heard him and continued with Her knitting.

Baz pressed a button and the screen hummed into life.

The screen filled with the same happy family, this time sitting down to a wonderful meal on a terrace overlooking a perfectly groomed golf course. Tinkling music played in the background as a deep, honeyed voice started to talk.

"When you arrive at Sweetwater Canyons you'll know right away that flunking out of 'Everlasting Paradise' may be the best thing you ever did! With its country club atmosphere, and carefully landscaped gardens, it's a real home from home for all the family. Choose from a range of architect-designed family homes set in five billion acres of lush greenery. Play our 180-hole, Bobby-Jones-designed championship golf course, swim laps in the sparkling heated waters of one of two thousand swimming pools, or splash in the abundant bubbling-hot natural spas. Work on your tan in the Fiery Pits of Hades, or cleanse your system in our 'natural-look' saunas and steam baths. Eat at award-winning gourmet restaurants. It's food to die for!

"And should Sweetwater Canyons become your eternal home, you'll be joining a growing band who know that when you talk about Hell, Heaven can wait!"

Baz looked up expectantly and smiled. "There's more, but I think you can see how far things have changed since we rebranded the old place 'Sweetwater Canyons'."

"You can call a pig a rose but it'll still smell the same," said God out of the corner of Her mouth.

"I don't know," said Mrs Moorcroft slowly. "Looks kind of nice to me. So clean. Not at all what I expected."

"Golf, too," Mr Moorcroft said, a wistful look on his face.

Mich looked puzzled. "I'm not sure I understand. Can we, like, *choose* where we end up? I thought that, er, God here said we were being assessed."

Baz smiled. "That's the line they give out, kid. There's more than one way to skin a cat, right? Right? The truth is they don't *wanna* let you know there's an element of choice. All you gotta do is decide if you want to be uptown with all those other holier-than-thou types strummin' away on those harp things, or whatever it is they do all day, or downtown with us in Sweetwater, doin' some serious partyin'! It all comes down to what you want; spiffy place to live, plenty of leisure time, lots of golf. . ."

Mich made a face at the mention of golf and Baz leaned in closer. Mich expected to smell something nasty but all he got was a near-choking cloud of expensive cologne.

"Yeah, I was forgetting, you won't be interested in golf." Baz snorted and a tiny dribble of unidentifiable fluid ran on to his goatee. His voice dropped even lower and he draped a conspiratorial arm around Mich's shoulders. "But there's plenty of hot chicks down at Sweetwater just *dyin'* to meet a good-lookin' young man such as yourself. I'm tellin' you, man, it's Babe City." He winked and smiled wickedly. Mich drew back instinctively and sat down on the coffee table.

"Tell them the bottom line, *Baz*," said God. "Show 'em the price list."

Baz shot Her a look and closed his laptop hurriedly.

"Er, we don't have to get into details right now, folks," he said. "Give yourselves a chance to settle in. Let's face it, you got nothing but time now! Question is: how are you going to spend it?"

God sighed heavily and got to Her feet, brushing toast

crumbs off Her lap. "I suppose that's one thing we can agree on, Baz."

She turned to Mich and the rest of the Moorcrofts. "Well, you've got our manual and Baz's 'material' should you decide to opt out of our 'programme'. There are maps and other essential information in the folders you're holding."

Mich looked down at his empty hands. "What folders?" he said.

"Those," said God, and yea, Introductory Information Folders did blossom forth in the hands of the newcomers.

CHAPTER 4

In October 1999, a twenty-three-year-old Finnish hunter shot a grouse as it flew overhead. The bullet went straight through the bird and fell to earth, killing the hunter's eighteen-year-old brother who was a mile distant.

Daily Record, 13 October 1999

After Baz and God had left, the Moorcrofts sat in uneasy silence for a while. After all, what was there to say?

"This is all your fault," said Dakota pointing at Mich.

"Me? How? How is this my fault?"

Dakota threw her hands in the air.

"I don't know! It just is! She, God-woman, probably got annoyed by that stupid T-shirt or something and *made* that car crash into us!"

"Hey, hey kids," said Mr Moorcroft. "If it's anyone's fault it's

41

mine; I was driving. . ."

"That's just typical of you. Always a martyr," snarled Mrs Moorcroft, dropping her cigarette on to the carpet and savagely stubbing it out with the heel of her shoe.

"Urma!" said Mr Moorcroft. "The carpet!"

"Oh, what difference does it make?" yelled Mrs Moorcroft, bursting into tears and running towards the kitchen.

"Look what you did now!" snapped Dakota, following her mother.

"Me?" said Mr Moorcroft and Mich in unison.

Dakota stopped at the door and looked at them.

"You're pathetic!" she hissed, then turned on her heel and banged into the kitchen, slamming the door shut behind her.

Mr Moorcroft looked at Mich and seemed about to say something. Instead he patted him absently on the shoulder and left the room.

Mich sighed and flopped into an armchair. He needed time to think. Absently he opened the Information Folder on his lap.

"You're late for school," it barked in a sharp, high-pitched voice as soon as he lifted the cover. "The bus is waiting."

"Jeez!" squealed Mich and dropped the folder.

"Ow!" came a muffled shout from the floor.

School? What was that all about?

Mich picked up the folder and considered his options.

He could simply skip school. What was the worst that could

 42

happen? Then he remembered God making the note about Dakota in Her little notebook. The little old lady had looked so relentless, and there was something about Her confidence that made Mich think twice about getting on the wrong side of Her. To be honest he hadn't given the existence of God a great deal of thought prior to this moment.

Mich had not been a regular church-goer for some time, ever since his parents had abandoned their relatively feeble attempts to get him to attend. At school, whenever the subject came up, Mich affected a bored, cynical disbelief which had seemed fine, in theory. But here and now, having seen the Supreme Being sitting on the couch in the living room, things looked a little different. A little more pertinent. A little more *real*.

Although the room seemed warm enough Mich shivered and the hair on the back of his neck prickled as the realization sank in. He had met the Supreme Being. *God!*

Mrs Moorcroft came back from the kitchen sniffling softly into a tissue. Dakota had her arm around her and darted nasty glances at Mich. Mr Moorcroft ambled back in, too. He seemed lost and kept scratching the top of his head and squinting through the window as if all this was a rather tricky crossword clue that would work itself out eventually.

One by one the family opened their folders.

The room filled with the chatter of the Information Folders

barking out instructions. They were a surly bunch.

The folders told Dakota she was going back to school too.

"Like, great," she said miserably, folding her arms across her chest and pouting.

Mr and Mrs Moorcroft were both given new jobs. Mr Moorcroft at The Ministry of Lost Souls working as an accounts clerk. Mrs Moorcroft, much to her surprise, had been drafted into the Purgatory Police Dept.

"But I was a *hairdresser*!" she protested. "What do I know about police work?"

"Hey, don't blame me, lady!" snapped the Information Folder. "I just deliver the freakin' info, capeesh? You got a problem, take it up with Head Office."

Mrs Moorcroft looked like she was about to say something else when the words died in her mouth.

"Oh!" she squeaked, looking down and dropping the folder.

"Ow!" it yelled. "Do you mind?"

"He did that to me too," said Mich's folder. "Buncha butterfingers, if you ask me."

Mrs Moorcroft wasn't listening. None of the Moorcrofts were listening.

Right in front of them Mrs Moorcroft's clothes were mutating. In a blur of movement the overtight sports top became a crisp dark blue shirt, complete with embroidered patches and a black tie. The gold stitching on the right arm patch spelled out "N.P.P.D. North Purgatory Police Department, Officer Moorcroft: 232444231". Another patch with a pair of crossed fiery swords and "Defender of The Kingdom and Loyal Keeper of The Gateway" embroidered in the same gothic script appeared on Mrs Moorcroft's left arm.

Business-like pockets and flaps emerged from the fabric with audible popping sounds. Dark blue combat pants, a single yellow stripe running down the outside of each leg, replaced her pink leisure slacks. The pants ran down into gleaming black boots.

Around her waist, a thick black leather belt appeared, from which dangled various clubs, sprays, radios and some items that Mich couldn't identify. Mrs Moorcroft's usually wild curls tucked themselves firmly under a sharp peaked cap with a gleaming black brim. A high-tech microphone stalk appeared and curled around to position itself in front of Mrs Moorcroft's mouth, now fixed in an "o" of disbelief. The whole transformation took less than ten seconds.

"Formidable!" gasped Mr Moorcroft.

Mrs Moorcroft reeled and staggered back, stunned. Then she looked at herself in the mirror and straightened up, admiring her new look. She seemed thinner, stronger, more authoritative than before. She smiled and had opened her mouth to speak when her radio crackled and barked out an indecipherable stream of electro-static. She gingerly placed it to her ear, listened wide-eyed to the message and looked out of the window. A dark-blue-and-white police cruiser screeched to a halt outside and a tiny policeman, no higher than sixty centimetres tall and with large pointed ears peeking out from under his cap, leapt down, sprinted up the path and rapped on the door with his billyclub.

Mrs Moorcroft opened it nervously.

"C'mon, sister," said the tiny policeman in a broad Irish accent. "We got a 498 in progress down in Little Disney!"

He turned and raced back down the driveway.

Mrs Moorcroft, unsure in her unfamiliar uniform, turned back to her family, shrugged, and sprinted out of the room.

Everyone listened to the sound of heavy boot-steps running down the drive, then a car door slammed and the police cruiser screamed away, sirens wailing.

There was a moment's stunned silence in the room.

Mr Moorcroft looked as if he was having difficulty breathing.

Dakota was looking at her own clothes, a nervous expression on her face.

Mich decided he needed some air. This would be the weirdest day of his life, he thought, except for the fact that he was dead. He flipped up his skateboard and went out of the front door.

Mich stood outside breathing in the air (it seemed pretty normal) and looked around, not knowing quite what to expect.

He'd often imagined what it would be like to be dead, but never in his wildest dreams had he imagined that death would be exactly like life in Communion (apart, obviously from God, the Devil, Elvis, the Roman centurion, the flaming rocks and his mother's mutating clothes).

He still couldn't believe that only yesterday they'd been on their way to Gamma's.

"What do you think?" said Dakota. She was standing behind Mich, leaning against the porch, an expression of utter depression on her face.

"Of what?"

"Of all *this*, moron!" There was a rising note of hysteria in her voice that was uncomfortably close to how Mich felt. It *was* all true. They were dead, all of them, unless you counted Alaska and he might just as well be, the shape he was in.

"I don't know," said Mich. "But look on the bright side, Dak, at least you don't have to worry about your weight any more."

Dakota pursed her lips but said nothing. She lifted her hands in a "why me?" gesture and sat down dejectedly on the steps.

Mich walked to the end of the drive and looked in the direction of the soot-streaked red sky. Things must be different over there, but right here the neighbourhood looked relatively unchanged. He bent and picked a handful of dirt from the edge

47

of the driveway. It seemed like real dirt as it crumbled beneath his fingers. Smelt the same too.

Next he examined the sidewalk closely, dropping down on one knee to inspect it. He looked around in case anyone was watching. The sidewalk appeared real enough on first inspection but after seeing what happened to his mother's clothes, he was taking nothing for granted. Feeling a little foolish, he rapped his knuckles on the roughened concrete.

Solid.

Standing, Mich brushed the dirt from his pants. He looked down at his hands and then checked the rest of his body. It all seemed intact. He gingerly touched the back of his head where the exhaust manifold had hit and his fingers found unbroken skin.

His head began to ache.

Mich made an executive decision to postpone thinking about all this until he'd had a chance to see a bit more of Purgatory, or perhaps until he grew an extra brain or two. No sooner had he come to this conclusion than a horn sounded in the distance, there was a sudden rush of air and standing at the end of the driveway was the school bus. One thing was certain: it wasn't like the buses back in Communion.

It sat, yellow, low-slung and threatening at the kerbside. Flames were painted on the sides and the engine growled threateningly under bulging air intakes. Flared chrome exhaust pipes ran along its length, skirting over the swollen wheel arches which housed fat race tyres. A wide flat spoiler jutted aggressively from the back. The windows were mirrored black. Pounding rap music throbbed from what sounded like a serious sound system and the whole bus bobbed up and down on its springs.

"Extra valid wheels," murmured Mich appreciatively.

As he approached the bus, the front of the vehicle lowered itself to the floor so that it appeared to be crouching. Its radiator grille smiled wolfishly. The door hissed open and Mich looked in.

"Step aboard, son," said the driver, giggling like a maniac and cranking up the volume on the stereo. "Let's put the pedal to the metal!"

Mich couldn't help but notice that the driver had to sit on a cushion to reach the steering wheel. He also noticed she seemed to be no more than three years old. He shrugged and stepped aboard. He turned in the doorway and shouted to Dakota. "C'mon, Dak! We gotta go!"

Dakota hesitated before walking down the driveway and stepping on board too. Despite being sixteen she held Mich's arm tightly as they walked down the bus.

It was full of kids. Mich had been half-worrying, half-hoping that they would look like something from one of those zombie movies, all green skin, blood and staring eyes, but most of them looked perfectly normal, if perhaps a little strangely dressed. He sat down in the first seat he came to and looked at the girl next to him. Dakota rolled her eyes before reluctantly letting go of his arm and finding a place three rows back next to a kid wearing a straw hat and spats.

Mich risked a look at the girl in the seat next to him and found she was very pretty. She was in fact the prettiest girl Mich had ever seen in his entire life. Or death for that matter. All thoughts of his circumstances were temporarily forgotten.

He considered his options.

The first, and initially most attractive option (and the one most often favoured by Mich when faced with a genuine babe, or by any member of the opposite sex younger than twenty-five and older than twelve) was to say nothing and rely on sheer, smouldering animal magnetism to cast them under his spell.

As a tactic it hadn't worked very often; in fact it had, so far, never worked and showed zero prospect of working at any time in the future. The only females Mich spoke to with any regularity were his mother and his sister, and then only out of necessity.

Option two wasn't much better. It involved getting hold of a replacement personality inside the next two minutes; one that combined the street-sexy cool of say, Eminem the popular rap star, with the urbane sophistication of James Bond.

"The name's Moorcroft," Mich could picture himself saying, "Michigan Moorcroft," and arching a single eyebrow in the completely irrestible manner of a practised babe-magnet. According to his extensive studies of the James Bond movies, everything would follow from there.

He tried it.

"The name's Moorcroft, sweet thing. Michigan Moorcroft. You can call me Mich."

It couldn't fail. Unfortunately what actually came out sounded nothing like his 007-ness. Instead of the ultra-cool, growling baritone Mich intended, Mich made a kind of high-pitched barking sound and waved his hands around limply in mid-air. He turned bright red and began to sweat furiously.

Fortunately the girl didn't seem to have noticed a thing and the bus screamed off at an incredible speed. Through the window Mich could only catch glimpses of row after row of houses, just like his own, whizzing past at what seemed like the speed of light. He forgot all about what tactics to use and concentrated on holding on to his seat and not whimpering.

"Why are we going so fast?" he shouted to the girl over the roar of the engine, his eyes wide with fear. The last time he'd been in a moving vehicle things hadn't turned out too well. Was that really only yesterday?

"We got a long way to go," she said, nodding her head in the direction they were travelling. There was a pause as she looked at him. It wasn't an altogether unkindly look, although the girl did have a forbidding and somewhat gloomy expression.

"First day?"

"Er, yes."

"How d'you like being a Bonesider?"

"Bonesider?"

"You know. One of us. Dead. We call ourselves Bonesiders here. The live ones, the ones back home, they're called Breathers."

Mich looked puzzled and the girl shook her head. "On account of them still breathing," she added, smiling as if she was talking to an imbecile.

At least she hadn't said "du-uh", thought Mich, the way that Kyleann Caverell and Lila Corcoran did last week when Mich had muffed a question in Math.

"Well, I only got here last night. I was alive . . . a Breather . . . until I woke up this morning." He wanted to say more but, as he thought once again about being dead, his throat seemed constricted. Tears sprang unbidden to his eyes and he pasted an emergency expression of total boredom on to his face. He couldn't believe he was embarrassed about being dead.

"So do you have a name, then?" said the girl. As he got to know her better he noticed that she had a talent for not noticing his embarrassment, for which he was pathetically grateful.

"A name? Oh. Yes. Sure." Mich coughed and laughed wildly at the idea that anyone could be so stupid as to actually forget their own name.

"Er," Mich hesitated. He had forgotten his name.

The girl rolled her eyes. Even the most patient had limits.

"Let me guess; you're a secret agent sent here by a foreign Government and you can only reveal your name under torture?"

"Oh, sorry, um no . . . my name's, erm, er . . . um, Moorcroft! Yes, Michigan Moorcroft. Call me Mich."

"Ouch," said the girl grimacing. "'Michigan'? Hippie parents?"

"Yeah," said Mich. "Sort of. Not now."

"Me too. My name's Patterson. *Rainbow* Patterson." She spat angrily on the floor and held out her hand. "You can call me Patterson."

Mich shook hands with Patterson. Her hand was warm, dry, nice.

"OK . . . er, Patterson, pleased to meet you."

Mich jerked a thumb in the direction of Dakota. "That's my sister, Dakota."

Patterson shifted around and looked back down the bus to where Dakota was sitting, her face a serene mask of been-there-done-that indifference. From experience Mich knew she was terrified.

"Seems kinda grumpy."

"She usually is," said Mich. "So, er, Patterson, why the long face? Apart from being called Rainbow, I mean. And being dead, obviously."

"Long face?" replied Patterson sharply. "You try going to school every day for the last thirty years."

"THIRTY YEARS?"

"You got it. I crossed over back in the 70s. Bike and truck collision. Guess who was riding the bike? Har har. I'm not the worst off though. Take a look at Grunt back there."

She flipped her thumb at a kid sitting in the middle of the aisle. Mich turned in his seat to look.

Grunt was dressed in scraps of filthy animal skins. He carried a dead goat slung easily across his shoulders and his hair hung in thick dirty ropes. He squatted on the floor of the bus building a small fire.

"We call him Grunt because he can't speak any language we can figure out," said Patterson. "He's been coming to school since the dawn of human time. Bummer, hey?"

Mich felt that "Bummer" didn't begin to get close to describing the situation Grunt was in and he shivered at the possibility that the same fate could happen to himself.

Mich had relaxed a little during his conversation with Patterson. The bus hadn't slowed down, not even by a fraction, but Mich was confident enough to relax his death grip on the armrest. He stretched his fingers to work some blood back into them (hey! blood!) and took a look around.

Although, at first glance, most of the kids on the bus looked fairly modern, there were plenty sprinkled around dressed in old-fashioned clothes. Patterson herself was wearing bell-bottomed purple flares, platform shoes, a hideous yellow nylon shirt and had a haircut of the kind usually reserved for German rock stars, but (thought Mich) still managed to look gorgeous.

He wondered where she lived. Did she live alone? Or maybe in some sort of grisly afterlife orphanage? Mich had a sudden image of a spooky old building with stone-cold corridors and food infested with weevils. He didn't know what a weevil was but it didn't sound promising.

"Don't feel too sorry for yourself," said Patterson, turning away from Grunt. "You might not be here very long. Some kids only stay a few days before getting kicked upstairs."

She looked at Mich's Alien Death Factory T-shirt. "Although I wouldn't bank on being one of those."

There was a pause in the conversation and from behind him Mich could hear Dakota talking to the kid next to her. She was asking him about shopping malls and he was nodding and smiling. It was obvious he didn't have a clue what she was talking about.

"I don't get . . . all this," said Mich. "How come you've been here thirty years? And what about Grunt? Are you guys real badasses or what?"

Patterson shook her head.

"I don't know," she said. "You'll find out what it's like here soon enough. They make a big play that it's all sorted out, no mistakes and so on, but it's all creaking around the edges. No one really knows how they decide, or when they decide. I've put in so many requests for a case review that I'm on first name terms with the clerk at The Ministry."

Mich wondered about asking about The Ministry, then decided it could wait. He was operating on information overload as it was.

Patterson continued. "This place is a nuthouse. Think of New York but a thousand times bigger. It's not like, oh here's some dead dude, better kick one of us out to make room. No, it's all kinda . . . *messy*."

She waved her hands around to emphasize.

"And think about all the people who work here; they're no different from the people down there who tell you you're in the wrong line, or you have the wrong form, or they lost the original, or the computer's down today, yadda-yadda-yadda. You know what it's like. And then they all report to one person. It's a real mess. I think that's why Sweetwater's doing so well. People just get bored waiting for a transfer and take the easy route out."

"What about you? Why don't you do that?"

Patterson paused. "It's tempting, don't get me wrong. But, I don't know, something just doesn't feel right about it. I never trusted the guy with the sales patter."

"Baz?"

"Yeah," said Patterson, meaningfully. "'Baz'. Gave me the creeps. At least the old lady was pretty straight down the middle."

Mich risked another look out of the window. They were still travelling at warp speed five but he was getting used to it. He caught fleeting glimpses of yellow cornfields, industrial waste-land, medieval castles and snow-bound villages. They were most definitely not in Kansas any more, or anywhere that looked anything like it.

"Jesus," murmured Mich. "I gotta get outta here."

"You aren't talking about crossing back, are you?"

Patterson looked at him curiously.

"That's probably not a great idea, Mich. You can't escape you know; they'd just send the Controllers after you."

"What are they?"

"Kind of like the police. Mostly they see to it that people get delivered to their Final Destinations. Not everyone is happy with their Final Destination. I mean it's OK if you want Sweetwater but plenty of people end up there who don't. So the Controllers see to it that they make it to the right spot."

"My mom's in the police!" said Mich. "She started today."

"Your mom? She's gonna have an interesting day with those dudes."

"Why, what are they like?"

"You're not going to believe this."

CHAPTER 5

Forty-eight-year-old Dwayne Carroll from Kentucky died from a heart attack in July 2001 as he prepared the ground on a plot of land he intended to use for his and his wife's final resting place in Floyd County Cemetery. On being told the news of her husband's death, Mrs Carroll, 49, died of shock. They were buried together in the grave he'd been working on.

Ananova, 11 July 2001

"Nobody messes with the Easter Bunny!"

The two-and-a-half-metre-tall rabbit (complete with whiskers, pink nose and long floppy ears) hoisted the regulation police issue immobilizer on to his shoulder and took aim. There was a measured confidence and professionalism to his movements as if this was something he did a lot. The crim, realizing what was about to happen, turned and sprinted off down the alleyway, still clutching the stolen harp (state of the art, dual synthesizers and twenty-four-track mix capability) under his arm. The rabbit fired and a fine mesh net shot from the barrel at an approximate speed of something very fast. It wrapped around the crim like a rocket-propelled octopus and he fell to the floor, writhing helplessly.

"These guys," said Officer O'Toole to Mrs Moorcroft. "They always forget they're dead, you see, then they see all this stuff just lying around and they can't help themselves, the wee tinkers."

O'Toole had been assigned to Mrs Moorcroft for on-the-job training. He was a big fella for a leprechaun, standing almost sixty centimetres high. He had a lined "seen-it-all-before" kind of face rimmed with an emerald-green beard. He'd explained that leprechauns on the force had been given special beard dispensation on cultural grounds. He and Mrs Moorcroft had dealt quickly with the 498, which turned out to be a particularly nasty traffic snarl-up on Donald Duck Boulevard.

The Easter Bunny, or Officer Grimes as it said on his badge, strolled over with the crim tucked firmly under his arm like a loaf of bread.

"Fishin's good today, I see," said Officer O'Toole.

"Never better," said the Easter Bunny, holstering the big immobilizer in a shoulder harness. He casually lobbed his catch into the back of his police cruiser like a bag of dirty laundry.

 60

"Lemme introduce a new recruit to you," said O'Toole, craning his neck upwards to the massive bunny. "Officer Grimes, this is Officer Moorcroft."

"A Norm," said Grimes. "Things must be gettin' desperate." He barely nodded at Mrs Moorcroft before jumping into his cruiser, gunning the engine and screeching away from the kerb.

"Charming," said Mrs Moorcroft.

"Oh, pay no mind to the Big Fella. He's been on the job jest a tad too long. And he misses the eggs, don't you know."

Mrs Moorcroft hadn't been too surprised to see a two-and-a-half-metre Easter Bunny dressed as a policeman. Back at the station she'd been given her initial induction, and she'd quickly realized that most of the Controllers were not "Norms" like her. The desk sergeant, for instance, was one of the many Tooth Fairies on the force. He was a big guy with a heavy five o'clock shadow and beetle brows; the only clues to his past as a Tooth Fairy the golden curls and the little pair of gossamer wings poking out of his back.

There were plenty of leprechauns, too ("The Irish connection," O'Toole had winked), and elves and pixie folk. She'd seen a squad of elves with special red berets trot past, grim-faced and determined looking, on their way to a 356 (a hostage situation) and O'Toole had explained they were an elite SWAT team made up of ex-members of Santa's Little Helpers. "Most of 'em passed away in industrial accidents," said O'Toole. "All that toymakin' can be real dangerous. But they make great Controllers; very disciplined, very secretive."

O'Toole had explained that all these fairies, and goblins, and pixies and suchlike made ideal cops up here in Purgatory. They were hard-working, trained in covert operations ("Particularly the Tooth Fairies,") and they stayed in Purgatory for ever because The Organization couldn't make up their minds where to send 'em. There were a few other Norms like Mrs Moorcroft working as Controllers, O'Toole had said; more since the supply of pixiefolk had started to dry up ("Due to the lack of belief down there, yer see?").

Mrs Moorcroft loved it all. She'd been issued her own badge and had her own locker downstairs in the station. And she loved the way she looked in the Controller uniform. It was so slimming and she looked powerful, commanding . . . *different*.

Now, out on patrol with Officer O'Toole, Mrs Moorcroft felt happier than she'd done since she could remember. She hadn't realized there'd be so much to do, she told O'Toole.

"To be sure, there's a tonne of it up here," he said. "What with so many Norms being dumber than a lump of Dublin coal, no offence, and with crowd control duties on special holidays and big events, and with guarding The Gateway, obviously."

"The Gateway?"

"You'll find out soon enough," said O'Toole as he peeled off into the traffic.

 62

Mrs Moorcroft reached forward and flicked the siren on. As they wailed through the Purgatory rush hour Mrs Moorcroft looked out of the window.

"I think I'm going to like this job," she murmured.

CHAPTER 6

Stephen Hyett, 38, of Haverhill, Suffolk, survived a number of dangerous organ transplants including the replacement of his stomach, liver, kidney, pancreas, duodenum and small bowel. Six years later, Mr Hyett died when he fell from a chair while replacing a light bulb.

Daily Express, 15 April 2000

The red truck pulled into the parking lot of the 7-11 and parked next to a double-wide pulling a trailer. It was a mid-sized place along the main highway, decked out in hundreds of tiny red lights for Christmas. They hung down in bunches from the overhanging roof frame. "Krazy Kristmas Special: $3.99!" screamed a dayglo banner in the window. Mitchell Freestone Moorcroft had almost forgotten it was the holiday season, but then, he wasn't really what you'd call a Christmas kind of person. He'd spent the last three behind bars.

He checked before he turned into the lot that there were no cops stinking up the place, taking yet another doughnut break, the fat-ass freeloaders. But as far as he could make out the place was cop-free, and Moorcroft relaxed, a smile still on his face.

He sat in the cab and finished his cigarette, listening to the radio. He'd been cruising along since the wreck, listening to an old Aerosmith tune on K-Rock Klassik 104 after finding the station hidden in a whole raft of those goddam rap stations they had up here. Moorcroft hated rap, and hip-hop, and R&B and the blues, and jazz, all that *foreign* music. Moorcroft didn't have any time for *foreigners*. In fact, pretty much anyone who wasn't an off-white pinky colour with a sunburnt neck was suspect in Moorcroft's book and Moorcroft hated plenty of folks like that, too.

He had a substantial hate list which included, but was not limited to, cops, teachers, probation officers, traffic police, security staff, doctors, dentists, hairdressers, guys wearing business suits, people from New York or anywhere in California, people who worked in banks, overpaid sports stars, that stupid dude reading the news with the big hairspray 'do, the guy at the motel who'd given him a hard time about paying with a bunch of quarters, old geezers, certain members of his own family, *teenagers*. Was there anything more repulsive on the face of God's earth than the average American teenager?

Jeez, he hated those dumb kids. Like the one in the car wreck. Moorcroft chuckled at the memory. Boy, did that kid get a surprise!

He let the song finish, snapped the radio off, killed the engine. He flipped his cigarette butt on to the parking lot and stepped down from the cab, the heels of his dirty tan work boots clacking on the wet tar. He coughed a little. He'd quit smoking one day. *Yeah*, he laughed to himself, *I'll quit on a cold day in Hell*.

The red truck was safe enough for a time. Moorcroft didn't think it had been reported stolen just yet on account of he'd buried the driver in a landfill site back in Roebuck and he wasn't going to be contacting the FBI in the foreseeable future. Jesus Hernandez Victor De La Cruz had not been married, did not have any children and was travelling from New Mexico to find work in Florida, when he'd had the bad luck to pick Moorcroft up at a truck stop in Louisiana. Jesus had told Moorcroft all of these things in the three short hours they'd travelled together. Man, that little fella could talk. At least he could before Moorcroft had shut him up for good with a heavy length of pipe he'd found on the floor of the cab.

They'd stopped on an empty stretch of highway outside Lafayette, when Moorcroft had told Jesus he needed to take a leak. While Jesus was checking something on the flat bed, Moorcroft had laid him out cold with the pipe and now Jesus was forty miles down the road headfirst at the foot of a locked-up landfill site.

No one would be finding that particular Jesus anytime soon.

Moorcroft smiled again at that even though he felt sorta bad about it too; he hadn't meant to put the guy's lights out for good, just give him a li'l' tap on the noggin and be on his way. But he musta overdone it a bit and needs must when the devil drives and all that.

The plan was to head north, up to Maine and lie low in a cabin he knew about up near Calais, right on the Canadian border. He figured if things got hot he could slip across and get lost in all that Canadian outdoors; he'd heard they had a lot of it up there. Moorcroft was en route to the cabin when he'd fatally intersected with the Moorcrofts travelling south on I-91.

Moorcroft went inside the truck stop and found a seat at a window booth where he could see anyone pulling into the parking lot. He ordered coffee and made sure he was good and polite to the waitress when she wished him a "Merry Christmas". "Right back atcha," he said with a soft smile; no point in drawing any more attention to himself.

Now, sitting in the booth with a hot cup of coffee, he had a chance to reflect on the car wreck. Man, that had been some-thing – hadn't it but? Moorcroft thought about the old lady he'd seen crossing right in front of the truck. He'd had time to see she was unconscious, or maybe she was dead; hey, that'd be rich, if she'd croaked before the wreck! She'd sailed past him and Moorcroft had given her rear end a little nudge with the fender of the red truck, just for a little wake-up call and because he was bored with all that driving and because he could never resist a little devilment when it came right down to it. Then he'd noticed the Chevy move across at exactly that moment, and before he knew it the old lady had slammed right into those suckers. Whooowheee!

Moorcroft had seen it all and had carved a path right through that whole mess like a thumb through a soft peach. He'd picked the gap in the whirling mess like a running back through a leaky defence, and gunned the stolen truck through with just a lick of paint separating himself from the smash, clean as you like. Like all Southern good ole boys, Moorcroft was proud of his driving, but he knew he'd been lucky this time. He smiled; someone up there must have been looking out for him.

He'd smiled as he'd drifted past that kid, too, and then with a sudden jolt, Moorcroft realized he might have a problem.

What if the kid had survived?

It *had* been a hell of a car wreck, and Moorcroft had seen enough to know that not many of the people involved, if any, could have come through still breathing. But it was possible, wasn't it? It was just possible that that punk kid was talking right now to some nosy cop who was wondering exactly who the dude in the red truck could have been, and why that fella didn't come forward as a witness? Moorcroft tried to recall the scene and remember if there'd been anyone else close enough to make trouble. He didn't think so, the road had been clear except for the old woman and the car the kid was in. Maybe the kid had got the licence of the truck. It was unlikely, but the thought settled in Moorcroft's brain like a tick on a cow and kept biting away at him. Moorcroft put down his coffee and cursed under his breath.

"What did you say, honey?" said the waitress and Moorcroft realized he'd spoken out loud. He smiled at her to show he was harmless but she backed off with a sour expression, seeing something in his eyes that she didn't like. Waitresses always knew; just like cops and bartenders, they could spot guys like him a mile away. Moorcroft felt the familiar hot rush of anger, and he had to force himself to relax. He didn't have time to get involved dealing with the waitress. Besides, she saw wackos all the time in here, and in ten minutes she'd have forgotten all about the guy talking to himself over his coffee. Not like that damn kid, though. No one forgets the details of a car wreck. Moorcroft threw down some bills and left.

He had urgent business to take care of.

CHAPTER 7

A macaque monkey dropped a plant pot from the sixth floor of a block of flats in New Delhi killing Arvin Jah, 48, instantly.

The Sun, 17 April 2000

Purgatory High was gigantic, enormous, stupendous and all the other words that mean "big".

It needed to be.

At the last estimate (and that's all it could ever really be) there were upwards of eight million students at the school. The original building had been constructed several millennia ago when demands on it were limited, but recently, over the last thousand years, it had expanded like some cosmic virus until the school covered a huge ill-defined area that no one, not even the School Managers, had ever managed to map. The building simply grew to cope with the tidal wave of new faces that threatened to swamp it, so that now it appeared to have a life of its own.

The additions had been piecemeal; a new tower here, a library there. Different eras left their mark, so that the building resembled nothing so much as a city constructed by a crazed student of architectural history. Soaring stone gothic buttresses the size of redwoods held walls as high and dramatic as the Hoover Dam; vast plains of smoked glass and polished granite marked more modern additions. Towers, their tops glittering with copper and bronze minarets, shining cupolas or fancifully crenellated edging, vanished into cloud.

Ornately carved fifteenth-century doors guarded by leering gargoyles opened on to 1950s-style hallways covered in shiny rubberized flooring. Classroom ceilings painted by Michelangelo and gymnasiums decorated by Picasso (Purgatory was full of artists, musicians, writers and other creatives; they seemed to prefer the uncertainty of death to Paradise or Sweetwater), jostled with stark utilitarian canteens and red plush staff rooms.

The school tunnelled below ground as much as it extended upwards and was riddled with interconnecting passageways and ducts so that if it was ever to be lifted clear of the earth (and who could say that that was not possible here, of all places?) it would resemble nothing so much as a monstrous plant, its labryinthine root system trailing brick and clods of earth.

On the ground the impression was simply of chaos.

Overpasses soared from one floor to another. Sleek modern glass elevators and simpler rope-and-pulley mechanisms from earlier times crawled up and down the outside of the school ferrying swarms of students from class to class.

Several different transport systems criss-crossed the school and it was a common sight to see new scholars standing on the subway platforms staring in bewilderment at the transport maps, which resembled the multicoloured scribblings of an infant. Strangely enough, that was precisely what they were; the transport system had been designed by Philomena Lutz, a child of two and a half mistakenly given the task sometime in the last century. The city engineers had built the subways according to one of Philomena's drawings, with the result that any journey meant the traveller circled violently, or deviated wildly off course along intricately winding rails before reaching their destination. The experience was so nauseating that vomitariums were situated at exit points throughout the system.

There had also been experiments with complicated Victorian-designed steam-driven hoverbuses, some of which still noisily buzzed along the hallways in a cacophony of iron, great white clouds of vapour trailing from the clanking rear-mounted engines. They would be a menace to life and limb if everyone wasn't dead already, and the hoverbuses were unpopular with all but a few die-hard enthusiasts.

Many of the school's walls still had the original iron rings set into the stone where previous generations hitched horses or mules. A few still preferred that method of transportation, although some amongst the School Managers suspected that might have more to do with avoiding lessons than any fear of travelling via hover, subway or the latest network of accelerated walkways.

The school kitchens were legendary. Only a few years previously they had been condemned by a review panel as being so unhygienic that they actively encouraged students to opt for Eternal Damnation at Sweetwater Canyons simply to avoid lunch. Then, luckily, a senior manager working for a well-known fast food chain was killed in a freakish and somewhat ironic accident (gored to death by a BSE-infected cow during a hiking vacation in England) and the school catering system had been radically overhauled. Now, two glowing golden arches towered above the entrance to what had become the afterlife's biggest burger bar. There were lines at the counters already as students piled their trays high with cholesterol-laden breakfasts.

Mich's bus pulled up with an ear-melting screech of brakes. Thick black smoke swirled from the tyres as they bit into the asphalt and the bus juddered to a halt. Mich had a million more questions to ask Patterson about the Controllers, about the school, about everything, but she reassured him that everything would be clearer once he'd had a chance to settle in. The doors hissed open and the students poured out.

Mich stood on the sidewalk in front of the school and gaped. Purgatory High was the biggest building he had ever seen.

"Welcome to Purgatory High," said a sign in front of Mich.

Mich jumped. He'd never heard a sign talk before, although he supposed he should be getting used to it after the Information Folders.

"Come on, come on!" it said, nudging him towards the school. "You're late." The sign butted him forward.

"Look at the size of this place!" said Mich, eyes wide.

"Yeah," said Patterson. "Eight million and counting."

"It sucks," said Dakota, stepping down from the bus and casting a sour glance at the school.

"Hey!" she yelled at the school sign which had turned its attention to her. "Quit pushing!"

Mich left her arguing and followed Patterson towards his new school. Patterson seemed to know plenty of people.

As they passed through the heavy doors he looked up. The top of the school disappeared into the red-tinged clouds high above him. Mich figured that Purgatory High must be situated close to Hell. Further away than his old school then, ha ha.

Inside the doors was a cavernous entrance hall. A full-size

airliner could circle overhead and, indeed, as Mich watched, one roared into the distance taking a class to one of the far-flung annexes. The din of eight million kids hurrying to lessons echoed painfully off the walls.

"Pretty impressive, huh?" said Patterson.

Mich didn't reply. There was too much going on around him.

"Mich! MICH!"

He heard Dakota's voice behind him and tried to turn back to her, but the press of bodies coming in was too strong. Patterson tapped his arm.

"She'll be OK, don't worry."

Dakota's voice grew fainter and Mich shrugged. He hoped that Patterson was right. This place was a zoo.

Mich was jostled by a large kid who looked like he had died sometime recently, if his hip-hop clothing was anything to go by. He was talking animatedly to a smaller kid wearing a 1930s-style three-piece grey woollen suit, his hair plastered in a greasy shine flat to his scalp. Both spoke with pronounced New York accents and gave Mich a hard city-stare as they passed.

A little way into the hall a crowd was gathered round something wriggling on the floor and Mich squeezed through to take a look. An escapologist, encased in a canvas sack bound tightly with chains, writhed furiously on the floor. He seemed to be having difficulty getting free. He was grunting loudly and cursing fluently in three different languages.

"'The Great Mondoli','" whispered Patterson in his ear. "Trainee escapologist with a Russian circus when he arrived here. Died in a bungled river escape."

She dragged Mich's arm as he hung back, gawking.

"C'mon, he never manages to get out."

Other street entertainers and hawkers seemed to be there simply through force of habit and the desire to entertain. Here and there columns of blue smoke rose into the air from camp-fires around which sat bands of strangely garbed and extravagantly ragged children roasting unappetizing hunks of meat for breakfast. Other children passed, munching on bacon McMuffins, and Mich remembered that he hadn't eaten. His stomach must still be working.

An ear-splitting blast from a whistle right behind them made Mich jump as a steam hoverbus rolled past, the crowds parting in front of it like water before the prow of a ship.

"Why dontcha watch where ya goin', ya moron!" yelled the driver, a kid of around eight who sported an eyepatch over one eye and a monocle in the other.

"Ah, sit on it loser!" shouted Patterson. "Goddam steam freak!"

Everywhere people were in motion; walking, running, riding on ancient bicycles, scooters, pogo sticks, skateboards, rollerblades, toy cars, donkeys, horses, even a camel or two. Mich spotted one group of students passing atop a stately elephant swaying from side to side, their noses deep in thick textbooks. Even the air above their heads was occupied as students buzzed past on elaborately decorated (and astonishingly noisy) personal jet-packs. Some looked like they had been built using cannibalized machine parts and dripped oil and water on to the heads of the throng below, others were sleek, streamlined craft with gleaming enamelled paintwork on their casings and shining chrome exhausts.

"Airheads," shouted Patterson above the drone. "Kind of a craze. You'll get used to them."

A street hawker with mottled skin and disturbingly hyperthyroid eyes thrust himself in front of Patterson and Mich. He jabbered excitedly in a language unfamiliar to Mich but sounding a little like Spanish, and moved the tray in their direction. Patterson rummaged through the jumble of objects on the tray and picked out an aerosol can with bright green markings. The hawker seemed satisfied and moved off towards another student.

"Don't you pay them?" said Mich.

"What with?" replied Patterson. "They do it because that's what they were when they died. Besides I needed some of this." She held the can out to Mich.

"What is it?"

" 'Wray-Go'," smiled Patterson. "Haven't you noticed those things buzzing around?" She pointed to a couple of mosquito-like insects trailing a tiny white vapour behind them. Mich had seen them everywhere but hadn't given them much thought.

"Mosquitoes?"

Patterson shook her head. "Wraiths. Spirits who have slipped through the cracks somehow. They're a nuisance." She pointed the can and sprayed it at one of the wraiths which disappeared in a tiny flash of dust.

"It just makes them disappear for a while," she said noticing Mich's look of concern. "It doesn't like, kill them or anything. They're already dead."

"This place is going to take some getting used to," murmured Mich.

"Try not to freak too much, sport," said Patterson. "You'll do fine. This is where I say bye. Catch you at lunch, OK?"

"Er, sure. So we still eat here? I mean, being dead and all."

"Of course," said Patterson, already walking away. "We got to fill the time somehow. See you."

"See you." Mich spoke in a small voice, watching Patterson walk away. She had a nice walk and he watched her until she melted into the crowd. He stood watching her, his mouth slack with love until he was jostled by a passing mule.

"Hey, Romeo!" yelled the mule's rider, a tough-looking cow-girl. "Give a gal some room! I'm comin' through!" She whistled expertly and the mule picked up the pace.

Mich shook himself and wondered what to do. He should have asked Patterson while he had a chance.

In the centre of the hall, about half a mile in the distance, he spotted a window with *School Office* written on it in glowing green neon. He dropped his skateboard to the floor and set out towards the office. A big sign barked, "No Skating!" at him as he passed but Mich ignored it and the sign couldn't keep up with him. It dropped back into the crowd, shouting at the other skaters.

By the time he neared the office, the crowd had thinned a little and, thankfully, there was no queue.

Across a shabby desk sat a large round woman reading the racing section of a newspaper. She was making notes in the margins with a tiny pencil. A small badge on her blouse said *R. Klebb, School Secretary*.

Mich waited for a minute without being noticed. He coughed.

The woman slowly flicked one eye up at Mich and regarded him much as one might look at a particularly ugly slug making an unscheduled appearance on a salad.

She held out a pudgy hand, palm up.

"Form," she said, heavily.

"I, er, don't have a form," replied Mich.

The woman shifted in her chair, put the newspaper down and clicked a key on the computer on the desk.

"Why me?" she sighed, although Mich didn't think she was asking him a question.

"Name?" she said. "You *do* have one of those, I presume?"

"Moorcroft. Mich Moorcroft."

She punched some more keys and looked at the screen, her nails tapping sharply as she waited for the information.

"Oh," she said, looking at the screen. "You."

She eyed Mich nastily. "I'm surprised that they let you come here at all. I'd have thought it'd be straight to Sweetwater Canyons for *your* sort. Kinda young-lookin', for this sort of thing, aren't you?"

Mich looked at her blankly.

"Well, I know I like some freaky music and I'm into skating, but I didn't think that was so ba—"

"I'm not talking about all *that*, Mr Moorcroft," said the secretary. "I'm talking about *the other stuff*. The gangs, the cruelty to animals, the lies, the guns, the fires, the *murders*. I suppose none of that's you, is it?"

"No!" said Mich, goggling wildly. "It's not! I haven't done any of that stuff! Well, maybe one or two little lies, one or two things I'm not so proud of . . . but none of the rest of it, all that guns, fires and stuff! And I *definitely* never murdered anyone! You must have me mixed up with somebody else!"

"That's what they all say, son," said the secretary. She pressed some keys and a desk printer rattled out a sheet of paper. "It's all right here in black and white."

Mich took the paper and looked at it. It was a report.

Mitchell Freestone Moorcroft, read the name on the top. A shiver of relief ran along Mich's spine.

"That's not me!" said Mich holding the paper up to the secretary. "See? Mich*igan*, not Mitch*ell*. And I'm Free*bird*, not *stone*. And look, he's older than me!"

"Whatever, kid," said the secretary. "I just work here. If you don't like it take it up with the Admissions Officer. You're in luck, it's his day today. He's just down the hall." She smiled nastily. "Next!"

There was no one waiting. The secretary picked up her racing paper and slid a frosted glass panel across the counter.

Mich grabbed the report and looked around. The school was quieter now, although there were still many, many kids wandering around. He supposed that most of the students had gone into class while he'd been arguing.

Mich looked back at the secretary, hidden behind the glass, and flipped her the finger.

"I saw that," she said, not moving a centimetre. "I knew I was right about you. Have a nice day, Mr Moorcroft."

Mich skated off. Dakota was right, this place *sucked*.

Finding the Admissions Office wasn't easy. Mich still had to negotiate the late-coming students hurrying to class. He remembered what Patterson had told him about Purgatory not

81

really working and, judging by the numbers of kids here, Mich could believe it. They streamed past him in their thousands. A tall, tough-looking kid, wearing modern style clothes and clutching a basketball like a teddy bear, stopped him and asked for directions in a shaky voice. When Mich said he was new here the kid burst into tears.

"Me too!" he wailed. "I wanna go home! Waaaaah!"

"You could ask at the office, dude," said Mich feeling uncomfortable.

"Office?" bawled the kid. "Waaaah!"

Mich didn't know what else to say. He patted the kid on the shoulder.

"Don't touch me!" he yelled leaping back. "You . . . *dead* zombie *freak*! Waaaaaah!"

Mich began to explain, then shrugged and skated past the howling boy. No one else in the streams of people brushing past gave the kid a glance. This kind of thing was obviously an everyday occurrence. The encounter shook Mich, but plainly he was coping with being dead better than some, and this gave him a renewed purpose.

Eventually he reached the place the secretary had pointed out. A small red sign hovered gently in mid-air. *Admissions Office* it read, above a flashing arrow. Mich looked where it was pointing and headed that way. As he moved off he noticed the sign drift to his left and point in another direction. He hesitated and the sign floated back to hover in front of him again. It motioned for him to move in the direction it had pointed him in first. He slowly skated that way and the sign waited this time. When Mich had gone five metres the sign nodded and then floated off, satisfied at a job well done.

Mich skated to where the sign had directed him. He stood uncertainly at the entrance to an enormous white corridor. It stretched away from him into what looked like infinity. Recessed strip lights bathed the corridor in a shadowless light. At intervals along the corridor were odd bits of furniture, the sort you find in swanky hotel corridors or conference centres; uncomfortable-looking designer chairs made from stainless steel and leather straps, dainty half-tables holding elegant high-tech vases with unusual, faintly repellent ice-blue flowers. The floor was white and was made of a slightly yielding rubberized material. It all had the shiny antiseptic tang of a laboratory and Mich hesitated, one foot on his board, suddenly unsure about taking his complaint further. A chill air-conditioned breeze blew softly towards Mich and he heard a faint electronic humming sound.

Mich blew out his cheeks and set off purposefully down the corridor, the soft rattle of the skateboard wheels echoing ahead of him. Once inside the corridor, the chill was intimidating. And there was something strange about it. Although ahead of him in a straight line lay what looked like miles of empty white hallway, Mich was certain of one thing: he was not alone.

Mich picked up the pace and concentrated on finding the Admissions Office. After a few minutes of skating he had begun to relax, when something ice-cold and unspeakably disgusting brushed against him. Mich yelped and looked around at the empty space.

"Who's there?" he squeaked.

He felt his legs go as adrenalin rushed through his system. There was nothing he could see, but to his left, just at the edge of his peripheral vision, he half-caught a shimmer of movement against the corridor wall, as if something large and transparent was sliding along it. What he saw had no shape, if in fact he saw anything. It was as if a lens had been passed across Mich's vision. His breathing grew shallow and he began to have doubts about going any further with this.

"C'mon, man, what's the worst that could happen?" he muttered angrily to himself. "Let's face it, you're already dead."

He pressed on.

Without quite knowing how, Mich knew that whatever it was back there wasn't following him now, it was hanging back, watching. Mich skated hard away from whatever it was.

In practically no time, twenty minutes, no more, Mich's heart rate stopped leaping around his chest like a trapped salmon and settled down to a manageable zillion beats a minute. The worst of his shaking had stopped and his breathing

 84

had slowed. If he could just manage to get his teeth to stop chattering he'd be in great shape.

Mich began to think about what the School Secretary had said.

That there had been a mistake Mich knew already. There was simply no way he could be dead, not yet, not with all those things he hadn't got round to doing in life. He didn't have an exact idea about the sort of things he would do if he hadn't been in the car wreck, but he knew they involved stunningly beautiful supermodels, parachute jumping, trekking through the Himalayas and becoming the new lead singer for Alien Death Factory . . . that kind of thing: you know, *stuff*.

No, there had obviously been a mistake, and he'd just have to set it right now he knew that another, *different* Mich Moorcroft had been due in Purgatory, a Mich Moorcroft who'd done some very bad things, someone who the secretary had thought would go straight to Hell, do not pass go, do not collect $200. And that could only have one meaning, couldn't it . . . that he, the *real* Mich Moorcroft, shouldn't really be dead after all. For the first time since finding out he was dead, Mich felt he had something to live for.

After a few minutes more he arrived at the Admissions Office. The door of the office looked out of place in the white corridor. It was large, at least three metres high, and very old. It was made of dark wood, studded with iron bolts and hanging on three monstrous, ornate black hinges in the shape of leering gargoyles.

Mich hesitated for a moment before reaching forward and rapping his knuckles against the wood.

"Come," creaked a low voice and Mich gently pushed open the door.

CHAPTER
8

Angler Anto Schwarz, 45, was killed in July 2000 when the fish he'd hooked in Eva Maria Lake, near Vienna in Austria, pulled him in. Schwarz could not swim. The fish was believed to have been a catfish, some of which can grow as large as three metres in length.

Daily Express, 26 July 2000

The room Mich stepped into was colder than anywhere he'd been in his life.

At the same time, though, and he couldn't explain how, he felt hot, feverish, his body insubstantial, inconsequential. Most of all, though, Mich felt scared.

An extremely tall, black-clad figure was stooped, his back to Mich, flicking through a folder in a filing cabinet in the corner of the room. There was something disturbingly familiar about the black-clad shape. The small, battered filing cabinet clanked and rattled as the figure shuffled the papers.

"I'll be with you in a moment," said a voice as dry as dust. "Please take a seat."

Mich looked around. It seemed like a fairly ordinary kind of place but on closer inspection there were one or two rather curious things about it. On one wall a small electronic display showed red glowing numbers ticking steadily up. "24,665,987,042" read the dial. Someone had written "and counting!" in marker pen next to it.

Mich read another small notice, this one fixed to the wall by a drawing pin. "You don't have to be decomposing to work here," it said in bouncy cartoon print, "but it helps!"

The desk was made from a single slab of very old wood, similiar to the door. There were huge numbers of tiny wormholes dotted across its surface and jagged scratches along the edges.

A shiny new computer sat on top of the desk in front of which was a small sign saying *Admissions Officer*. As Mich looked, a shiny, jet-black cockroach scuttled out from behind the sign, ran across the desk and disappeared over the edge. Behind the desk was an expensive and complicated-looking black leather office chair. Propped in one corner stood a strange wooden pole with a gleaming, curved blade arching viciously down.

"Now," said the figure. "What can I do for you, Mr Moorcroft?"

Mich started to ask how he knew his name, when the figure turned and the words died in Mich's throat. It wasn't the first time the tall figure had had that effect on visitors.

At first glance the Admissions Officer appeared to have no face, just two eyes glowing deep inside the tattered folds of a black hood. Scraps of fabric fluttered in a breeze that Mich couldn't feel. He towered terrifyingly over Mich for a moment before settling into the chair with a little sound of pain.

"Thank God for this chair," said the figure. "She OKed it out of petty cash. I don't know what I'd do without it. It's my back: I'm a martyr to it."

He glanced over to the scythe in the corner and extended a skeletal hand towards it.

"Humping that thing round all day, I suppose. Purely ceremonial these days, of course. We've had to modernize, use more up-to-date technology, but I sometimes miss the old ways."

He eyed the scythe lovingly and seemed lost in memories for a moment.

Mich said nothing. He couldn't because all his breath seemed to have been sucked from his body as he remembered where he'd seen the Admissions Officer before.

It was on the cover of Alien Death Factory's last CD: "Meet The Boss". It was a mega-cool cover, remembered Mich. And the guy he was looking at now had been on it. Except that on the CD cover he'd been screaming into a microphone while holding a battered silver guitar and balancing a bikini-clad woman on his knee. But Mich knew who he was.

Sitting across the desk from Mich was the Grim Reaper; Death himself. Mich swallowed.

This was scary. Serious scary.

The Admissions Officer placed the folder he'd collected from the filing cabinet in front of him and slowly opened it. From his seat across the desk Mich read *Mitchell Freestone Moorcroft* on the front. The Admissions Officer pushed his hood back to reveal a skeletal white face, bloodless lips and those red-rimmed eyes.

He flicked a bony hand at the computer.

"I'm supposed to get all your details from this thing. Latest departmental instructions," he said. "But I just can't get the hang of it. So until I do, I have to rely on the old ways."

He moved the file up a centimetre or two.

"Got all the same information in here, whichever way you look at it," he said. He looked at Mich and Mich felt ice float through him.

"You look younger than I'd have expected, Mr Moorcroft," said the Admissions Officer. "With a file like this." He hefted the weight of the file in his bony hand and put it down on the desk. "But my eyes aren't what they used to be. No, back in the old days I could pick out a coffin-dodger at three miles in a heavy fog. Happy times, happy times. . ."

There was a pause as he drifted away into his memories before sitting up straighter and looking at Mich once more.

"Now, what can I do for you?" he said leaning back in his orthopaedic chair and sighing pleasurably.

Mich coughed but before he could speak there was a knock on the door.

"Come," said the Admissions Officer and the door opened. A bone-white skeleton with bulging eyes and a manic grin poked its head around the corner. It was spotted with what looked suspiciously like blood.

"Oh," it said, catching sight of Mich. "Didn't realize company you had, amigo. I go, leave you chop-chop."

The Admissions Officer waved a bony hand.

"Sure, Mike, let's grab a coffee. Catch you later."

The skeleton grinned at Mich.

"Don' get him talking my frien'," he said in heavily accented English. "He will bore you to death, I think! You get joke, yes? Is funny, I think!" He cackled and snapped the door shut.

The Admissions Officer turned back to Mich.

"Sorry, don't mind Mike, he's such a kidder. . ."

"Mike?"

"'Mictlantecuhtli'," said the Admissions Officer. "Aztec Lord of the Underworld. He's been on secondment here

91

for the past thirty years or so. Part of the department's multicultural studies programme; you know the kind of thing. He learns a little about me, the scythe, God and all that; I swap back and study his wind of knives, how to deal with human sacrifices (not that's there's much call for that kind of expertise these days). Anyway, where were we?"

He sat back comfortably in his leather chair.

"Er, I think there's been a m-mistake," said Mich, pointing at the file. "That's, erm, not exactly, how can I put it? That's not me, you see. Sorry."

"Really," said the Admissions Officer.

"Yes, really!" said Mich.

"You know things will go much more smoothly if you drop this nonsense, Mr Moorcroft and simply accept your fate," said the tall figure, sighing. He tapped his long bony fingers on the file. "Do you know how many people try and wriggle out of this Admissions Office?"

"No," said Mich.

"Er, well it's a lot, I can tell you. And what do you think would happen if I let all of them out? It'd be a very crowded world, wouldn't it? No, you are Mich Moorcroft and I'm afraid that's the end of it."

"But I'm not Mich Moorcroft! I mean, yes, of course I *am* Mich Moorcroft but I'm not that Mich Moorcroft, the other Mich Moorcroft, the one who did all that bad stuff! He's

 92

the one you want! I mean look at me! Do I *look* like a violent psycho killer?"

The Reaper gazed at him thoughfully.

"Hmm. Quite."

"But I'm not!" shouted Mich. The Reaper raised a mouldy eyebrow.

"Sorry," said Mich. "It's just that I really am not the Mich Moorcroft you lot think I am! His name is Mitchell Moorcroft. Mine is Michigan Moorcroft. Different, you see. And he did all those bad things, right? Look at me, I'm only fourteen! The worst I ever did was some computer hacking, and even that wasn't any of the really bad stuff."

The Reaper leaned forward across the desk.

"It's not really very convincing is it, though, Mr Moorcroft? Your story, I mean. All that about not looking the part of a psycho; I've seen plenty of people who had done much worse than you look like butter wouldn't melt in their mouths. And being fourteen doesn't mean a thing; I've seen some very nasty teenagers in this office, believe you me. No, that sort of thing simply won't wash. And, by your own admission you say you've been one of those 'hackers'. You may not think that's so bad, but we take rather a dim view of it here. As for your idea about there being a mix-up, perhaps if you had any evidence, any documentation to support your claim, there might be a tiny, minuscule chance that I'd be able to think about taking another look."

"Documentation? What documentation?" said Mich.

The Admissions Officer heaved himself wearily to his feet and for a moment Mich thought he was about to fetch his scythe, but instead he reached into the filing cabinet and shuffled through the drawers.

"I knew I had them somewhere," he said turning and blowing a large quantity of dust from a sheaf of papers. "Departmental Error Form 7655555644XC. There's a way of doing these things. Fill these in and I'll add them to my pending tray."

He gestured towards a yellowing stack of dog-eared forms propped half in and half out of a battered cardboard box in one corner of the office.

"What about an appeal? A pardon?" said Mich. "There must be someone else I can talk to about this."

"Someone else?" said the Admissions Officer, chuckling. "I'm afraid there's no one else, Mr Moorcroft. I am the Admissions Officer and I take my responsibilities very seriously indeed."

Mich slumped dejectedly in his chair.

"Look, the best I can do is to make a note on your file," he continued. "If by any miracle you *do* run across this other 'Mr Moorcroft' (and that, let me tell you, really *would* be a miracle), then there's a faint chance we may be able to look at your case again. But it's up to you. I'm afraid that my department is tremendously short-staffed, what with budget cutbacks and organizational reshuffling. We're snowed under down here at the moment. We don't simply deal with school matters, you know; I'm only at the school one day a month. You are very lucky to have caught me in at all. No, you must file a request with the proper authorities." He lifted the forms, shook them by way of demonstration, and continued speaking.

"But, as you can see, we simply don't have any spare time for wild goose chases. That's life, I'm afraid. Or not, in your case, har har!" The Admissions Officer chuckled softly and Mich could hear a bell tolling somewhere in the distance.

"Just my little joke, Mr Moorcoft. Now if you don't mind I have an appointment to keep; little typhoon in the Philippines. Always means a bit of supervisory overtime for yours truly. Don't *have* to be there, you understand, just like to drop in unannounced now and again to keep everyone on their toes."

"Everyone?" said Mich.

"Well, we have to subcontract you know. Far too many croakers for just me to deal with. Worked out a nice deal with Santa's Little Helpers, Inc. Very reasonable, and far more efficient than you might think."

He thrust out a hand and gave Mich the forms.

"You'll need to fill these out and drop one copy with me and one at the correct department at The Ministry."

"The Ministry?" said Mich.

"The Ministry of Lost Souls," said the Admissions Officer.

"Big building on Red Tape Square, can't miss it. Everything in Purgatory is dealt with at The Ministry. They deal with all administrative matters and many other things that, quite frankly, are simply not your concern. A pleasure meeting you, Mr Moorcroft. Good luck with the quest."

"What about the Controllers?" asked Mich. "Do they have anything to do with mistakes like this?"

"I'm afraid you'd have to take it up with them, Mr Moorcroft," said the Admissions Officer. "Not my department. I've already explained to you that there hasn't been a mistake. Now, I really must be getting along, I need to catch that typhoon before it blows itself out."

He rose once more and pointed towards the door.

And, without actually moving, Mich found himself back in the corridor.

Uncertain of what to do next he opened the Information Folder.

"You're late!" it yelped.

"Is that all you can say?" snapped Mich. "Late for what?"

"Time," said the folder. "It's your first lesson."

CHAPTER 9

November 2000: German tourist Hermann Roag fell from his eighth-floor hotel window in Lausanne, Switzerland. He survived with only a broken ankle. Roag died when he fell from the ambulance taking him to hospital and was run over by a bus.

Guardian, 23 November 2000

With the increasingly short-tempered help of his Information Folder, Mich found his way back to the main school hall (thankfully there was no repetition of the Thing in the Corridor this time) and on to the first lesson of the day for which, because of his interview with the Admissions Officer, he was late.

He pushed open the door of the class and walked in.

Like everything in the school, the room was enormous. It was a semi-circular lecture theatre, with steep rows of desks stretching upwards from a central platform. There must have been close to a couple of thousand students.

Near the front sat rows of attentive kids, scribbling furiously in neat white notepads. As Mich looked further back he saw kids asleep, watching TV on hand-held monitors, even one or two cooking over small campfires. Clouds of white smoke drifted around at the top of the lecture theatre. It was too dark to see what was going on right at the back of the class, but if it was anything like his old school, Mich knew it'd be full of all the rejects, bullies, punks, freaks and the plain loons. Back amongst the living Mich would have parked himself right in the middle of those guys in an eye-blink and felt right at home. Here, in this place, Mich wasn't so sure.

At the front of the room, standing on a desk, was Mich's teacher. He was very small, maybe a metre high, and dressed in a soft black rubber suit, a bit like a diver's wetsuit. Mich wondered why and could think of no ready explanation. A sign on the desk read *Mr Morphail*. Behind the dais, a huge old-fashioned grandfather clock stood, softly ticking.

The professor looked at Mich and he wondered if he'd be on the receiving end of a tongue-lashing from the little man. It wasn't his fault he was late. He had just been in a car wreck, for cryin' out loud. And he was *dead*, in case anyone was forgetting. He wasn't going to apologize to anyone.

"Sorry I'm late," said Mich, inwardly cursing himself for his spinelessness.

"Late?" said Mr Morphail. He had a reverberating deep bass voice, like a bear shouting from the bottom of a deep cave.

"On the contrary, you are early, Mr, er. . ." Professor Morphail looked down at a sheet of paper on the lectern in front of him. " . . .Moorcroft. It all depends on how you look at it. For example, while you may technically be 'late' for this lesson, you are clearly very early for my lesson on Tuesday. Please take a seat."

He gestured towards an empty chair near the middle of the class about thirty rows up. Many of the students at the front of the class tutted as he passed and pointedly looked at their watches.

"Yeah," muttered Mich. "Like you don't have all the time in the world."

The steps were steeper than they look from the floor of the room and Mich was slightly out of breath by the time he reached the empty seat. Morphail watched him the whole time, a not-unpleasant smile fixed on his features. On the way up he noticed Dakota sitting over to one side. There were no seats available next to her and Mich made a "what-do-you-make-of-all-this-face" at her. She shrugged and rotated a finger next to her temple. Mich felt the same way; this place was a nuthouse. He nodded back to his sister and found his seat.

Once Mich had taken his place Morphail continued with the lesson.

99

"We were discussing the varied nature of time, Mr Moorcroft," said the miniature teacher. "I was about to explain the difference between 'active time' and 'round time'. Most of the time we operate on 'active' time, except when we are waiting 'round' when we enter 'round' time, with a corresponding expansion of 'inactive' time. When you add in the Fooblebaum Principle of Diminishing Pleasure/Expanding Time you begin to grasp the. . ."

The little professor babbled on and Mich was quickly lost. He tuned out Morphail and took a deep breath. So much had happened to him so quickly that he hadn't really had a moment to sit back and catch up with himself.

He began by facing the most depressing thing about the situation.

He was dead. Extinct. No more. Passed on. Gone to sleep. Kicked the bucket. Bought his last ticket. Call it whatever you like it all still meant the same thing: no more Mich Moorcroft. Not on earth at least.

There was no getting around that, thought Mich, glumly.

The next thing, and it was slightly more encouraging, was that at least now he knew there had been a mix-up. And, although everything was very (very) strange in Purgatory, there was a kind of crazy logic to the place which meant that there might be a chance he could fix this thing. He was *not* the Mich Moorcroft that everyone thought he was. *The problem is,* thought Mich, *how am I going to convince anyone else?* It wasn't going to be easy.

One more thing: were all the lessons going to be soooo boring?

He sat back, deep in thought.

"Why don't you do something to liven up the place?" said a voice in his right ear. "You *are* bored, right?"

Mich looked around to see who had spoken and found himself face to face with a little devil floating above his left shoulder. He was just twenty centimetres tall with a tail and horns and dressed from head to toe in red satin.

"Like the outfit?" he said, noticing Mich looking at him. "Versace ran it up for me himself. I think it takes grams off me." He pirouetted to let Mich get the full effect.

"Who *are* you?" said Mich, his mouth opening and closing like a fish.

"He's trouble. Nothing but trouble," said a second voice close to his left ear. "Don't speak to him, he'll just go away."

Mich whipped around and found another small figure hovering just above his right shoulder. This one was dressed more conventionally in jeans, boots and a camouflage jacket. He wore his hair in a ponytail and a loop of gold glinted when he smiled. A small golden harp dangled carelessly from an extended finger on his right hand and a pair of white wings sprouting from his back gently flapped the air as he hovered.

"You're an . . . an angel," said Mich.

"No kiddin', Einstein," said the angel, before hoisting the harp in a swift fluid motion and cracking it down hard on the head of the little devil.

"Ow!" the devil cried out.

"Hey!" said Mich.

The angel looked at Mich. "Lemme just deal with this sucker and I'll explain everything."

With a face twisted in fury, he hurled himself at the devil, who was reeling in mid-air, hands clutched to his head. The angel managed to get a nasty headbutt in and the devil jabbed a retaliatory fork into the angel's eye, before Mich grabbed both of them and pulled them apart. He held them by the backs of their necks about thirty centimetres away from each other.

Mich looked around but no one else in the class seemed to have noticed anything out of the ordinary.

"Oh, Cranborne, man, you are one sneaky son-of-a—" said the devil, breaking off as the angel threw his halo at him. It skittered harmlessly off his fork and fizzed softly into a cloud of golden sparks. Instantly another halo appeared above the angel's head.

"C'mon, chicken!" yelled the angel, rolling up his sleeves, his face a bright red. "I'll have yer, ya yellow-bellied skunk! Anytime! Let's finish this, right here, right now, *mano a mano*!"

 102

"I'm waitin', altar boy. Bring it on."

The angel's legs thrashed helplessly in the air.

"Hey! Cranborne!" hissed Mich. "Quit it. You'll get me in trouble; more trouble I mean. What's going on?"

"What?" said the angel. "Oh, I get it. You don't think that this is the way for angels to behave, do you? We should be all nice and white and sweet, right? Well up here that's not the way we play it. This is more a gloves off, no messing about, real down and dirty kind of deal we got going. There are millions, billions of those nasty little red suckers we got to deal with. This is Good against Evil man! We're the front line, the ones who—"

"Oh spare us the soapbox speech," said the devil, feigning a yawn. "We've heard it all before. And frankly it is boring the ass offa me."

He looked at Mich.

"I'm a devil. Your devil to be precise. My name's, er, Marion."

He shot a venomous glance in the direction of the angel who had snorted derisively at the word "Marion". The devil looked up at Mich and shrugged.

"It's one of the things we have to put up with here. We get silly names."

Marion glared at Mich, as if expecting a snotty remark. Mich said nothing. He knew all about silly names.

"Well, anyway, I'm Marion, and this psycho is called

Cranborne. Don't ask me why. We are your personal advisors while you're here."

Mich became aware of someone calling his name.

It was Professor Morphail.

"Mr Moorcroft! *Mr Moorcroft!* Perhaps you'd be so kind as to let me have your answer?"

All two thousand students turned in their seats to check out Mich. Even the guys at the back of the class had put down their victims and were waiting to see what happened.

Mich didn't have a clue what Morphail had been talking about. He'd been too busy sorting out the fist fight between Cranborne and Marion.

"And you can put your hands down now, Mr Moorcroft," said Morphail. "One would be more than enough."

With cheeks burning Mich inspected his hands. The two visitations had disappeared, leaving only the faintest traces of golden sparks and red smoke hanging in the air. Mich quickly put down his empty hands and sat on them.

"Thanks for nothing, guys," whispered Mich.

"Well?" said the professor from down below, his voice booming up across the galleries.

"Er," said Mich. "Erm—"

"Yes!" shouted the professor, beaming triumphantly. "At least *one* person has been paying attention! The correct technical name for a pause in time is an

'Equidistant-Repeatable-Millisecond; or, in layman's terms, an 'Erm'!"

Just then, a tremendous, ringing, vibrating sound crashed through the room; a deep, reverberating sound that loosened the fillings in Mich's teeth and shook the chair he'd been sitting on.

The lunch bell.

CHAPTER 10

Inside the Food Hall it was sheer pandemonium. The noise, worse even than the din in the entrance hall that morning, echoed from the clatter of thousands upon thousands of metal trays and plates and knives and forks and spoons.

Mich found the place with some difficulty. Thank God he'd brought his skateboard with him. If he'd walked to the Food Hall he was sure he'd have starved on the way, his bones discovered years later by some afterlife archaeologist, covered in dust in some long-forgotten corridor.

Then Mich remembered that he was already dead and therefore starvation was not high on the list of things to worry about. Depression settled on him once more, like a cloud on a hill. When he'd been alive he had had something of a fondness for feeling miserable – when he had no money for example, or his PlayStation went on the blink, or his mother served up corned beef hash again.

But not now.

No, not now he was actually *dead* and actually here and was never going to do any of the things he'd imagined he'd do when he grew up. A sudden wave of overwhelming self-pity crashed over him and Mich began to calculate all the various experiences he'd never have.

He'd never grow that oft-imagined face furniture for a start, because he was never going to get any older, or at least he assumed that he'd never get older. He'd have to check that one with Patterson, but from what he'd seen already people didn't get any older in Purgatory. When you thought about it, it was pretty obvious. Ageing is a sign of decay. Decay leads to death and as everyone here was by definition already six feet under, then ageing was off the agenda as far as Purgatory was concerned. If he wasn't going to get any older then he'd be stuck with this meagre wisp of bum-fluff for eternity.

107

And tattoos were probably out of the question up here (unless he got sent to Sweetwater Canyons, he thought miserably). Again, he made a mental note to check that one with Patterson.

He'd never visit Europe. Not unless Purgatory High had some kind of spooky school exchange thing going on. When he'd been alive, Mich had harboured a secret desire to go to Europe. Things looked so much more interesting over there. Maybe, Mich thought, now he was dead Europe had come to him, if what he'd seen from the school bus window had been anything to go by. Mich was sure he'd caught a fleeting glimpse of the Eiffel Tower and spotted some street signs in German on the way to school but he couldn't be certain; they'd been travelling so fast it was only at intersections and bends he'd had a chance to see anything.

He'd never become a famous Nu-Metal Hero of Rock. This one hurt. Mich didn't actually play a musical instrument, but he knew he would have done if he'd been alive. He'd had his eye on a jet-black guitar in the window of DuPont Music down at Communion Mall. He would've taken some lessons, or maybe just picked it up by himself, how hard could it be? Touring the world by seventeen, a superstar by eighteen. He'd figured that three or four years at the top would be enough, before he started getting too old for music, say twenty-three or four. Mich already had the name of his band: Rancid Green. He had

 108

all the details worked out including an imaginary playlist and a complete list of backstage demands: red jelly beans, yellow M&M's, chilli dogs, groovy chicks (of course), a skate park, some cool arcade games and things like that. It wasn't going to happen. The world would just have to survive without the musical legacy of Rancid Green.

Then there was the colossal disaster regarding Veronica Whitelake. He'd never get to ask her out on a date now.

Another, more shocking thought occurred to him: he'd never have *sex*! Not that Mich knew if he'd really like sex, or anything, it was just that, you know, sex was something that happened to you as you got older and now it wasn't. Going to happen to him, that is. Because he wasn't going to get older. Ever.

Unless . . . unless he managed, "by some miracle" the Admissions Officer had said, to find this Mitchell Freestone Moorcroft, the guy who *should* be here, and get all this sorted out. Despite his feeling of elation at the discovery that there had been a mistake, Mich couldn't see how he was going to do anything about the situation. Purgatory was confusing enough without having to deal with all this as well.

Mich sighed. Death *sucked*.

He looked around the hall.

Thousands of kids sat wolfing their lunches on long rows of formica-topped tables. For some reason the fact that there was formica in Purgatory struck Mich as faintly ludicrous. Was there a formica supplier in town? A formica mine maybe, where crews of dead, down-trodden formica miners carved out raw formica from the soil?

"Pull yourself together, man," he said to himself. "You're losin' it."

He needed a friendly face. He needed information. He needed to find Patterson.

Patterson sat down in front of him.

"How did you find me?" Mich asked, startled, as she settled into the seat opposite. "There must be twenty thousand kids here."

Patterson opened up a lunchbox with a picture of a cartoon dog on the side. "I dunno," she said. "It just happens like that round here. You don't really think about it, but somehow it all hangs together."

She bit into a peanut butter sandwich.

"So, how did it go?" she said, through a mouthful of bread. "Your first day and all."

Mich told Patterson about his morning. He told her about the other Mich Moorcroft out there, the Evil Mich Moorcroft enjoying life to the full, while he, Totally Innocent Mich, was stuck in Purgatory.

"Bummer," said Patterson, stifling a yawn.

"Aren't you surprised?" Mich was outraged. "They got the

 110

wrong guy! I should still be walking around out there, smelling the flowers and, and, and . . . er, watching sunrises and stuff!"

"You watched a lot of those, did you, when you were alive?" said Patterson.

"Thought not," she continued, seeing Mich's face. "Couldn't see you as the flowers and sunrise type, somehow. Listen, Mich, don't get me wrong but almost everyone in here has a sob story: 'It wasn't my time, there's been a mix-up, I'm a twin and he's the one who was sick, not me, not me!' Blah blah blah."

"But there *has* been a mix-up!" exclaimed Mich. "I *shouldn't* be here!"

He looked at Patterson hard and leaned in closer.

"And what's more, you're going to help me get out of here and sort this mess out."

"Excuse me?" said Patterson, coughing out a sizeable chunk of part-digested peanut butter sandwich on to the formica. "The acoustics in here must be worse than I thought; for a moment there I thought you said you were going to get out of here and I was going to help you."

Mich moved closer, propped his chin on his hands and spoke in an urgent whisper.

"I'm not talking about escape! I'm talking about putting something right . . . or something, I don't know! That's exactly the point; *I don't know*. I need someone who knows their way around this place. You've been here long enough to know the ropes, Patterson. You know the system. You can help me."

He sat back and eyed Patterson slyly.

"Who knows? Helping me may help you get moved upstairs more quickly; kind deeds and all that. You've been waiting thirty years, maybe there's a reason for that, maybe you need to take some like, positive action . . . maybe all those forms you're putting in down at The Ministry are never gonna work. You don't want to end up like Grunt, do you?"

Mich knew he'd scored a hit with that last suggestion when Patterson started talking animatedly to the empty spaces above her own shoulders.

"You have them as well!" said Mich.

"Of course I have them," said Patterson. "Everyone does. Now clear off!" Patterson glanced at Mich. "Not you, them. You learn to live with them after a while," she added.

"And you only see your own?"

"That's right. They're yours, personal as underwear."

"Do yours argue all the time? Mine do."

"You have to get them trained up. Get them to sort out their differences, so they can give you good advice. It'll happen. And you'll learn how to control when and where they pop up. It can be quite embarrassing before you manage that."

She looked at Mich.

"But all this is besides the point. You can butter me up all you like about getting out and all that, but the fact is that *you* don't know what happens to people who try and rock the boat."

"No," said Mich. "I don't know, but I'm going to try anyway, whether you help or not. Don't you see? I'm not supposed to be here! And someone else, someone who's a whole lot worse than me, is walking around quite happily back down there amongst the living. It's just not right! And what about Alaska? If I don't get back there what will happen to him?"

Patterson looked at him thoughtfully. He was talking complete drivel about the mix-up, of course. Every new Bonesider went through the same routine when they arrived here and Patterson had been dead long enough to know that being here was never a mistake; there *are* no mistakes in death, that was the awful, final bottom line. But he had struck home with that Grunt gag. She considered the prospect of several millennia getting the bus to Purgatory High and shivered. It couldn't be considered. Thirty years was almost too much to have endured and besides, what had she to lose by helping Mich? She liked talking to the awkward new kid. He *was* kind of cute in a scuffed-up, mumbling way, and he *had* only just crossed over. Patterson had an insatiable curiosity about the world she had left behind. Mich could help her with that.

Across the table Mich held his hands up and imitated a puppy begging for a treat.

"Please?" he said. "Pretty please with sugar sprinkles and a cherry on top?"

Patterson laughed and shooed him away.

"Things can get a whole lot worse than this, Mich," she said, waving her apple around to include the entire school. "Trust me. But what the hell, let's give it a shot. I'm bored stiff of this place: maybe it's time for a change."

Before lunch was over they arranged to meet after school and make plans.

"See you later," Patterson said as she turned and began to walk away. Mich wanted to say something to her, something snappy and memorable that would make her instantly worship him for ever. He thought furiously and opened his mouth.

"Uh . . . OK," he said. He dropped his head to the table and let out a long low groan.

Idiot.

CHAPTER 11

A twenty-five-year-old Mexican man died when he was hit by a woman's leg as she was travelling on the "Top Gun" roller coaster at the Paramount Great America Theme Park in September 1998. He had jumped into a restricted area to retrieve a hat. Police identified him as Hector Mendoza, only to discover the real Hector Mendoza alive and well in Mexico. The dead man had taken over Mendoza's identity and was never identified himself.

Associated Press, 7 September 1998

The rest of the day passed quickly enough.

There were lessons in Astral Projection. In Astral Projection, or AP 101, Mich learned how to move from place to place on something called the Astral Plane, which, it was explained, was a way of whizzing all over the place without actually physically moving at all. The teacher talked about neural connectors and cranial nervosa, the system of internal cosmic highways down which Astral Projectors could move, and all about how AP could only connect you with people and places that have some emotional link.

Mich didn't really understand much of what he was told but he found, after several abortive attempts when he just sat at the desk feeling stupid, that to his surprise (because normally he didn't believe in all that sort of garbage) he was pretty good at Astral Projection.

During his first "voyage" he found himself looking down at his mother at work. On a busy intersection somewhere in the city, she was wrestling a huge bull of a man to the floor with a group of other Controllers. After subduing the prisoner, Mrs Moorcroft stood him up and briskly cuffed his hands behind his back. "Book 'im," she snarled, passing the captive over to another cop, before adjusting her belt and giving the cop standing next to her a high five. The cop was the one who'd whisked Mrs Moorcroft away that morning and he had to jump in the air a little to reach Mrs Moorcroft's outstretched palm.

She looked like she'd been in the job for a couple of years, never mind a couple of hours, thought Mich. He gratefully returned to the classroom, a little unsettled by what he had seen.

Other lessons included Metaphysical Education (like Physical Education except you just thought about doing it),

Seance Etiquette ("It simply does not do to pretend to be a Breather's long lost second cousin just to liven up a dull Wednesday. . .") and Algebra.

Mich was astounded that Algebra was on the curriculum. Surely there was no need for this sort of cruel and unusual punishment? *I mean*, he thought, *it's not as if we're already in Hell, is it?*

When the school bell tolled to signal the end of his first day at Purgatory High, Mich felt as though he'd been there for months. He had enjoyed parts of it too, even meeting the Admissions Officer; pleased that he'd handled meeting the Grim Reaper (not to mention his weird Aztec buddy) without dissolving into a puddle of naked fear. Wouldn't do to get too complacent though. He *had* had a supremely creepy moment or two in that Admissions Office corridor. He shuddered as he remembered the sensation of something brushing past him, and the way the hair on the back of his neck had bristled as if warning him of something dark and horrible.

With a shock of recognition he realized that he *wasn't* remembering that feeling, he was experiencing it, fresh and new, right now. An icy vibration ran like liquid nitrogen down the centre of his spine and brought goosebumps out along his arms. The hairs on his neck tingled and he gave an involuntary gasp.

Mich whirled around and scanned the school. Around him

the throng of dead children streamed past, heading for the vast fleets of schoolbuses lined up in the parking lot. He couldn't pick up anything unusual from the crowd but he *knew*, just knew, for the second time that day that something was watching. Something was waiting.

He picked up his pace and arrived at the gate a little flustered. Patterson was there, leaning against a wall and chewing gum.

"What's up?" she said catching sight of Mich's face. "You look like you've seen a ghost. Apart from me, I mean." She laughed and suddenly looked so attractive that Mich just nodded blankly and made a kind of barking sound in his throat.

"Aaark!" he said. It sounded like a young sea lion was wedged in there. "Let's find our bus," he eventually managed to croak. "Do you know where it is?"

Patterson didn't seem to notice Mich's seal impression and explained that they could get on any bus, it would still end up taking them home.

"Don't ask me how it works," she said, once they were seated. "It just does. There's a lot of things around here that work that way. Pretty much everything works like that."

She had a way of gazing directly at him that Mich was beginning to find very unsettling. Back in Communion, back amongst the Breathers, most of the girls Mich knew were dumb as fence posts, in his opinion. This opinion had a great deal to do with the fact that not many of them had time for Mich or any of his skanky skate friends. They wore clean, fresh clothes and all wanted to be Britney Spears and say "whatever" a lot. But Patterson was different. She was more like a guy.

Except for being pretty. . .

This time, the bus was driven by an elderly man wearing a hospital smock. As they drove through Purgatory Mich noticed plenty of similarly clad people. Patterson explained that for some unknown reason most people in Purgatory wore what they died in.

"Jeez," said Mich.

"Don't be too sorry for those guys," said Patterson, and pointed out of the window. "It could be worse."

A group of pedestrians were waiting to cross a busy road. Traffic was at a standstill so Mich had plenty of time to see that three of the people were completely naked. They didn't seem embarrassed by it at all.

"They're used to it," said Patterson. "But can you imagine anything more cringe-making than having to walk around naked every day for maybe thousands of years?"

She sat back and crossed her purple polyester bell bottoms over her brown platform shoes.

"Oh, I don't know," said Mich slyly, once he'd recovered from hearing Patterson say the word "naked" out loud. "I could think of one or two things."

He looked at her bell bottoms.

Patterson lobbed her bag at Mich's head.

"You pig, Moorcroft!" she yelled. "I'll have you know I was one of the best-dressed kids at Little Neck High."

"In 1972, yeah!" said Mich and the two of them dissolved into laughter at the back of the bus. After a few minutes they fell silent until Mich asked a question that had been nagging at him since he'd met Patterson that morning.

"Where do you live?" he said quietly. "I mean, most of my family got wiped out in the crash. But what about you? I mean, you don't have to tell me if you don't want to."

Patterson smiled.

"It's OK, Mich. I'll show you."

CHAPTER 12

Lisbon, Portugal, November 1998: While demonstrating to his class the easiest way to keep your head in the correct high position for the tango (by keeping his eyes fixed on the ceiling), Alberto Fango danced straight out of his fifth-floor studio and fell to his death.

Sunday Independent (Dublin), 15 November 1998

He supposed it wasn't too bad. He'd been half-expecting the kind of place you'd see Scooby Doo and Shaggy getting chased by evil swamp monsters or loopy janitors. He sat in the pink string hammock which stretched between two fibreglass palm trees and watched as Patterson stashed her books somewhere in a large gunmetal-grey office cabinet almost covered in plastic toy figures. Mich had inspected it when they arrived and saw that Patterson (at least he imagined it was Patterson, it had her character stamped all over it) had glued them on feet first so

121

that they jutted outwards at odd angles: plastic wrestlers, dinosaurs, soldiers, dolls, action figures of every description. The cabinet now resembled a rectangular piece of plastic coral.

Mich looked around. Every centimetre of wall space in the room was concealed by something; pictures, stickers, feather boas, PVC cushions, a full-size cut-out of a singer Mich didn't recognize (*David Cassidy* said the type at the base of the cut-out), a TV set, its innards scooped out and replaced with a fish tank. There was barely space to move, but the overall effect was cosy, comforting, and Mich relaxed into the hammock as Patterson fussed around an old coffee percolator perched precariously on a gigantic stack of books.

"I'm addicted," she said looking up. "Never drank the stuff Down There, but can't get enough of it now." She hoisted a cup in the air and nodded towards Mich.

"Want some?"

He nodded back, although he hated the taste.

They were in Patterson's room at Paradise Postponed. Once they had stepped off the schoolbus after the now-familiar white-knuckle ride Mich found himself standing in front of three gigantic concrete towers, their tops too high to see, sticking up out of what must have once been a landscaped park. As they walked towards one of the towers Mich saw that the ground nearest to the buildings was littered with crushed

 122

debris: mangled refrigerators, televisions, old boom boxes, electrical products of every description, all smashed, mangled and exploded into their component parts. Some of the wreckage looked like it had been there a long time. Weeds and grass almost covered some of the rusting hulks.

Patterson said nothing but Mich noticed that she kept looking upwards as they neared the door. Over to their right a TV set fell from the sky and crashed with a glassy whoomp into the floor.

It was only after Patterson had dragged Mich through the doorway that she seemed to relax a little. Mich opened his mouth and then closed it again. It seemed rude to ask Patterson about the falling TV.

They crossed a large hallway towards a bank of elevators across what had once been carpet but was now only odd tufted islands standing in a labryinth of puddled water and unidentifiable goop. The soles of Mich's shoes stuck tackily to the floor as they walked to the elevators. Patterson was quiet and neither of them spoke. Above their heads came the soft pounding of music played very loud a long distance away.

Mich hadn't seen a single person since getting off the bus.

Patterson lived on the 326th floor. The elevator was surprisingly clean and efficient and they were at Patterson's door in what seemed like no time. She opened the door with a set of five keys, each key setting off a series of heavy clunks

123

before she pushed the heavy metal back and they stood inside her room. She turned and carefully locked all five bolts before taking off her jacket.

"Take a seat," she said. "I'll get the coffee on."

The towers had once contained a Ministry headquarters, but had long since been given over as housing for the expanding child population in Purgatory. Each floor, Patterson explained, sipping her coffee (black as pitch, three sugars, noticed Mich) was supposed to have a supervisor to help the younger children and keep order amongst the older ones. They did have supervisors still, but the problem was they kept changing, getting pushed into Paradise or to Sweetwater Canyons. The result was complete anarchy.

"There's a backlog in the processing system or something, I guess," said Patterson. "Most of the kids are supposed to go directly to Paradise, I think, but here we all are. Maybe we're too hard to process. I don't know really."

Mich gingerly took a sip of coffee. It tasted foul but he resisted the urge to spit it out. Not cool. Before he could ask any more questions there was a knock on the door.

"Inspection!" yelled a high-pitched voice before bursting into song. "La-la-la-la-la-la-la-laaaaa!"

Patterson groaned.

"Not now, Overta!" she said. "Can't you come back later?"

"I must insist," sang the voice operatically. "My contract clearly states/ As clear as night follows day/ That though formerly one of opera's greats/ My duties for me to discharge this way/ Are there in paragraph three, subsection eight!"

The last words were trailed out in a long vibrating trill of notes that rattled the glasses on Patterson's kitchen counter.

Patterson flicked back the bolts on the door and opened it.

An immensely fat woman stood in the hallway occupying almost all the available space. Her face was plastered with stage make-up and she was dressed for a performance. A blonde wig, plaited into two pigtails, peeked out from under a horned Viking helmet. Her cheeks were heavily rouged and she wore a laced bodice with full sleeves and a flowing skirt. In her left hand she carried a trident.

"O Rainbow," she sang, one hand pressed against her gigantic bosom. "O Rai-ai-ai-ai-nbow/ What treachery is this?/ A stranger in your room behind my back?/ You know the score/ Now skedaddle, Jack!"

She pointed dramatically at Mich and rolled her eyes towards the ceiling.

"This is Overta Von Shtempling," said Patterson. "She used to be an opera singer. . ."

"Simply the best!" screeched Overta. "Better than all the rest!"

Mich felt she'd stepped a little off track, musically speaking.

125

"Does she always do this?" he said. "Sing, I mean?"

Patterson nodded. She stepped back as Overta lumbered into the room and peered down the slope of her bodice at Mich who was backed up against one of Patterson's palm trees.

Overta seemed to fill the room. She shook her trident angrily and it caught on one of the feather boas that hung from the ceiling.

"She died during a performance," whispered Patterson. "After getting booed. I don't think she ever got over it."

"Perfidious oafs!" yodelled Overta, stretching out the last word to a good twenty-eight seconds.

"Those fools wouldn't know/ A talent like mine/ If it came right up and bit 'em in the ass!"

She flashed her black-ringed eyes at Mich as if daring him to argue.

"I was the best Brunhilde ever seen/ I'll bet/ At La Scala or the Met/ How was I to know/ That jealous witch/ Had spiked my drink to itch my throat so I'd get ditched?"

She didn't seem to require any answer. She drew another gigantic breath that quivered her nostrils like a thoroughbred horse and began singing again.

"You'd better go," shouted Patterson over the din. "When she's like this she can go on for hours. Last year I had to sit through the entire performance of *The Barber of Seville* before she'd leave." She shuddered at the memory. "I'm still

 126

getting flashbacks about it. I'll catch up with you at school."

Mich shrugged. The noise from Overta was making it hard to think straight.

"How do I get home from here?" he roared.

"Just jump on a bus," Patterson screamed. "And watch out for people dropping stuff when you leave the building. They do that whenever they need a bit more space, the little darlings."

Overta was still wailing about being stabbed in the back by her understudy at the opera house and Mich was getting a stabbing pain all of his own. He grabbed his board and waved to Patterson.

"Thanks for the coffee!"

"Out, out! / You damnable scoundrel!" trilled Overta waving her trident.

She lunged at Mich and he jumped towards the door. He caught a glimpse of Patterson laughing and waving before Overta slammed the door shut behind him.

CHAPTER 13

Terrence Adams, 55, of Brooklyn, USA, was killed by his own sweater as he burgled a Brooklyn shop named the Dum Dum Boutique, in April 1999. The sweater caught on a piece of metal as he broke in and he was strangled.

Reuters, 12 April 1999

The winged messenger rounded the corner of The Ministry of Lost Souls: Incoming Department 3 (Western Reaches) at an approximate speed of two thousand miles per hour and a height of eight centimetres above the floor. Paper scraps and balls of dust whirlwinded behind her as she passed. A clinging, black, specially designed neoprene suit and mask were protection from the worst of the G-forces which would otherwise have torn her apart. As she approached Mr Moorcroft's desk she flipped a switch on her workbelt and decelerated expertly in an instant. She floated easily a few centimetres above the ground, her head bobbing from side to side as she listened to something on her headphones. The visor on her mask slid upwards with a softly efficient electric hum.

"SIGN HERE!" she said, thrusting a clipboard at Mr Moorcroft and tipping a ten-centimetre stack of Ministry memos on to his desk. She hadn't turned the music down and her voice was unnaturally loud.

Mr Moorcroft signed and handed the clipboard back.

"THANKS! HAVE A NICE DAY!"

She nodded to Mr Moorcroft, popped a gum bubble and zipped soundlessly away, the visor sliding back into place as she picked up speed, her movements fluid and practised with a nonchalance that came from long days spent delivering paper from department to department inside the labryinthine Ministry. The WMs (Winged Messengers) recruited mainly from recently deceased sports stars and athletes, were a familiar sight around the building, but Mr Moorcroft watched her go, a wistful expression on his face. He wished he was a WM. It looked fantastic. It looked like fun.

The messengers were needed at The Ministry. It was a fantastically large place; so large that had the paperwork been delivered by walking staff it would have taken weeks for a simple memo to travel between, say, the Department of the Waking Dead (Monitoring) over in the new part of the building, and the Department of Religious Intolerance Section buried deep in the bowels of the original Ministry building on floor minus 544. So there was a constant stream of WMs, travelling on specially-designed ankle-clip "angel" wings. Constructed of micro-fibre titanium-strengthened polymer wings and powered by powerful nano-drive turbo-particle-stream motors which utilized top-secret military individual personnel flight devices, the wings had been developed by a military scientist blown into oblivion (and hence to Purgatory) when a propane gas cylinder ignited during an M.I.T. reunion barbecue ten years previously.

Mr Moorcroft turned back to the stack of memos and sighed deeply. He wondered why, if the Powers That Be could rig up something like the angel wings, they couldn't just devise an easier way of getting messages around. He guessed that the messengers, like the creaking air-conditioning which needed constant maintenance, the old-fashioned steam-powered ducting which routed bigger parcels around The Ministry and the super-abundance of paper, were all designed for one reason: to give people something to do.

Look at the Cube, for example.

The Cube hung in mid-air above Mr Moorcroft's desk. It gave off a soft, somewhat granular white light and held all the information that the paper ledgers held. There was no reason why the ledgers had to be kept at all; everything was safely stored on the billion-gigabyte hard drive on the Cubes.

But the ledgers *were* kept, religiously.

A stub of pencil bounced cleanly off the top of his head and landed neatly on the desk in front of him. Mr Moorcroft picked it up and it joined the other pencil stubs, rolled-up balls of paper, large paper clips and an off-white piece of dried chewing gum arranged in a neat line to one side of Mr Moorcroft's workspace.

"Nice shootin', Rocco!"

"Four and zip to me!"

Mr Moorcroft waited until the laughter died before turning and smiling through gritted teeth at Vincenzi and Brown, the self-designated office jokers leaning on a desk over to his right and currently giving each other high fives.

"OK guys," said Mr Moorcroft. "F-f-funtime's over!"

There was a second's pause and Vincenzi, and Brown doubled up with laughter once more.

"N-n-n-no problem, M-M-M-Mike!" snorted Vincenzi, his eyes fluttering as he made a "funny" face.

Mr Moorcroft carefully took out an imaginary baseball bat, hefted it until it sat comfortably in his hands and beat both of them to a highly satisfying imaginary bloody pulp before waving weakly and returning to his work.

"Work".

That was a laugh. The truth was that Mr Moorcroft almost

welcomed the odd pencil stub coming his way from the two morons. At least it broke the monotony. The huge ledger lay on the desk in front of him, the list of names, dates and personal information blurring in front of his eyes. It was all kind of depressing when you came right down to it. So many dead people. All those names; dead people like him. Or, to be more precise, people who were about to be dead.

Mr Moorcroft worked in the Incoming Department (Western Office) and his job was to double-check the list of Soontas (as in "Soon To Be Deceaseds") against the daily quota set by The Organization. The daily quota varied from day to day but was always close to the half million mark.

The Office Manager, Ms Sluman, a jumped-up little squit of a woman with bad breath and hair that appeared to be made of wire wool, had explained it all to him on day one. Mr Moorcroft hadn't followed all of the details, chiefly because Ms Sluman's head was on back to front which proved extremely disconcerting. When she spoke her body faced away from Mr Moorcroft, giving him the impression she was talking to him over her shoulder as she walked away. Someone in the Ministry canteen told Mr Moorcroft that Sluman was a mistake, that Breathers were supposed to revert back to their normal body shape on death, but, now and again, and with shocking results, this sometimes didn't work.

"Gets kinda messy when there's been a bad road smash,"

132

Peggy Fourmile, the co-worker who'd told him the Sluman neck story, had said.

"Oops," she had added remembering Mr Moorcroft's own death. "Sorry."

Mr Moorcroft hadn't responded. He wasn't sensitive about the crash. He didn't remember a great deal about it, to be honest, and, unlike Ms Sluman, he didn't have a scratch on him. He did worry constantly about Alaska and felt he should be doing something to help. But for the life of him he couldn't see what he could do.

Sluman didn't let her 180-degree neck-twist worry her, although Mr Moorcroft wondered if perhaps at least some of her foul temper couldn't be put down to spending eternity with her head on backwards.

There were about fifty people working in Mr Moorcroft's section and, apart from the head-on-backwards thing, most of them were identikit versions of people that Mr Moorcroft worked with back in Communion. Same business suits and ties, same office jerks, same stale coffee and jokes. He had been excited when he arrived for work at The Ministry and his first impressions had done nothing to alter that. The size of the building, the ancient stone walls and mysterious corridors, the winged messengers. Everything fresh and new and not like home. But the feeling evaporated as quickly as bubbles in champagne, and now, only a few short days into the job,

133

something unfamiliar was stirring deep in the belly of Mr Moorcroft, something he hadn't felt for a very long time: rebellion.

CHAPTER 14

An eighty-nine-year-old Welsh man, Dennis Verity, died from daffodil poisoning when he fried and ate some daffodil bulbs, mistaking them for onions.

Wales Echo, 29 June 1999

Drops of water fell to the floor as the smaller of the two gates to Communion Cemetery swung open. Mitchell Freestone Moorcroft, hunched into a thick parka, closed the gate behind him and trod hurriedly across the soft turf. He coughed, stopped, then coughed again, this time long and hard. He'd been coming down with a cold since Loiusiana. He ached for a cigarette but he was all out.

Rain bounced down around him with the force of bullets. The cemetery was usually quiet, but at this early hour, in the time between waking and sleeping, it was utterly deserted.

135

The only sound was the soft drumming as rain fell against the chimney and roof of the unlit crematorium. The building, silhouetted against the distant sodium lights of Communion Chemicals, gave Moorcroft the creeps. He hated graveyards.

Communion had once been a busier town than it was now, and there were many hundreds, maybe thousands, of stones and memorials. They lay in precise ranks as far as the eye could see. Even small towns produced plenty of grave-stones if you waited long enough. The stones nearest to the crematorium were the oldest, going back some sixty years. Massive black granite angels impassively guarded the tombs of the richest; plainer stones for most. Here and there white marble cherubs, signalling the graves of children, wept as the water streamed down.

Moorcroft knew what he was looking for and was in a hurry to get this over with. He'd read in the newspaper that some-one had survived the wreck, but he didn't believe in leaving anything to chance. He wanted to see for himself; to know that there was a need for him to get involved. Five graves would tell him for sure that he could just move on, all witnesses silenced. Four, and he might have a problem.

To the east of the crematorium splashes of colour shone through the grey-blue half-light. Fresh flowers – roses, carnations, lilies – signposted new graves.

 136

As Moorcroft approached the eastern end of the cemetery he cursed. Even from a distance he could see just four graves almost covered in fresh flowers.

From the relative shelter of a nearby tree, a solitary magpie shrike watched as Moorcroft squatted to read the names, wiping the water from the inscriptions. He straightened and walked along the graves bending to each one carefully, his lips moving a little as he read.

"Michigan Freebird Moorcroft RIP" said the fourth stone, and then below: "April 10th 1988–December 23rd 2002. Dearly beloved son of Michael and Urma, brother of Alaska and Dakota, now sadly passed from this vale of tears. God rest his immortal soul." The other stones contained similiar messages, none of which made pleasant reading for the visitor. Seeing a name so near to his own on the stone gave Moorcroft the shivers, and he pulled his coat closer.

Moorcroft rummaged in his pocket and produced a folded newspaper. He looked at the story and read it again, checking the details, even though he'd known what he needed to do as soon as he'd seen the four graves. He looked down and counted them one more time before hurling the sodden news-paper to the floor. The paper caught in a swirl of water running along a cemetery path, the words of the headline fading as the water soaked in: "Family of 4 Perish, 1 Child in Coma After Interstate Car Horror".

The shrike watched as Moorcroft howled, loud and long, stamped on the graves and danced a dance of anger and hate; a crazy, looping jig of undiluted evil.

CHAPTER 15

July 1999: Frank Gambalie III, 28, parachuted illegally from the top of El Capitan, a large rock in Yosemite National Park and survived the difficult leap. In an effort to avoid park rangers, Gambalie dived into a river and drowned.

Associated Press, 16 July 1999

Time passed. Death went on as usual.

"Just look at this, pumpkin," said Mr Moorcroft, pointing at something in the newspaper he was reading. The paper was *The Purgatory Record*, and Mr Moorcroft spent most evenings reading it from cover headline ("Ministry Ups Quota Levels") to the sports pages at the back ("McIntyre Inks New Deal For Anaheim Angels"). It was the jobs pages that were occupying Mr Moorcroft right now.

Only Dakota and Mr Moorcroft were in the room. Mrs

Moorcroft worked long hours on patrol with her new job, and with Mich frequently sequestered in his room with Patterson, Mr Moorcroft and Dakota found themselves alone together more often than either of them would have liked.

Dakota was finding death in Purgatory difficult, and she had spent most nights since the crash painting her nails, doing half-hearted aerobics and looking after her hair, or otherwise avoiding thinking. She had half-convinced herself that this was all some sort of nightmare and she wanted to look her best when she woke up. In her heart of hearts she knew that they really had been in a car wreck, it was just that Dakota thought it might turn out that Alaska was the one who was dead and the rest of them were in a coma from which they would wake up peacefully (and very much alive) in a clean white antiseptic hospital with all limbs and faculties intact, and preferably in the care of a good-looking young doctor.

Another thing which was proving to be a major source of irritation to Dakota was the quite remarkable shortage of good-looking guys at Purgatory High. To say that most of the boys in her classes did not achieve the required standard was putting it mildly, in Dakota's expert opinion. They were, she thought, as complete a set of gargoyles you would find outside Notre Dame Cathedral, even allowing for the fact that they were dead. It wasn't simply what they looked like, it was what they wore. The freakiest clothes, no sense of style at all, or

 140

worse, no clothes at all, just a few scraps of fur. Dakota strongly objected to fur, except on animals. She'd had a run-in with one guy in her Time class who'd been positively *swathed* in all kinds of rare and endangered-looking animal skins; when she tried to lecture him about the correct attitude towards animals he'd just grunted, and *pulled her hair*, would you believe? It was becoming obvious to Dakota Moorcroft that some people here obviously didn't bathe at all. It was all so completely depressing, not to mention unhygienic.

Dakota sighed heavily and headed upstairs for a shower.

Mr Moorcroft shuffled his newspaper and craned his neck forward to read an advert asking for experienced wraith-handlers to apply for positions with Purgatory Pest Control. Dakota, fresh from her quickly taken shower (she had developed a morbid fear of her "angel/devil" apparitions turning up unannounced and copping a free eyeful; she could now shower and dress in under forty-eight seconds), regarded her father as though he'd recently crawled out from under a rock. She shook her head pityingly. Pathetic. Were all men as clueless as her father and brothers, she wondered?

She turned back to the TV where an ad for Sweetwater Canyons was playing.

"Call us now on 1-800 666 2003 to make an appointment with your personal Sweetwater counsellor today!"

As the ad faded into one for a brand of afterlife toothpaste ("Just because you're dead doesn't mean you shouldn't keep those teeth shiny white!") Dakota picked up a pen and jotted the Sweetwater number down. You never knew when it might come in handy.

Satisfied that Dakota wasn't paying attention Mr Moorcroft also picked up a pen and turned back to his task. It was time for action, time to take some decisive steps in making a new death for himself. His motive, apart from the fact that he didn't like his job at The Ministry was his bafflement at why, of all the Moorcrofts, *he* was still in Purgatory. He didn't wish any ill for any of his family, but once he had discovered they were all dead (well, apart from poor Alaska, of course) he *had* thought that with his track record he'd be going directly to eternal Paradise, no questions asked, none of this pointless waiting around nonsense.

Mr Moorcroft had had plenty of time during the last few days to think about his life and wonder where he'd gone wrong. Apart from one or two youthful indiscretions (and who didn't have those?) he felt that, on balance, all things considered, he'd led a pretty blameless, if mainly tedious, sort of existence. On the other hand maybe they just *observed* pretty much everyone up here, with only saints and Mother Theresa and Billy Graham going straight through in the express lane? That must be it.

 142

Mr Moorcroft worried about Alaska, too; but, like Urma and the rest of the family, he wasn't sure which result would be better for Alaska. If he survived the crash, he'd be on his own and would have to go to Gamma's to live.

Mr Moorcroft shuddered at the thought. Three days at Christmas was more than any human being could stand at his wife's parents. Still, life was life, he supposed. As soon as Mrs Moorcroft had discovered what Mr Moorcroft's job was she had pestered him to do something on behalf of Alaska. He'd tried to find out more at work, but with little success. Alaska's death date was marked as "pending" and nothing Mr Moorcroft tried on his Cube got him any further than that. Maybe Urma would have more luck with her contacts among the leprechauns and Easter Bunnies down at the Controller HQ.

Mr Moorcroft hadn't talked all that much about his new job at home. Because there wasn't really that much to say, he thought sourly.

He hadn't told anyone this (and he found it difficult even to admit to himself) but part of him was *glad* he'd died. At least now there might be some colour, some adventure in his life. Or death, to be strictly accurate.

All the early days (amazingly, it was still less than a week) *had* been an adventure. Meeting God and Baz and all that had been truly unbelievable. Elvis! Mr Moorcroft was a big fan of

Elvis. He'd plucked up the courage to stop him one morning and ended up having a long chat about why the King was still down here in Purgatory. Elvis had winked lazily and told him, "there's more'n a few chickens still loose in the henhouse, if y'all know what I mean." Mr Moorcroft hadn't known, not exactly, but he nodded, thrilled to be talking to the King of Rock 'n' Roll over the trash. Meeting Elvis had impressed him a little more than meeting God, if he was honest with himself. Maybe that was one of the reasons he was still in Purgatory; he wasn't showing enough respect to the little old lady?

Mr Moorcroft shook his head and tried to concentrate. No use letting himself be distracted by the likes of Elvis and the rest of that kind of glitz, if he wanted things to change he'd have to take some real decisive man-type action. In this respect, it has to be said, Mr Moorcroft didn't have a good track record. He had never been able to do it (take decisive man-type action that is) in the living world, never been able to make the leap from accountancy to being a lion-tamer or lumberjack or one of those guys called Red, or Slim, who capped out-of-control fires on oil rigs, no matter how much he ached to. It had all seemed too difficult somehow; life was safer, easier behind the desk at Gimlet & Hawke. But being dead had had a strangely liberating effect on Mr Moorcroft, and for the first time ever he felt that maybe he might, just might, be able to do something about his circumstances. He bent back over the employment ads with fire in his belly and change in his heart.

Up in his bedroom, Mich sat on the floor with Patterson in front of the TV and munched steadily on a bag of Doritos they'd liberated from the kitchen. Since the first visit to Patterson's place they had been spending a lot of time at Mich's. Patterson seemed happier with this arrangement, although Mich was keen to pay a return visit to Paradise Postponed. He was thrilled at the idea of having your own place. Still, if it meant spending more time with Patterson, Mich was prepared to put up with his family indefinitely.

A large pile of paper was spread out in front of them. Mich brushed a wraith away from his face. To Mich the wraiths were more evidence that in Purgatory mistakes *did* happen.

"Lemme just see if we got all this straight," he said. "Purgatory is really big. Like, *really* big, right?"

Patterson nodded. They'd been over all this before.

"And it's like some big old computer, or machine or something that is supposed to sort out where everyone ends up. Except it's too old and mistakes keep happening. Like you, for example."

"White man speak plenty wise medicine," said Patterson flicking a Dorito at Mich's head and stifling a yawn.

Mich ignored her and continued.

"And that little old lady—"

"God."

"Yeah, God. She's in control of all this except that perhaps She's gettin' a little fuzzy around the edges. You know how all those old geezers get."

"I'm not sure you should refer to the Supreme Being as a 'geezer'," said Patterson. "She might not like it."

There was a pause and Mich looked around the room.

"See?" he said. "No thunderbolt. I'm tellin' you. She's taken her eye off the ball, man."

He smiled. "This may be our window of opportunity."

Patterson rolled her eyes.

"This is getting us nowhere," she said. "Why don't you just try those forms they gave you at school?"

Half an hour later the Admissions Office forms lay in an untidy heap around Mich and Patterson as they struggled to make sense of the strange information the documents were asking for.

"It says here: 'Describe the subject you wish to trace'," said Mich. "How'm I gonna do that when I don't even know who it is I'm looking for? I only have the guy's name!"

"There's something at the bottom of that page," said Patterson. "It says: 'Feel The Force'. Now what could that mean?"

"'Feel The Force?' That's from *Star Wars*."

"Star What?"

Mich was about to say something when he remembered that Patterson had died a few years before the first *Star Wars* movie had even been released. He explained how the wise old Obi-Wan Kenobi instructed the trainee knight to trust his instincts and use "The Force" to guide him. He had to admit it sounded pretty thin but Patterson seemed to like it.

"That's it," said Patterson. "Let's try this 'Star Wars' way."

"How do you mean?"

"Just concentrate on what you think this other Mich Moorcroft looks like and maybe, erm, maybe something will happen."

"'Something will happen?' Is that the best you can come up with?"

"You got a better idea, Thomas Edison?" said Patterson.

Mich didn't have a better idea and they *were* really struggling with this set of forms. They seemed to have been devised by a lunatic. Questions kept trailing off into cul-de-sacs of nonsense, random lines of poetry popped up in the middle of a dry piece of legal jargon. There were no numbers on any of the sheets yet they kept saying things like "refer to sheet 66b", or "add figure from column 4, paragraph 6, page 10 to column 23, paragraph 55, page 34" only for Mich to find there was no page 34. Or there'd be a 34 but no column 23. It was incredibly frustrating. Patterson thought that it was deliberate,

147

that the Admissions Officer was setting Mich (and Patterson) a lateral thinking problem, that Mich had to *earn* his right to ask for a review of his case.

Mich felt silly sitting back and closing his eyes, holding the form in front of him, but Patterson insisted.

"That's right, Mich," said Patterson. "Just let it all flow. You know what this guy looks like, you just have to bring it to the front of your brain. Or what's left of it at any rate – *ow!*"

The last bit was because Mich leaned forward and jabbed Patterson in the ribs.

"Shuttup will you!" he said. "Can't you see I'm trying to concentrate?"

Mich had no idea what he was concentrating on. He just felt stupid, sitting there breathing deeply and pretending to be Luke Skywalker. Patterson wasn't helping the atmosphere by noisily munching her way through the last of the Doritos. The crunching loomed louder and louder in Mich's hearing until, quite suddenly, it stopped annoying him and somehow began to help. The rhythm grew steadily lower in tone until, after several minutes, all Mich could hear was a sort of low booming sound repeated over and over. In his head a few details began to appear in the darkness, tantalizingly close, like figures in the fog. The shape of a face, the colour of an eye, the look of a patch of skin. The pieces were there, if Mich could only

 148

assemble them. But they wouldn't come, no matter how much like Luke Skywalker he tried to be.

He opened his eyes and sat up in frustration.

"Nothing!" said Mich. "A few bits, nothing else. This is a dumb idea."

Patterson didn't reply. She was holding the sheet of paper in front of her and looking at it intently, an expression of bewilderment on her face.

"What?" said Mich, rubbing the side of his head. He had a headache the size of Texas. "What is it?"

Patterson held the sheet of paper up and Mich reeled back.

In the centre of the sheet a full colour, three-dimensional image of a man's face had materialized. It was perfect in every detail. Mich could see the individual hairs on the man's whiskery chin, the blemishes and pockmarks in his skin and, most disturbingly of all, the man's eyes seemed to be tracking him around the room from under their lazy, tough-looking lids.

As Patterson moved the sheet, the face altered angles and Mich saw the face from the side, the back. He looked at Patterson.

"It's him," said Mich in a low voice.

"What, the real Mitchell Freestone Moorstone-croft whatsit?"

"No! I mean, yes, I mean, I don't know!"

"Well, what *do* you mean?"

Mich looked at the man's face.

"I mean that I don't know if this is the real Mitchell Moorcroft, but I do know one thing," said Mich, turning to Patterson. "I've seen him before."

He looked once more at the face on the paper and the image of two tattooed hands sprang into his memory, clear and sharp followed by a quick ripple of detail: a lazy wink from a heavy-set man. A checked shirt.

He saw a man driving a red truck.

It was the guy he'd seen driving right through the centre of the Moorcroft car crash.

"Wow," said Patterson after Mich had explained. "But do you think this is him, the real Mich, I mean?" she asked.

"I don't know," said Mich whose headache was now assuming the proportions of the entire continental United States. "Maybe I just came up with a face that I associated with the crash? I *don't know*."

"It's got to mean something," said Patterson. "I don't think that this form would allow you to imagine a face that didn't belong. Think about it; the information that appears on this form could be very important. Maybe only the real guy's face could appear in this space, like some sort of cosmic key was needed."

Mich looked at Patterson doubtfully. It certainly was peculiar that of all the people that could have appeared on the sheet, it

 150

was the face of someone who had come within a gnat's lip of getting creamed themselves.

"Maybe it is the right guy!" said Mich, excited again. "And he was supposed to be the one who was killed, not me! That might have been why he was at the crash, maybe the Admissions Officer got confused because of the coincidence; you know . . . 'Mitchell Moorcroft', 'Michigan Moorcroft'."

"Maybe they did make a mistake, after all," said Patterson. "Everyone makes mistakes, don't they?"

"So what do we do now?"

"We fill in the rest of this stuff," said Patterson waving a hand at the forms. "And then we try and put this right. We'll cross you back!"

Mich looked at her.

"What do you mean, 'cross me back'?"

"I heard rumours about it," said Patterson. She hesitated. This kind of thing wasn't really talked about in Purgatory. No one actually told them not to, it just didn't seem . . . *wise* somehow.

She continued speaking.

"Some of the other kids, the ones who've been here for longer than me, say there's a Gateway, where everyone passes through when they arrive. It's the only point where the two worlds intersect. Now, the rumour is that it's a two-way street: you can cross back through The Gateway."

"Well, that's great!" said Mich.

"Easy boy," said Patterson holding out her hands, palms out. "Not so fast, there are one or two things to consider."

"Like what?"

"Like the fact that in millions of years no one has ever crossed back. Well, maybe one. And He had permission." Patterson halted. "Add the fact that The Gateway is heavily guarde. . . Hey! Are you actually listening to any of this?"

Patterson broke off. Mich was looking past her left shoulder at the TV screen, an expression of pure horror on his face. He lifted a trembling hand and pointed.

Patterson turned to look at the familiar image of Alaska in the hospital bed. A white-clad figure was bent over the motionless child.

"So?" said Patterson. "It's just a nurse, or an orderly, or something."

Mich shook his head violently.

"*Look*," he said.

Patterson squinted more closely at the screen. The orderly seemed to have finished whatever he had been doing and slowly turned to face the camera. He looked straight into the lens, his face close up and expressionless as if he was studying what type it was.

Patterson looked down at the Admissions Office form with

the 3D face on it. The man on the form was the same man looking out at them from the TV screen.

It was the man in the red truck.

CHAPTER 16

Samuel Strickson, 39, of Nebraska died when his feet became entangled in a clothes drier. He had been stamping on the clothes in order to force them into the drier when it accidentally turned on.

Mail on Sunday, 22 August 1999

The only sound in the small, warm, antiseptic room was the tiny electronic bleep from Alaska Moorcroft's heart-rate monitor. His breathing was too shallow for it to make any impact on the noise levels.

There was a small click as the door opened, and Mitchell Freestone Moorcroft padded into the Intensive Care Observation Unit at North Morton Teaching Hospital. His hands were covered in a pair of surgical gloves which served a dual purpose: they prevented him leaving fingerprints and they covered the tell-tale prison tats he wore on either hand,

 154

left-overs from his period up at Joliet.

He wore the uniform of a hospital orderly, which sat easily on his big frame, and he carried a plastic bag containing a length of thick dressing-gown cord. He had found it when he'd stashed the orderly whose uniform he'd stolen in a supply closet on the floor below this. Moorcroft had figured to improvise something when he got here, not being able to risk getting picked up by hospital security carrying an obvious weapon. He hated leaving his gun behind, but it was traceable. The cord would get the job done.

Moorcroft took his time, making sure that he was alone in the room with the unconscious child. He looked at the injured boy, feeling nothing except a growing irritation that, once again, he'd been inconvenienced. Christ, it wasn't his fault that those dumb hicks had been wiped out, he'd only barely touched the old lady's car, a little nudge was all. But to let himself be identified by one of the brats was dumb. He'd even winked at the little freak!

And now the cops were looking for the mysterious third driver. They wanted to speak to him about the crash, he knew, but he couldn't risk them picking up his sheet from the wires and finding out he was long overdue a spell inside, on account of him absconding from the tail-end of an eight-to-fifteen in Georgia State.

Besides, he hated talking to cops just on principle.

Back in his motel room the previous evening, Moorcroft had seen the fat patrolman on the flickering TV news asking for information about the red truck. His red truck. He'd had to dump the truck and lift another, all of which meant more aggravation, more stress. After a restless night, Moorcroft tuned in again to check the details of the crash. "Family Interstate Car Horror: 4 dead, 1 In Coma," the talking head had said before turning cheerily to news of a double homicide. Moorcroft lifted his coffee to toast his bad luck. A survivor, just what he needed.

To make sure, he'd tracked down the graves and seen for himself that the TV had got it right; there was a witness, or at least someone who could be a witness, which was close enough for Moorcroft. Too close. There was a good chance it wasn't the kid he'd winked at, something about the age felt off to Moorcroft, but it *could* be the kid and that was close enough to make it a flyer. The paper put the kid at ten and Moorcroft felt that the kid with the black T-shirt who'd seen him, he seemed older than ten . . . but, but . . . he couldn't be sure. No, there was only one certain way to clean the house. He'd have to do it himself.

Moorcroft winced at his own stupidity in winking at the kid in the car wreck and reminded himself why he was here. He had a job to do. It was the job he'd been born to do, as surely as a gifted athlete was born to run and leap and throw, he was there to wreak havoc. The master of mayhem, that's what he was, answerable to no one, captain of his ship, lord of all he surveyed, the. . .

Moorcroft checked himself and let out a controlled slow breath the way that quack shrink had showed him. He had been in and out of prison therapy so often he could recognize and diagnose for himself the onset of one of his grandiose manic phases. Phases when he knew, he just *knew*, he was invincible. Trouble was, *they* all thought it was a mental abberration, a disease that could be controlled with drugs and treatment. Moorcroft flushed with anger as he recalled the mealy-mouthed psychiatrists and social workers down the years who tried to harness and control the Mighty Power of Moorcroft.

They wanted to turn him into one of those dried-out little *ordinary* people, one of those tiny-minded drones whose idea of a thrill was to leave the lawn for another week.

Goddammit, he had more in common with Superman, or better yet, that bald dude from the X-Men movie. That guy was righteous, immaculate. Moorcroft raised his head and thrust out his chest. He flared his nostrils and breathed deeply. He was a king, an emperor, a god!

With an effort, Moorcroft let himself settle back into the world of the hospital. His breathing slowed and he turned his attention to the boy. As Moorcroft bent nearer the still figure,

157

he couldn't swear it was the boy who'd seen him on the freeway, not with all that freaking tubing spaghetti coming out of his nose and mouth. But he couldn't be sure it *wasn't* the kid, and, after all, what sort of life did the boy have waiting for him even if he did pull out of the coma? His family'd been wiped clean off the face of the earth.

Moorcroft chuckled at the delicious irony of his own narrow escape and the astonishing coincidence of the names.

That had shaken him, he to admit it, when he'd read the names on the tombstones. At the graveside, seeing what was so close to his own name there on the stone, Moorcroft had been childishly thrilled, in the way he'd last remembered feeling on the ghost train at the State Fair at age eight. In prison, he couldn't remember which one, he'd found a book in the library one time which had been full of coincidences, weird tales, alien abduction stories, all that crazy stuff. Moorcroft loved it, particularly the true stories about people who died strange deaths. He remembered a couple he liked; the one about the children's entertainer who was killed by an inflatable elephant which accidentally inflated while he was driving. Or how about the patient who died when a cleaner unplugged his life support machine so she could use the vacuum cleaner? You had to laugh at that, Moorcroft certainly did and it all confirmed his philosophy: Life Sucks.

There was a soft whirring noise from the corner and

Moorcroft turned to see where it was coming from. Up in the corner of the room, the security camera swivelled on its plastic gimbal. The camera! Moorcroft cursed under his breath. He'd almost done it again, through a dumb, greenhorn mistake. Why hadn't he checked the room for cameras?

He steadied himself. Chances were no one was watching. Moorcroft knew from experience that most security cameras were window dressing, making whoever installed them feel better, without actually being safer. Still, he'd have to get that tape and disable the camera before he could deal with the boy. He could wait a few days, thought Moorcroft. It wasn't as if the kid was going anywhere. He made a note of the camera number and walked from the room without a backward glance.

CHAPTER 17

A flying cow weighing approximately 340 kg killed a driver in California. The cow, disorientated during a storm, had wandered on to the road and been hit by a car, flinging it into the air where it collided with the dead man's pick-up, which was travelling in the opposite direction.

Reuters, 26 February 1999

If Mich had been keen to try and find a way out of Purgatory before, it was nothing compared to how he felt now. Seeing the man in Alaska's room simultaneously chilled him to the bone and fired him with an angry energy he hadn't known was in him.

He *had* to get back into the living world, not simply for his own sake, to see if he should still be alive, but to protect his brother. Until he'd seen Moorcroft pacing around Alaska's

160

hospital bed just now Mich hadn't known that he even *liked* the little geek, but he did know one thing: he was not going to stand by and watch the last remaining member of his family get wiped out like a bug on a windshield. He considered telling his family, and then thought better of it. His father wouldn't do a thing and his mother worked for the Controllers. As for Dakota, well. . .

Patterson's doubts had vanished. She knew that it was too much of a coincidence for Mich to visualize the face on the Admissions Office form, and then have that same face turn up in Alaska's hospital room. Something was happening.

"We have to do something," she said, grim and determined.

Mich looked at her. "It's all at The Ministry," he said. "Everything goes through there; you said so yourself. . ."

"Well, mayb—"

"Maybe nothing. It's the only thing we can do. Besides; I've got the keys."

He smiled and nodded towards the hallway.

"Or I know a man who has."

"What are we waiting for?" said Patterson, rising and dragging Mich to his feet.

Creeping into the hallway, Mich ducked his head into the kitchen where his dad stood at the sink, his wrists plunged deep into the suds. The radio was on and Mr Moorcroft was singing tunelessly to an old song.

161

"Please allow me to introduce myself," sang Mr Moorcroft. "I'm a man of wealth and taste."

Mrs Moorcroft was still on duty. She'd been working late since she'd started as a Controller. They would have plenty of time.

In the hallway, Mr Moorcroft's jacket hung on the coat rack, the heavy keys to The Ministry dragging one of the pockets down. Patterson kept an eye on Mr Moorcroft while Mich anxiously lifted the keys, careful not to let them clink.

"You do know that that's highly illegal, and very dangerous, don't you?" said a snappy high-pitched voice. Mich yelped and spun round. It was Cranborne.

"Now?" hissed Mich. "You have to pick *now*, to start with this again? You must have seen that psycho in the hospital: Alaska needs our help."

"What better time for me to speak up than when you are about to do something like this?" said Mich's angel piously, folding his hands over each other and lowering his eyes. "You can't do anything to help your brother anyway. You'll never make it through The Gateway."

Mich gave a snort of anger and made a grab for him but the apparition vanished and his fingers clutched the empty air.

"Never mind him," said Patterson. "The keys!"

Mich slipped the keys into his pocket, hoisted his board on his back and they headed for the door.

 162

The two of them slipped out into the night. In the hallway, Dakota Moorcroft moved from her position in the stair shadows where she had been watching everything. She moved towards the kitchen and then stopped. She hesitated, as if making her mind up about something, before slipping her coat on, opening the front door and stepping into the cool night air.

The Ministry was a lot further than Mich had imagined. They jumped one of the circular buses that made constant return trips from the city to the outlying suburbs. In the few days he had been there, Mich had come to realize that Purgatory must be vast, far bigger than he could begin to comprehend. Patterson had explained that since everyone has a personal Purgatory, the city and its suburbs were almost infinite.

"Think of it like this," she had said. "When you died you found yourself in a place that was pretty similiar to Communion, the place you'd left. It helps make people more comfortable."

"More comfortable with being dead, you mean," muttered Mich who was still having difficulty with the odd idea that he really was not alive.

Patterson ignored him and continued, "So everyone who has died since the beginning of time has gone to their own personal Purgatory. Even allowing for everyone who's passed through the Furry Gates or gone to Sweetwater that's still a whole bunch of dead people. Just think of how many neighbourhoods that means."

It was true; no sooner had Mich been told this than he began to notice that every time he travelled into the city to school, the neighbourhoods had shifted, altered slightly to accommodate new arrivals or recent departures. Just yesterday, Mich had seen Victorian English cobbled streets rubbing up next to Swiss Alpine villages, and fourteenth-century Irish peat-cutting settlements cheek by jowl with upmarket Connecticut clapboard. All in one trip to Purgatory High.

"There are more than twelve billion separate communities, with new ones starting up and old ones fading away as fast as people are landing in Purgatory," said Patterson. "A kid in my Sin and Sinning class told me that he'd heard from another kid that The Organization is running into memory problems with them all. When it was first built they didn't know there'd be so many of us."

It seemed to Mich that the bus must have gone through pretty much all twelve billion districts by the time they pulled up in Red Tape Square, the vast open area flanked by The Ministry for Lost Souls and other Organization buildings. They stepped down from the bus (a flame-red customized fifties-style cruiser) out into the steady beat of the rain which fell straight down from a green-black sky. In front of them was The Ministry, instantly dwarfing the two friends.

Neither of them noticed Dakota stepping down from another bus some four or five hundred metres distant. She slipped into the shadow of a wall and watched. She was beginning to regret her decision to follow.

Looming out of the darkness in front of them, The Ministry for Lost Souls sat, heavy and brooding, running the entire length of one side of the square. Thick granite columns the size of lunar space rockets stood in an imposing line supporting an overhanging flat roof. Black shapes loomed over the edge of the building. Squinting up through the rain, Mich could make out streams of water, black in the fading light, cascading from the faces, claws and wings of dozens of elaborately carved gigantic stone gargoyles peering malevolently down into the square. He had the very real impression that they were watching everything he and Patterson were doing.

"Who lives in a house like this?" said Mich, in an attempt to lighten his mood. It didn't work.

They looked at one another.

"Where do we start?" said Mich. "It's so *big*!'"

Patterson was shivering. "I dunno. But whatever we're doing, let's do it quickly, I'm soaking."

"There!" said Mich, pointing through the murk.

At the base of one of the columns, almost unoticeable through the rain, a faint blue neon light glowed weakly from the shadows of The Ministry's walls.

They hurried across the square and Mich experienced a strange sensation of moving without travelling, as they seemed to grow no nearer to the great building. He had underestimated its size and it took them two full minutes to draw close enough to the light. It shone a weak cone of blue on to a narrow side entrance set back down a short flight of steps. As he drew closer they could see that the light was coming from a sign above them.

The sign spelled out the words *In Here*, and Mich looked at it, puzzled. Was someone, something helping them? Or tricking them? Or was this kind of thing just everyday nonsense, the kind that Mich was coming to regard as normal around here?

"What do you think that means?" he said.

Odd, metallic-sounding little insects scuttled away into the darkness as Mich and Patterson came down the stairs. Up close the walls of The Ministry were ancient, pitted with an infinitesimal number of strange hieroglyphs. Mich looked at them closely and shrugged. He was about to speak when Patterson tugged his arm impatiently.

"Did you feel that?" she whispered.

"Yes. You're tugging my arm."

"Not that, you cretin!" Patterson said, shaking her head. *"That."*

She stood very still and cocked her head to one side.

Mich listened for a few moments and then shrugged. He heard nothing except the sound of the rain against the stones.

"Just feel it," said Patterson softly.

Mich tried again and this time he picked it up. A deep, low murmur, somewhere between hearing and feeling, seemed to seep out of the very walls of The Ministry for Lost Souls. It was faint, almost imperceptible, but once he picked it up Mich wished he hadn't. It was an awful sound, a desperate keening wail filled with bottomless, rancid energy; part machine howl, part electro-static. It was a sound that Mich knew he didn't want to hear too often.

He and Patterson glanced at each other and moved to the door.

Mich hesitated.

"How do we know this is the right door?" he said.

"I don't know," Patterson said, shaking the rain from her hair. "But I'm getting the weirdest feeling that if you want it to be the right door hard enough it will be."

Mich looked at her.

"It's not something I've thought through completely," she said, seeing his puzzlement. "It's just a feeling I've got that all this is what we make it, you know? Sort of like a big test. There are too many coincidences happening for it to be accidental. The guy with almost the same name as you being in the same car wreck; your dad getting a job here right where The

Gateway's housed; finding this door, I dunno, lots of stuff. . ." She tailed off into an embarrassed silence.

When she spoke again it was in a stronger voice. "Sometimes, when I've had some problem to solve, I've felt like I could *make* things happen, move events along simply by wanting them to happen. It's like you are in control, just for a few moments at any rate."

Mich couldn't really follow all of what Patterson was saying but there was something in what she said; he *had* felt like that himself at times during the past few days.

"Maybe it's just when you are upset, or angry," he said. "Maybe the system responds to energy levels." He stopped and coughed, embarrassed. He sounded like one of his mother's old New Age creep friends. They were forever sitting around in the living room, cross-legged and talking about crystals, or colonic irrigation, or energy lines in carrots or some such bilge.

He turned to the door and looked for a lock. It was perfectly blank. He produced the ring of keys and looked at them stupidly. So much for their theory that this was all some grand design. Come on, there must be a way to figure this out. Think. *Think*.

"Look again," said Patterson, pointing to the door. Mich turned and saw a fresh keyhole in the door. When he had first looked, he was certain, the door had been blank.

 168

Mich frowned. He lifted the ring of keys and suddenly just *knew*, the way he knew that his hand was attached to his arm, that it didn't matter which key he used, the door would open. He began to feel that Patterson might be right about them being able to shape events a little. Maybe it was all about faith, belief, confidence.

He grabbed a key, any key. The one he picked was a large rusting old-fashioned key that was way too big for the sleek new keyhole in the door.

The key slotted in perfectly, the mechanism clunking solidly as the metal slid home.

He was getting the hang of this.

CHAPTER 18

Italian Salvatore Chirilino leaned over to pick a lucky four-leaf clover, slipped on the wet grass . . . and fell fifty metres to his death from a clifftop in Vibo Marina, Italy, in 1992.

Daily Mirror, 20 November 1992

Inside, the sound was louder, more insistent. Mich could feel it deep inside his bones before he heard it and he suddenly felt very much like a little boy, it was only with a huge effort of will that he stopped himself turning straight round and running flat out for the exit. As if sensing what was going through his mind, Patterson slipped her hand into his, and Mich felt a thrill of electricity run through his body. While he didn't exactly feel anything even in the neighbourhood of brave, he knew he was going to move forward not back.

They were standing in a long low corridor painted a drab

170

institutional green. Mechanical cleaning drones hummed busily along the corridor. They had a sinister, shifty appearance. One approached and bumped into Patterson's foot. Annoyed, it reversed and slid off in the direction it had come from. To judge from the dust and small pieces of trash on the floor, the drones weren't particularly effective.

Softly buzzing, fluorescent strip lighting ran along the centre of the corridor ceiling in either direction. To their left, in the distance, one of the strip lights was broken. It flickered irritatingly.

Mich and Patterson looked at one another.

"Any ideas?" asked Mich.

"I'm beginning to get the feeling that one direction is as good as another."

"Only one way to find out. Let's try this way."

They set off left, in the direction of The Ministry's main entrance. Up ahead the broken strip light flashed on and off, on and off.

"You know," said Patterson. "We shouldn't expect to find The Gateway *too* easily, Mich."

Mich nodded. He had been thinking the same. If you looked at what had happened to him from one angle you could say it was a series of tragic, unconnected coincidences. It was the Butterfly Theory.

He'd first heard of the Butterfly Theory in an interview with

171

the Shock Warriors, one of his favourite bands. The singer had been saying that everything was connected if you looked back far enough, in the same way that a butterfly beating its wings in California could cause an earthquake in China. Mich didn't really understand all of this, but he instinctively knew what the Shock Warriors had been talking about, kind of. *If* they hadn't been travelling up to Gamma's place, *if* that lady hadn't been driving towards them, *if* they'd stopped for gas a few seconds earlier or later . . . if, if, if.

And before that, if Mr Moorcroft hadn't met Mrs Moorcroft, then Mich wouldn't even exist.

But he *had* existed, and all those little different decisions and accidents had created a delicate, gossamer-fine web of connections which had landed him here. With every person having literally billions of these tiny connections and coincidences making up their lives and deaths, the permutations were mind-boggling. It was like thinking about outer space; you couldn't really comprehend how much of it there was out there. It was the same with this connection stuff. *The real question, though*, thought Mich, *is was it meant to happen, or was all this just a meaningless series of random events?*

He shook himself, at the moment all this was simply fogging the lens. There was work to be done and all this hot air wasn't helping Alaska.

They walked as far as the broken strip light. Patterson took a few steps past the buzzing lamp before realizing that Mich had stopped directly beneath it.

"What?" she said, turning back towards him.

"This is it," said Mich. "I don't know why, but this flickering light is pointing the way for us. It's almost like something is guiding us to finding out where The Gateway is."

Patterson looked at him steadily and seemed about to disagree. Instead she narrowed her eyes and shrugged.

"Seems as good an idea as anything else."

This feeling had been steadily growing in Mich; the sense that some sort of guiding force was nudging them towards *something*, towards, he hoped, Alaska.

The door nearest to the flickering light was, like all the other doors they'd passed, closed tightly. It had no windows, locks, or hinges that Mich or Patterson could see. Mich stepped forward nervously and tapped the door gently.

"Hello?" he said.

There was a laugh from Patterson.

" 'Hello'?" she sniggered.

Mich was about to argue with her when Patterson brushed him aside and, drawing back one of her platform shoes, kicked the door wide open.

Smiling sweetly, she gestured to Mich.

"After you," she said. "There's no need to look at me like that. You would have taken for ever."

They ducked through the doorway into a completely different world. The institutional green, the fluorescent office lighting had gone. Instead, the friends found themselves inside an enormous, dimly lit stone-walled chamber, its roof lost somewhere high in the shadows. The sound in here had a subtly different quality, echoing and vibrating off huge swathes of cables, pipes and ducts hanging down in heavy snaking coils. Peering through the gloom Mich could see many of the pipes ran into power points and ports set into the desks, while others snaked off into the indistinct corners of the room. Lazy flickers of electricity darted here and there in the gloom like shining fish in a darkened aquarium. Steam drifted from an unseen vent and a series of dull orange oil lamps cast softly leaping shadows around them, giving the place the disturbing appearance of being alive.

The chamber was full of desks, high wooden objects with tall, straight-backed stools behind each one. On every desk lay an enormous ledger, stiff parchment pages bound in some sort of dusty leather. Beside the ledgers, strange glowing Cubes floated gently, the front face of each one giving out a dull, icy-blue glow. The low wailing noise was louder here in the chamber.

They approached one of the desks. It was as tall as Patterson, and slightly taller than Mich. He could only see over the top by standing on tiptoe. Close up they could see that

174

each of the desks had been personalized by whoever worked there. Photographs were taped on work surfaces, some of the Cubes had small cuddly toys balanced on the tops, others had plants in small pots arranged around the edges; all the things that people do to make their work-space more like home. Each desk had a small name-plate bolted to the front.

Mich closed his eyes and frowned, concentrating. He was sure he could feel something.

"Feel the force," he muttered to himself a little self-consciously. "C'mon, you dipstick, feel it!"

He whirled around and pointed at one of the desks.

"This," said Mich dramatically in a voice he thought sounded like Luke Skywalker, "is the desk of Michael Moorcroft!"

He checked the name-plate: *Frank Mazevski*.

"So much for that theory," muttered Patterson, moving to check the names on some of the other desks.

"Oh," said Mich, disappointed. "I was certain this would be the one."

He felt the presence of Cranborne itching to pop out and offer some unwanted advice. Mich didn't feel like giving him the satisfaction so he strained and managed to push Cranborne back. Immediately, Marion popped up over his left shoulder in a fizz of golden sparks.

"Attaboy!" he said, smiling broadly and twirling his fork. "Don't give that creep the time of day! If I had a nick—"

"Oh, you can shut it, too!" said Mich. "I don't need either of you right now."

"Suit yourself," said Marion, folding his arms and pouting sulkily. He faded slowly from the feet up until only his face was left. He poked his tongue out and disappeared with an angry pop. Mich sighed.

From the darkness to his right, he heard a shout from Patterson.

"Over here!"

She stood in front of a desk and pointed at the name-plate.

"This is your dad's desk, Mich."

Mich hadn't thought much about what his father was doing down here at The Ministry. He'd imagined he'd be sitting at some antiseptic computer desk, very much like the one he'd sat at for the past ten years at Gimlet & Hawke. This was a very different kind of workplace. He looked at the ledger on his father's desk and carefully opened the heavy cover. Patterson craned her neck over his shoulder to see. The book was full of names and dates, thousands of them in tiny, precise hand-lettering running down page after page. Each name had a birth date followed by a place name, followed by a second date. This column was headed *Date of Death*.

"Look."

Patterson pointed out one of the names near to the top of the list.

 176

"Bryony St James," read Mich. "And?" The name meant nothing to him.

"Look at the date," said Patterson, digging Mich in the ribs.

"Ow!" He rubbed his side. "What about it?"

"It's next *week*," Patterson said as if speaking to a child of four. "As in, this person isn't dead yet!"

Mich looked at the list. He wasn't sure if this was good news or bad. Obviously, he thought, it was fairly terrible news if you happened to be called Bryony St James, and he grew cold at the idea of Bryony (whoever she was) going about her business quite happily, while all the time the remaining seconds of her life were trickling away. He imagined her as a teenager, maybe sixteen, meeting her boyfriend and not quite knowing what had happened as the car ploughed into her at the intersection, or the killer struck from behind the trees, or the disease found a home in a lung or kidney, or the bomber chose just *that* moment to detonate, or any one of the thousands and thousands of ways that death snuck up and took you as casually as a shoplifter swiping a carton of milk.

On the other hand, from his own point of view the end of Bryony was a very encouraging bit of information. After all, he reasoned, if your last breath is pre-recorded here at The Ministry, by people like his *dad*, who (it seemed to Mich) had trouble putting one foot in front of the other, then surely that

177

meant that mistakes *could* be made. He flicked down the list of names trying to find his own, but quickly realized it was a waste of time. They had no way of knowing how the ledgers were organized. They didn't appear to be in any kind of order and Mich couldn't figure out what system they were using. There were people who'd snuffed it back in the twelfth century right alongside some poor stiff who had been walking around the shopping mall yesterday. Add the fact that there were at least 500 ledgers in this chamber alone, thought Mich, his heart sinking, and it became obvious that tracking down a single entry would be as difficult as finding a yellow tooth at a convention of boy bands. Plus they had no way of telling how many other chambers just like this there were.

Then he slapped the side of his head.

"Doh!"

"What?" asked Patterson, confused. "'Doh'?" She was unfamiliar with the Simpsons.

"I'm so dumb," said Mich. "Maybe we don't need to use the ledgers. Let me check something."

Mich looked closely at the side of the Cube and fished out the ring of keys he'd taken from Mr Moorcroft's jacket. He examined them one by one until he found a small key that looked different from the others. He moved towards the Cube and slotted the key into a small port on one side. Immediately the Cube glowed brightly and the screen flickered into life.

Mich grinned, turned to Patterson and polished his fingernails on his T-shirt.

"Very impressive, Sherlock," said Patterson. "I think they're running two systems here. The ledgers are the way they've always done things, slowly, by hand; that's why they keep them. But things have changed and I reckon these things –" she waved a hand at the Cube – "are a more up-to-date way of keeping the information. You should know more about this kind of stuff than me; the only time I've seen a computer was on a school trip to the Smithsonian Museum in 1974 and it was the size of a Mack truck."

"Things *have* changed since then," said Mich hoisting himself up on to the desk and flexing his fingers.

"Stand back. Watch and learn."

There were no buttons on the Cube and no keyboard. Mich touched the glowing screen, guessing correctly that it was a touch-screen system. There was a slight hum and a keyboard appeared on-screen. Mich punched in his own name and pressed *search*. The Cube buzzed softly and the screen changed colour rapidly. After a couple of seconds a message flashed up.

No results found.

Mich punched the air. This was the first solid confirmation he had had that they were on the right track. If there was no entry on the system under his name then that could only mean one thing, surely? They'd got the wrong guy!

"Of course they might have just missed putting you on the new system," Patterson said.

"Thanks," said Mich, his face sinking. "But that's not what I want to hear."

"You have to at least face the possibility that it's only a clerical error."

Mich grew quiet and Patterson knew she'd said the wrong thing.

She put her hand over his. It was hot and dry and it felt wonderful to Mich.

"I'm sure it'll be OK," she said in a small certain voice and kissed him softly on the mouth.

Mich forgot all about the Cube and Purgatory and the mistake (if that's what it was). He forgot about where he was. He forgot his name for a second or two.

They pulled away from each other, red and flustered.

Or, at least Mich was red and flustered. Patterson seemed to take it all in her stride.

How do they do that? thought Mich. Girls seemed to have some sort of secret way of knowing stuff that boys didn't.

"Er, thanks," said Mich who, not having kissed anyone properly before, didn't know what else to say.

Patterson said, "You're welcome."

They sat next to each other, Mich awkward and unsure

 180

about what to do next. He coughed and began typing again on the screen.

"What now?" said Patterson.

Mich typed in the names of his family and hit the *search* button.

"Look," he said.

Patterson bent across and looked. On-screen next to all the Moorcroft family's names, with the exception of Alaska, was the same number: 12/23/2002.

"That means that you were all supposed to die, I guess," said Patterson softly.

Mich looked at the screen blankly. He had been sure he was on to something. "There has to have been a mistake. There just has to."

"How about punching in the other guy?"

"What?" said Mich, confused.

"The other guy, the other Mich Moorcroft. How about putting his name into the computer?"

"Oh. Him. Good idea."

He turned back to the Cube and touched the screen again. He keyed in *Mitchell Freestone Moorcroft* and pressed *search*. This time the screen filled with text and it took them a few moments to read what was there. Words jumped out. Murder. Theft. Extortion.

And a date. Moorcroft's death date.

"The twenty-third of December!" said Patterson. "That's when. . ."

"That's when I died," said Mich.

CHAPTER 19

Prophet of doom Jose Ricart, 53, of Burgos, Spain, was killed by a truck in September 1998 while crossing the road. Ricart was wearing a banner which read: "The End Of The World Is Nigh" when he was struck.

The Sun, 18 September 1998

Moorcroft took the lemon-yellow metal box of lighter fluid from his pocket, flipped the spout forwards and sprayed a fine jet of clear liquid over the video cassette lying in the gunmetal trash can at his feet. From his other pocket he produced a book of matches and tore one free. With a practised gesture he'd perfected during one of his spells inside, he flicked his thumb against the sulphur, and watched as the match caught and then sputtered into life. He smiled and looked down at the trash can before dropping the match on to the cassette. With a familiar whoosh, the tape caught light, blue-white flames licking hungrily around the rim of the trash can. The cassette gave off acrid fumes as the plastic bubbled and cracked. Moorcroft watched as the label browned and read the words *North Morton Teaching Hospital, Ward 18, OBS TAPE 4: 12/26/2002*, before they faded to black and orange, consumed by the flames.

He opened the motel room window and let the fumes blow into the wet parking lot. The rain was sleeting diagonally in from somewhere out in the Atlantic and the room temperature dropped as soon as Moorcroft opened the window. The plastic video cassette crackled and hissed as the odd icy raindrop fell into the can, and the acetate tape inside curled and twisted into a sticky black mess.

Moorcroft closed the window and turned back to the bed. He checked his kit, neatly laid out on the orange-checked counterpane. White orderly uniform. Fake laminated hospital staff pass. Toolkit in a Velcro-tabbed webbing belt. Moorcroft paid special attention to the toolkit. It would come in handy if a little problem cropped up.

He checked his watch. Two-fifteen. It was only a twenty-minute drive to North Morton where the boy lay in a coma. Moorcroft had visited the hospital three times since his first, ill-judged trip. He'd been stupid then, and had compensated by being more careful with this one than ever before. His hospital

 184

visits had established the nursing shift pattern: they changed at four pm and there was a fifteen-minute period during the ward rounds when the boy was left unchecked. This period coincided with a change of shift for the security staff. Moorcroft had gone by the security office several times and knew that he could disable the video surveillance before he visited the boy's ward. It was tight, it was risky, but he'd taken risks bigger than this before. He'd gotten away with it more than he'd been caught, that was for certain.

Besides, thought Moorcroft, *the kid would probably be a drooling vegetable the rest of his life if he did live, and what could be worse than that?* Certainly not the quick and easy end that Moorcroft had in mind for him. This was virtually a mercy killin', when you came to think of it.

He stood and began to dress. Suddenly a great series of hacking coughs rocked him backwards and forwards and he fell on to the bed. It sounded like something was ripping his lungs out in there, something shaking loose. He wheezed desperately for breath and eventually it came, leaving him red-faced and wet-eyed. The room was cold, and Moorcroft had been getting colder ever since the crash. Even when he was driving with the heat cranked up high and with a thick wool coat and hat, Moorcroft was cold. *It isn't just the weather*, he thought, *I must be sickenin' for something*.

CHAPTER 20

Vlad Cazacu, 43, a Romanian fire-eater, died in March 1998, when he inadvertently swallowed some of the flammable liquid, belched, and then exploded.

The Parrot (Accra, Ghana), 2–8 June 1998

Outside The Ministry, Dakota Moorcroft stood by the door she'd just watched Mich and Patterson slip through.

She looked up at the dank, black walls and cursed her stupid little brother. This was like, *so* not her scene! But she knew she had to follow him, if only to make sure the little creep didn't screw up her own chances up here, down here, wherever the hell it was they were.

Now, she shook her head angrily and pushed open the door of The Ministry. It opened easily enough, even though she hadn't thought about whether she might need a key or not. Up ahead of her in the corridor, she spotted Mich and Patterson standing under a flickering strip light. She opened her mouth to shout when Patterson kicked the corridor door and the pair of them disappeared through the opening.

It took Dakota a couple of minutes to get within fifty metres of the flashing strip light. As she neared the entrance to the chamber she stopped, picking up a flash of something moving. Something big and powerful and moving with a purpose. She didn't see whatever it was, she sensed it like a white-hot needle point of fear right inside her guts. It terrified her.

Adrenalin poured through her system, weakening her knees, and bringing her breath out in short, ragged gasps which she fought to keep quiet. A frantic cold sweat sprang out in tight little beads over her face.

She risked a look forward. The corridor seemed quiet enough; just the faint hum and buzz of the strip lights. Then she saw something.

It was as though the entire wall of the corridor had rippled like the skin of a heavily muscled snake, or as if something transparent had passed in front of the wall, slightly altering its appearance as it did so.

Instinctively Dakota pressed herself tighter against the wall even though she knew it was pointless here in the brightly lit space. If whatever she had seen looked this way down the corridor she would be as visible as a bug on a window.

187

Whatever it was hadn't seen her, or at least it hadn't so far made any move towards her, she wasn't certain which. She wanted to run, bolt, now! Instead she stayed where she was, paralysed with fear, and tracked the . . . *thing* as it slid along the ceiling, over the broken strip light and into the chamber beyond.

A minute passed. Then two. Gradually her breathing returned to something approaching normal and she relaxed her grip on the wall of the corridor. Several of her fingernails were broken where she had dug them into the wall. Stepping carefully she looked both ways down the corridor.

Nothing.

She moved slowly, scarcely daring to breathe, towards the opening up ahead, expecting "it" to leap on her and eat her, skin her, whatever the hell it wanted to do, at any minute. It didn't and, after what seemed like for ever, she reached the broken door. A faint slab of blue light from the chamber lay across the corridor floor.

Dakota slowly moved into the doorway and looked inside.

At the door to the chamber, her nerve failed. She tried to move into the room but found she couldn't. Her feet refused to move. She had seen too many spooky slasher movies to take another step. Ahead of her in the dark she saw Mich and his little friend illuminated by some sort of blue ball of light. She saw the light bob away into the darkness and then she saw that *thing* drop down from the ceiling and move after them. It was this that rooted her to the spot. She simply couldn't go on.

Dakota ran back down the corridor and banged open the door leading to the outside. She raced into the square, putting as much distance between her and The Ministry as she could. The electro-static wailing faded as she ran. A bus in the shape of a giant gherkin (but with chromed alloy wheels) was waiting at the other side of the square and she gratefully jumped aboard.

Gradually her heart rate slowed, her breathing eased as the bus pulled away from The Ministry and she began to think about what she was going to do. What had started out as idle curiosity had gone wrong. She wanted to run, to hide. She didn't want to get involved. Maybe she could just forget about the whole thing, let Michigan and his friend deal with whatever it was they were involved with, leave them to whatever mess they'd gotten into.

The simplicity of this tempted her, pulled her in, whispering how easy it would be to do that. *And it would be easy*, she thought. *Who would know?* Just then Dakota's own angel and devil popped up and began a furious argument about what she should and shouldn't do.

"Shut up!" she wailed, and the other passengers turned briefly to look at her before realizing she was only talking to her visitations. It was a common sight and no one in Purgatory took very much notice.

Dakota turned back to her problem but she knew, deep down, that she couldn't just walk away from Michigan. Horrible ugly grungy little squit that he was, he was still her little brother. She would have to do something. Dakota thought about it for a moment, her teeth chattering as her clothes dried slowly, and then the answer came. She would do what she always did when Mich was being a royal pain in the rear.

She would tell her mother.

CHAPTER 21

An Indian man, Khandal Tripura, 35, of Chinchharipara village in the Ramgararh district, Bangladesh, was bitten on the hand by a cobra. The bite might not have been fatal, but Mr Tripura then bit the snake back, causing it to bite him again. He died the next day.

Independent, 22 July 1998

"Ask it about The Gateway," suggested Patterson. "It can't hurt." They were kneeling side-by-side on the stool, their elbows on the desk.

Mich turned back to the Cube and keyed in the words.

RESTRICTED ACCESS flashed angrily on to the screen.

"Oh well," Patterson said, sighing. "So much for that."

"You think that's gonna stop me?" said Mich flexing his fingers. "There isn't a computer made that can keep me out." He started tapping in sequences so fast that it was difficult for

191

Patterson to follow what he was doing.

"If this is a new system, it stands to reason that someone from down on Earth designed it, right?" says Mich, his eyes never leaving the screen.

"I guess," said Patterson.

To Patterson computers were still something of a mystery. Mich, on the other hand, had spent every waking moment since the age of four plugged into some kind of electronic gizmo or another. And almost every night, for the past two years, he'd been playing a dangerous game from the small Mac in his bedroom. Mich was a hacker. Not, it has to be said, a very bad hacker, but certainly enough to have got him in trouble if he'd been caught, and more than bad enough to cause him a few nasty moments at the Admissions Office.

Mich had joined a webring of juve hackers playing an escalating game of hide and seek amongst bigger and bigger secure computer systems. There had been quite a few scares and Mich had been terrified when one kid up in Oregon had been jailed for hacking into a military computer. Since then he'd back-pedalled, targeting TV stations and burger franchise systems. He'd once altered eighteen million sachets of burger ketchup so they contained excess sugar, simply by hacking into the condiment control computer at the manufacturers. Him and a couple of friends had had a ball the following week, spotting the tampered sachets from the expressions on

 192

customers' faces at the local grease pit. Man, that had been a blast!

But the hacking *was* wrong, Mich knew. Worse, it was dumb, but while he'd been alive and fourteen years old and indestructible, he couldn't have cared less. Now he was dead it was another story, and it was something he'd been worrying about since he'd woken up in Purgatory that first morning and the old lady had eyed him up so keenly.

This, however, was an emergency, and Mich didn't hesitate in trying to break every security measure The Ministry had put in place.

"This is too easy," he said, his fingers flying across the keys. "These guys don't have a chance. Bow to the might of The Flash, oh puny mortals!"

" 'The Flash'?" said Patterson, giggling.

"Well, yeah," said Mich, his cheeks flushing. "That's my, erm, handle: 'The Flash'."

Patterson collapsed into a fit of laughter and Mich turned back to the Cube.

"No one messes with The Flash," he muttered.

A few moments later there was a satisfying click from the Cube and an intricate web of blue-lined graphics appeared onscreen. Mich sat back and smiled.

"What is it?" said Patterson turning her head this way and that.

193

"The whole set-up," said Mich sitting back and folding his arms across his chest. "Plans, directions, everything."

He reached forward and pressed the Cube again. A flat disc about the width of Mich's hand slid smoothly out from the Cube. He pressed it and a three-dimensional plan similiar to the one God had produced from Her handbag formed in the air in front of them.

"Wow," said Patterson. "Now I'm impressed . . . *Flash*."

Mich opened his mouth to snap back a reply when there was a small brushing sound from the direction of the doorway. The room, already cool, grew suddenly colder, and Mich shivered involuntarily.

"What was that?" whispered Patterson, looking round into the darkness. Her breath hung white in the air. The only sound came from the low wailing that was as much a part of The Ministry as the dripping black walls.

Mich hadn't so much heard the sound, as felt it. Something had slithered into the chamber and up into the black nest of cables and ducts above their heads. The cables trembled a little and moved back and forth in the dim light.

They both looked slowly up towards the ceiling. Something was up there. Something big, angry, slithery and invisible. It wasn't a good feeling.

Mich glanced at Patterson and signalled with his head for them to move back from the desk. Whatever had come in was

 194

definitely above them, Mich was sure, although he felt that it was a little to one side, nearer to the door.

"Pat," whispered Mich. "My super-spidey sense is telling me something."

"What?"

"There's something in the room with us and I don't get the feeling it wants to play catch. We need to get out of here, quick." He looked carefully at the 3-D hologram in his hand. "This way."

Patterson backed away from the desk into the shadows, Mich following close behind. He darted nervous glances over his shoulder and up into the darkness. He held his hand out in front of him with the hologram vibrating slightly as they moved. The light from the hologram was giving their position away but without the plans they would be running blind. Whatever had come into the chamber was moving towards them, he was certain. What wasn't certain was what it had in mind for them. It wasn't the first time that Mich had encountered this . . . thing. If it had wanted to harm him surely it could have done it at any time? It was all very well reasoning it out like that, but Mich had seen too many spooky alien movies to feel anything but complete fear. *Any minute now*, he thought, *a hideous alien face will appear above me dripping goo before it snatches me up into its vast, teeth-filled jaw*s. It was all he could do not to scream.

195

Somewhere in the darkness behind them Mich felt a weight drop to the floor. He risked a look, turning and peering into the shadows. He almost swallowed his tongue as he saw a clutch of desks shimmer. Something big, something transparent, had moved in front of them. They heard a new noise, a low growling, or perhaps it was breathing, rising in pitch. Whatever it was was getting closer. There was a sense of barely repressed malevolent anger in the chamber, although Mich had an odd feeling that it wasn't himself and Patterson that the anger was directed at, although he couldn't put his finger on why.

"Where?" said Patterson. "Where do we go?"

Mich looked at the plan and forced himself to concentrate.

"Down there!" He pointed at an L-shaped bend in a corner of the chamber. They raced around the corner and found themselves in a circular space. Twelve huge tunnels radiated out from where they stood, like giant spokes. The tunnels sloped down at a terrifyingly sharp angle. Each of them was as black as pitch.

Behind the two friends, the growling was now drowning out the other noise. Patterson clutched Mich's arm, her eyes wide with fear. Mich's theory that the thing might not be chasing them seemed ridiculous now.

"Which one?"

"There!" said Mich dragging Patterson towards one of the

 196

tunnels. They ran into the darkness, the massive stone arches soaring above them. As soon as they reached the tunnel mouth, they were running full pelt down the slope, out of control, their legs windmilling frantically beneath them as they fought to slow down. The ground underfoot was too slippy, treacherous, wet with some sort of strangely glowing, rust-coloured moss, and their feet slithered on the slick surface. They stumbled, Patterson screaming as her knee painfully rapped the stones, a stab of pain shooting up her leg. Mich banged his hand as he fell, but managed, somehow, to hang on to the disc. The back of his head cracked against the floor and for a moment he didn't know which way was up.

"I can't slow down, Mich!" shouted Patterson.

"Just hang on!" he screamed.

And then they were falling through space, faster and faster, into complete and total darkness.

CHAPTER 22

In February 2000, Anton Brieszov climbed into the lions' enclosure at Moscow Zoo to retrieve a child's toy. He escaped the chasing lions by leaping into the moat, only to drown. He was a non-swimmer.

Guardian, 15 February 2001

The thing drew near to the sleeping figure and stood over it. The shape, at least twice the height of the boy, bent and sniffed. As it did so, to an observer it would look like Mich had been folded in a clear jelly. It sniffed him all over and probing, transparent fingers slithered around and inside his ears and nostrils. Whatever it was, it examined him for a full minute before slowly reforming into its original shape. It would wait, they weren't there yet. Mich coughed, and the shape softly slithered back into the mist, watching and waiting.

 198

* * *

Mich woke slowly, conscious at first of a sharp, acidic burning sensation in the fingertips of his left hand. He opened his eyes and found himself lying awkwardly, his head lower than his feet. He had no idea where he was and his head ached worse than it had done that time he and Cary Foster swiped some of his mother's cherry brandy and drank it at summer camp. In a sudden rush he turned and vomited violently. His throat burned as he retched. When it had stopped he gasped for air like a landed fish and he let a few minutes go by before he tried carefully to lift his head again. Carefully, tenderly, his head pounding, Mich raised himself up on to one elbow and looked around. An eerie phosphorescent green light was drifting on banks of low mist all around him. Mich wondered for a moment if he was somehow outside, then realized that they were in an underground cavern. He couldn't make out any kind of ceiling, but the sound echoed back from the stone somewhere in the gloom high above.

He gently touched his ear and felt a tickling wetness. When he drew back his hand it was damp. A small blob of completely colourless jelly, almost invisible, rested on the tip of his index finger and Mich looked at it with a strange tickle of recognition somewhere at the back of his mind. It reminded him of something, but the memory stayed tantalizingly just out of reach.

199

The noise in the tunnel was astonishing, a mix of howls, screeches, cries, screams, the scraping of fingers on stone, slithering, sucking, watery sounds, all mixed in a hideous din which rose and fell like demented rock 'n' roll feedback.

Still only half-conscious, Mich became aware of pain, lots of it. He looked down at his left hand and saw that his fingertips were dangling in a fast-running river. It took him a moment to realize that they felt like they were on fire and Mich jerked them out of the water with a yelp of pain. He looked at his fingers and gagged reflexively. Three of the fingertips had been burnt as if they'd been dipped in acid. There were no fingerprints left and the skin that was there bubbled and popped as Mich watched in horror.

He leaped to his feet, tucking the fingers underneath his armpit and doing a ducking, bowing, circular dance in a futile effort to dull the pain. His thinking was coming back now and he remembered his fall down the black tunnel.

He had come to rest on the banks of a mighty river, at least the width of a football pitch and looking both deep and fast. Low green-tinged mist lay across it, softly swirling in the thin light. Mich looked into the waters of the river and glimpsed movement below the surface. His stomach heaved once more as he recognized the shapes in the river.

It was a river of human beings, twisting, screaming and writhing in agony.

 200

Hundreds upon hundreds of them rolled by him in a few seconds. Occasionally the surface of the water broke and a gnarled claw clenched and unclenched before sinking back down. The noise, the sound he'd been hearing all the time he'd been in The Ministry, was coming from this river.

Mich puked again in a bitter torrent until there was, surely, nothing left.

He coughed and wiped his mouth with the back of his sleeve. And then suddenly, like a punch in the stomach, he thought of Patterson: what if she'd rolled straight into the river? He whirled in a panic, searching the ground frantically.

"Patterson!" he screamed. "PAT!"

He found her about ten metres away, half hidden by some of the green mist. He raced over and to his relief saw that she had missed rolling into the poison water by a whisker. The sole of her shoe dangled in it and part of it had been eaten away, just like Mich's fingertips. As Mich bent to lift her clear, a bone-white hand lurched up from the water and grasped his wrist. He screamed as his skin burnt under the touch. For one sickening moment he felt himself being pulled into the water. In a blind panic, he scrambled back, kicking out at the hand. It broke its hold and sank back beneath the surface. Mich's breath came in short, ragged bursts and he looked wide-eyed at his wrist. There were the fingermarks of the hand clear and visible. He dragged Patterson back from the edge and began to check her breathing before he relaxed a little: she was *already* dead, he remembered and he waited for her to come around, his heart still thumping.

After a few moments she awoke, and Mich held her as she too vomited.

Over his shoes.

As she recovered she looked around.

"I'm OK, sport," she said, her eyes wet and red. She looked down. "Sorry about your shoes."

Mich shook his head.

"Don't worry."

"What is this place?" She had to shout to make herself heard over the noise.

Mich looked closely at the hologram again.

"I think it's flowing down from The Gateway," he shouted, pointing up river. "This place is The Ministry of Lost Souls, remember? I know that it deals with everyone who comes through Purgatory but I think this river is the main reason The Ministry was given its name. I think that maybe that's what these guys are: the lost souls."

"Jeez," said Patterson.

"C'mon, let's go." He helped Patterson to her feet. "If I'm right this should lead us to The Gateway."

They held hands without thinking about it as they set off along the river, making sure they stayed well away from the bank. Occasionally, on a sharp bend, the river ran faster and the water slopped on to the bank and burnt as it splashed, a plume of steam rising from the acid-scorched earth.

"I had the strangest dream," said Patterson after about twenty minutes of walking. "I dreamt I was drowning in some kind of thick goop. It was gross. I couldn't breathe, my mouth and ears and lungs were full of the stuff."

Before Patterson spoke Mich wasn't aware that he'd had any kind of dream while on the river bank, but now it all came rushing back to him; the sensation of being enveloped, the feeling of suffocation.

"I had that dream too!" he said. "Kind of, anyway. It was close enough."

They fell into silence as talk was proving difficult with the howl from the river.

The cavern widened the further along they walked until they could no longer be sure they were in any kind of enclosed space at all. Certainly there was no roof they could see, or any walls at either side.

Strangely twisted trees, with gently glowing rust sticking to their trunks and branches, began to appear along the banks. Stunted vegetation, clinging vines and spiky leaves, grew heavier. Once or twice Mich glimpsed soft green phosphorescent lights moving deep in the undergrowth. Above them they heard odd rustlings and occasionally the flap of something big passing overhead. It wasn't long before they saw what was making the sound.

Ahead of them, on an escarpment made from a bend in the river, a group of six or seven black shapes were bent over something on the bank.

"They're vultures!" whispered Patterson.

They did, at first sight, look like vultures, but as they drew closer Mich saw that they weren't. They were bigger, for a start. Each was as tall as a large man and black as shadow, with great leathery wings folded across their muscular backs. The creatures' wrinkled necks bobbed and lengthened as they hopped around, pulling at some sort of unspeakable mess on the floor. The scratching of their claws and the soft ripping sounds as they feasted were audible above the noise from the river.

Although Mich and Patterson stayed silent and motionless, one of the creatures turned and looked at them.

Cold green eyes glowed nastily and a hooked beak dripped fluid to the river bank. As the drops hit they hissed and released small clouds of vapour. The creature regarded Mich and Patterson and then turned back to its meal.

Mich and Patterson skirted around the gathering through the thicker undergrowth. It was darker here and they jerked nervously as unseen things slithered and hissed away from them as they passed, but eventually they found their way back

 204

to the river. The vulture creatures were behind them, still feeding, and Mich and Patterson were glad to leave them.

They walked for what seemed like hours. Imperceptibly the river noise rose, the air became damper.

"That sounds like a waterfall," shouted Patterson. Mich could barely hear her.

The river opened out here and the water bubbled furiously into a large pool below a dark opening high in the cavern wall. Through this opening the river poured in a thick steady stream, boiling white-green and angry, as it smashed into the water below. Tiny stick-figures briefly appeared out of the mist and spray, then fell back, wailing, into the river.

"That has to be it!" shouted Patterson. "The Gateway!"

"It doesn't look as though it's guarded," replied Mich, cupping his hands to make himself heard. "Look."

He pointed up towards the dark opening. There appeared to be nothing there except a small building perched precariously on a stone ledge at the very lip of the falls. As they drew closer a flight of stone steps, dizzyingly steep, climbing up towards the little building came into view.

An official-looking sign stood at the bottom of the steps. It looked as though it had been there for ever. *Maybe it has*, thought Mich.

There were words on the sign, but neither Mich nor Patterson could make sense of them. They appeared to be in some kind of ancient language. There were several diagrams on the sign and they did little to reassure them. They showed images of screaming people pierced by lightning, being eaten by large animals, getting disembowelled and generally having a lousy time of it.

"Maybe the words say something like: 'Don't worry, if you pass through The Gateway, none of this kind of thing will happen to you'," suggested Patterson, shouting.

Mich looked at her and raised his eyebrows. He turned and stood directly in front of Patterson and shouted.

"Look, Pat, you don't have to come with me through there. There's no telling what could happen. Take the disc and head back. I'll do this myself."

Patterson shook her head and cupped her hand to her ear.

"I can't hear you!" she mouthed, smiling.

Mich smiled back and they turned towards the steps.

CHAPTER 23

Switzerland, April 1998: a nine-year-old boy was killed when the large snowball he had made rolled down a slope and crushed him.

AFP, 20 April 1998

Mr Moorcroft beamed with delight as the ball sailed up the fourteenth fairway straight as a die. It carved a white line against the blue sky and fell softly to the grass 200 metres dead ahead. A perfect drive. It was Mr Moorcroft's first of the day.

"Way to go, Mike!" said Baz Rheingold from the golf cart parked a couple of metres behind the tee. "Nice draw!"

Mr Moorcroft fairly bounced back to the cart and bagged his club like a gunslinger tucking away his 45 after a shoot-out. He hopped on to the cart and Baz gunned the electric motor. They peeled off up the fairway, squishing a small rodent too slow to get out of the way. Baz clapped Mr Moorcroft on the shoulder.

"You ever play pro?" he said. "C'mon, you didn't get that style in a cereal box!" As Mr Moorcroft made suitable noises of modesty, Baz lit a cigar the size of a dwarf torpedo and drew in deeply. He was clad from head to toe in matching golf togs: pastel yellow sweater over a pale yellow shirt. Canary yellow slacks, with creases sharp enough to slice salami, ran down to lime-green alligator-skin golf spikes. A flat yellow cap sat at a jaunty angle on the back of his huge head. Mr Moorcroft wore a similiar get-up all in tones of peach and aqua that Baz had presented him with at the clubhouse.

"So, Mike," said Baz, puffing on his stogie. "How do you like Sweetwater Canyons?"

Mr Moorcroft had called Baz a couple of days before and nervously asked him about membership at Sweetwater Canyons. Baz had been all ears and invited Mr Moorcroft for a no-obligation, low pressure sales presentation at the old West Course. "The best one," Baz had said, "but that's just between me, you and the four walls, capeesh?" Oh, and had he mentioned that this Friday there was going to be an added attraction at the course? Great news! An entire troupe of Dallas cheerleaders had been wiped out in a plane crash last weekend and they had taken a block visit booking at the Sweetwater Canyons course. Would Mr Moorcroft care to play a round at the same time as the cheerleaders? No need to mention it to the missus, Baz had whispered. She'd only worry about it. Besides, this was man-talk, right, feller? Important stuff, stuff that only guys could talk about, guys out playing golf (and lookin' at cheerleaders) in the sunshine, right?

"Well, I don't know. . ." Mr Moorcroft had begun but Baz had steamrollered him like a fly on the roadway.

"Meet at nine," said Baz. "In the clubhouse for coffee and doughnuts before we play, right? Right?"

And here they were. Mr Moorcroft had to admit, it was much better than he'd expected. He'd never been what you might call an overly religious man; not unless you counted that three-day Zen retreat in Florida, back before the kids came along. So when Urma had pitched in with all the warnings about Baz Rheingold and Sweetwater Canyons he'd just nodded along. But he'd secretly wished he could give it a try at least. What could it hurt? Besides, he liked to play golf, and he sure hadn't seen any other courses in the week or so he'd been here. And Baz had definitely delivered on the cheerleaders; Mr Moorcroft had noticed a large number of attractive blonde players wearing short skirts around the course.

All this made a nice change from his job at The Ministry; all that wailing was enough to send anyone loopy. Mr Moorcroft was ready for a change and it wasn't like God was making a decent pitch for his business, was it? At least Baz Rheingold was putting a bit of elbow grease into attracting the punters.

If only Baz would quit flashing those membership forms around in front of him every time he so much as moved. The first time he'd done it, Mr Moorcroft had waved them away, and for a flash he could have sworn that Baz's eyes had spat out little red sparks of fury. But they'd died away so quickly that Mr Moorcroft was unsure as to whether he'd seen anything in the first place.

The clubhouse had been nice. Kind of an odd roaring sound coming from somewhere underneath, but Baz had mentioned something about the underground train line running through the place and the subject was dropped. The sand traps had been a bit hairy the first time he'd gone near them, erupting in a small geyser of molten lava. But Baz had explained they were an unusual design feature of the course and Mr Moorcroft had adjusted his game accordingly.

Now they were nearing the end of the round and Baz had those damn membership forms out again. Mr Moorcroft was beginning to think that maybe he'd sign them just to get some peace on the rest of the trip. He remembered he was a highly trained accountant just in time and came to his senses. He needed to bargain. To make certain he was getting a good deal.

"How much does it cost?" he said, setting his face in a "I-can-play-hardball-too" kind of expression. Mr Moorcroft looked as though he had haemorrhoids, but Baz decided not to mention that.

"How much, he says! How much!" Baz threw his large head back and laughed. Mr Moorcroft noticed that there were some quite large bits of meat lodged in between Baz's big white teeth. And the smell! For a guy who wore so much cologne Baz had breath that could strip lead off a church roof.

"It's completely free, Mikey baby!" Baz laughed. "That's the beauty of it! You pay nothing, zip, zilch, nada, absolutamento notheeng, senor, and it's golf and country club living for as long as you like. The only thing we *do* ask for is a little old loyalty agreement. But a man of your business sense would know that a loyalty agreement is standard practice, right? Am I right?"

"I – I guess. I mean, sure, of course. Standard practice."

"Attaboy, Mikey babes!" Baz lifted the forms up to Mr Moorcroft's nose and thrust a pen into his hand. "That's the spirit! Faint heart never won fair lady, eh? Who dares wins, let's go, let's go, let's do this thing, right? Right?"

He leaned in closer and Mr Moorcroft wrinkled his nose. *Baz could really do with some dental hygiene*, he thought.

"I've just indicated where you need to slap your John Hislop. . ."

"John Hancock," said Mr Moorcroft, absently.

"Yeah, yeah, yeah, whatever, Hislop, Hancock, Shmancok; just sign the freakin' thing will ya. . .!" Baz broke off from the negotiations, breathing heavily, his reddening face clashing horribly with the yellow golf sweater, and suddenly there was

211

something about him that made Mr Moorcroft shrink back on the golf cart seat with a girlish squeak. Baz took a deep breath and smoothed a hand over his brow. As he did so a dazzling smile was instantly pasted in place.

"Look, Mike. I'm gonna level with ya here, *mano a mano*. If you sign the membership forms you'll be doing Ole Baz a real big favour. A *real* big favour. I'm talking brontosaurus-size favour. The real skinny is that I need to make a monthly nut on memberships. Correction: I *hafta* make that nut. We're talking sales quotas here, buddy." Baz choked back a big salty tear and put an arm around Mr Moorcroft.

"And the Boss; he's a *real* hardball. Old school. He upped my quota last month and if I don't make it . . . well, I just don't wanna think about my future if I don't manage those figures." Baz cocked an eye at Mr Moorcroft. "I can't bear to think what'll happen to little Baz Junior if I don't make that target."

He paused.

"So whaddya say, old buddy, old bean, old feller? Hm? Hmm?"

Mr Moorcroft picked up the pen.

"I've always prided myself on being a good judge of character, Baz," said Mr Moorcroft. "And I hate to see you getting punished just because you have a boss who doesn't give us working guys an even break. I'm gonna sign your forms and Urma can just. . ."

He stopped in mid-sentence. From overhead came a sound familiar to Mr Moorcroft from movies about the Vietnam War. It was the *whump-whump-whump* of helicopter rotor blades. A shadow passed over the golf cart and Baz and Mr Moorcroft looked up.

Leaning out of a large blue police chopper was Mrs Moorcroft. She had hold of a megaphone attached to the inside of the machine. As it hovered above the course, Mr Moorcroft heard his wife's elecronically enhanced voice cut through the din from the chopper.

"Michael!" she bellowed. "Michigan is in trouble! Hop in right now! That's an order, soldier!"

Baz punched the steering wheel of the cart in frustration. Mr Moorcroft gave him an apologetic shrug and stepped off the cart as the chopper touched down twenty metres away.

"Wait," said Baz clutching at Mr Moorcroft's shirt. "What's the rush?"

Mr Moorcroft prised Baz's hand off his shirt and trotted away. Crossing the devil (or the devil's Chief Sales Officer) was risky, but crossing Mrs Moorcroft, Mr Moorcroft knew, was downright suicidal.

"Sorry," he mouthed to Baz as he ran towards the helicopter door.

But Baz wasn't listening. He was too busy smashing each and every one of his golf clubs into tiny pieces.

CHAPTER 24

Jizan, southern Saudi Arabia, September 2000: a camel, savagely beaten by its owner, got revenge by waiting until the owner was asleep and then trampling and biting him to death.

Adelaide Advertiser, 27 September 2000

Mich paused halfway up the flight of crumbling stone steps and gasped for breath. Patterson stopped too and the pair leaned on their hands to suck in great lungfuls of the cold air. Forty minutes' hard climbing had got them this far up the stairway.

Far below them the River of Lost Souls boiled furiously. As they looked down it seemed to be dragging the friends towards the void. Mich felt dizzy and stepped back. The urge to just drop over the side and into the river was strangely tempting. As if realizing his thoughts Patterson tugged at his sleeve and

214

nodded up ahead. Mich looked up and started to climb again with Patterson at his side.

After what seemed like for ever they reached the top of the steps and paused, exhausted. The noise up here wasn't as bad. It was possible, just, to hear what the other was saying.

They reached the stone platform perched precariously just above the lip of the falls. Here, before it plunged dizzyingly down, the surface of the water was silky smooth and looked deep and heavy. It moved with tremendous power and purpose and seemed to gain speed as it approached the edge. The two friends watched in fascinated horror as writhing, wailing figures emerged from the water spilling over the lip of the falls, before vanishing into the abyss.

Further back, behind the small building, the river flowed through a wavering, shimmering skin stretched across the mouth of what Mich assumed was The Gateway.

The building was over to one side of the platform, leaning into an overhanging rocky wall. Close to, it looked shabby, temporary, but very old, as though it had been placed there centuries before with the intention of replacing it and somehow no one had got round to it. The walls had been repaired here and there, quite sloppily, with planks of raw wood just nailed across places that had cracked or flaked. It had a corrugated tin roof, mottled and scarred with rust and encrusted with what looked like algae, bright green, thick and furry.

"Mich," said Patterson. She peeped in at the window of the small building which was too grimy to see through. She wiped the window only to find that the grime was on the inside. Mich looked around and then pointed at a sign. *Enquiries* was hand-drawn on a piece of brown card and taped to the door with some grey duct tape. Patterson shrugged.

"What the hell?" said Mich, and pushed the door open.

The small building was no smarter once they were inside but for the first time since falling through the tunnel, the noise from the falls faded to a bearable level. The relief was instant. Faint music tinkled from a battered, paint-spattered old radio propped on the window ledge. A counter ran across the centre of the room, its surface covered with short stacks of yellowing forms and leaflets gathering dust. The only light came from a bare bulb hanging down in one corner. It cast a surprisingly gentle light across the room, making everything look like an old, sepia-tinted photograph. A thick layer of undisturbed dust lay on the floor.

On a chair behind the counter, his feet propped up on a small cushion, sat a balding, bespectacled fat man, wearing a dusty grey suit and stained dark blue tie. He was fast asleep and his long resounding snores filled the room. His half-moon glasses were pushed back on to his forehead and a newspaper folded open at the crossword page lay neatly on the counter. A Detroit Lions baseball cap several sizes too small for him sat perched on his head and gave him the appearance of a clown.

Mich walked to the counter and looked at Patterson for confirmation. She nodded at the dusty bell sitting at one end. *Ring for attention*, said a notice next to it.

Mich brought his hand down on the bell and it gave a loud *ping*.

In a panic the man behind the counter woke and almost fell off his chair. He coughed loudly, rubbed his eyes and looked at the arrivals in disbelief.

"Oh!" he said. "Oh!"

He stopped and blinked.

"Who are you?" he said. "What do you want? Where did you come from?"

"Which question first?" said Patterson.

"We're here to go through The Gateway," interrupted Mich. "And we are going to get through that Gateway whatever you might s—"

"Oh," said the man, adjusting his tie. "Let me get the forms." He scrabbled around on the desk and produced a sheaf of grubby forms and a business card. He handed this to Mich, who read: *J. Fleetside, Guardian of The Gateway*.

"Forms?" Mich mouthed the word at Patterson.

She raised her eyebrows but said nothing.

"So there isn't a problem about going through The Gateway?" said Mich.

"Problem? Of course not. It's just that there's not much call for travelling through The Gateway on account of the side-effects."

"Side-effects?" said Mich and Patterson in unison.

The Guardian of The Gateway stopped rummaging. "Ah," he said, eyeing them carefully. "Hasn't anyone told you?"

He saw their blank looks and began to tut.

"It's really not good enough," he said. "You really need to have prepared a little better for an undertaking of this magnitude. . ."

"Never mind all that," said Patterson impatiently. "What's all this about side-effects?"

"Well, for a start," he said, regarding them from behind his spectacles. "There's no telling if you'll ever be able to get back. You could be doomed to wander the earth for all eternity, denied rest in an endless, painless, pointless quest for a path back to Paradise."

"And the downside?" said Mich.

The Guardian ignored him.

"It's no joke, young man, I can assure you," he said. "There's also the little matter of your mortal flesh."

Patterson nodded. "Yes?" she said. "What about it?"

"Well, it's going to decay, isn't it? Bits of you will start to fall off. Not a pretty sight, I can assure you," said The Guardian. "Once you go back into the mortal world you are subject to their laws and physics. You will be back in your fleshly state. To

 218

put it bluntly, you will start to rot. On account of you being dead. Your soft tissue will go first, then the muscles. . ."

"Yeah, we get the picture," said Mich, noticing Patterson beginning to go green.

"Yes, well, it's something you should know about," said The Guardian, a little huffily. "Only trying to help."

"Do many people go back through The Gateway?" asked Patterson. She had heard enough about the side-effects.

"Oh yes, quite a few down the years, my dear, quite a few."

"Really?" said Patterson. "That's not what we heard. We were told that it's very rare."

"Oh no, my dear," said The Guardian. "There have been quite a few. Not many recently I'll admit." He looked around at the dusty office.

"But go back a few years and there was a fair amount of traffic through this little office. We were promised bigger premises in 1945." He sighed and tailed off.

"So all these people who crossed over," said Patterson excitedly. "Did any of them come back?"

"Well, strictly speaking . . . er, no. But that's not to say that it's impossible!"

"No," said Mich, looking at Patterson. "Just not very likely."

The Guardian turned and began to put the sheaf of forms back where he'd found them.

"Wait up," said Patterson. "Don't we need to fill those out?"

219

* * *

It took more than an hour to complete the forms. Like everything else in Purgatory the system was slow and old-fashioned. Mich and Patterson had to sign waivers and consent forms and receipts and fill in address after address before The Guardian was satisfied. On the whole Mich wondered whether a fire-breathing demon guarding The Gateway might have been preferable to wading through this lot.

But eventually all the forms were complete and The Guardian beamed happily from under his ridiculous baseball cap.

"You know we don't get that many visitors up here. Most of my work is just loose paperwork and throwing the odd soul back in every now and again. You two seem like nice people — for children that is — are you quite sure you want to go through with this?"

They nodded in unison.

"Very well," said The Guardian. "Come with me."

He opened the door and instantly recoiled in alarm.

"What is it?" said Patterson.

"I'm afraid it's the Controllers," he said. "Look!"

The three of them stepped through the door and looked back down the path of the river. In the distance high-power searchlights cut through the darkness and the sound of helicopters could be heard clearly above the falls.

 220

"What have you two done?" said The Guardian.

"Nothing!" said Mich. "Nothing!" He wasn't sure that The Guardian quite believed him but the man didn't say anything. Mich wasn't even sure if they had done anything wrong himself.

The helicopters hovered close by the edge of the platform, their searchlights trained on the three figures standing outside the doorway, frozen in the harsh beams.

"Michigan Moorcroft!" barked an amplified Irish voice from one of the choppers.

Mich was rooted to the spot.

"Michigan Moorcroft. Do not move! You are in contravention of –"

The voice faltered.

"You are in contravention of . . . what the hell *is* the little scallawag in contravention of, exactly, if you don't mind me askin'?"

There was the sound of a scuffle and a new voice came over the speaker.

"Michigan! This is your mother! Stop whatever it is you are doing and wait right there! You are in big trouble, young man!"

"Mom?" shouted Mich, stunned.

The choppers touched down on the platform apron and eight or nine Controllers leaped out, Officer O'Toole and Mrs

Moorcroft at the front. Mr Moorcroft stepped down behind them and waved to Michigan.

"Mom? Dad?" Mich couldn't believe what he was seeing. "What the – what are you doing here?"

Behind Mr Moorcroft Dakota got down from the helicopter with her fingers in her ears. She looked at Mich guiltily. Her face gave the game away.

"You grass!" shouted Mich, correctly guessing Dakota's part in the arrival of the Controllers.

"I had to tell," said Dakota. "You might have been ki. . ."

She tailed off, realizing what she was about to say.

"Anyway," she continued peevishly. "I didn't wanna be left here all by myself."

"Oh, be quiet," said Mrs Moorcroft and picked up the megaphone again.

"MICHIGAN!" she yelled. "Come here at once!"

Mich turned to Patterson and held out his hand. She nodded and took it.

Mich grabbed the arm of The Guardian who was standing nervously watching the helicopters.

"How do we get through?" said Mich, urgently.

"Well, this is all most irreg—"

"The Gateway! How do we get through it? *Now!*"

The Guardian pointed at the shimmering skin sealing the mouth of the falls and then made a diving motion. Mich looked at him, disbelieving and the man nodded. "Oh yes, straight through. But I'm not at all sure you shou —"

Mich looked at Patterson.

"Ready?" he asked.

"Ready, sport," replied Patterson.

They turned and sprinted towards the falls.

Officer O'Toole sprang forward.

"Now wait jest a minute, young feller," he said.

"Michigan!" said Mrs Moorcroft. "Don't you dare!"

"Er, Mich. . ." echoed Mr Moorcroft, holding up a finger.

"You little cheesebreath," yelled Dakota. "I hate you!"

Mich shouted back over his shoulder.

"I have to! *We* have to. I'll explain when we get back. Dakota, I forgive you. Watch the TV!"

Mich and Patterson sprinted for the edge of the platform. As they neared the membrane above the falls, the platform tapered, and sloped down towards a narrow strip of crumbling concrete, scarred by acid burns, which ran directly into the dark opening. Behind them, Officer O'Toole was sprinting too.

"Oh no you don't; not on my watch!" he spat and increased his efforts. For such a small policeman he showed an astonishing turn of speed and seemed to be gaining on the pair.

Mich glanced over his shoulder and flipped his board down to the floor as it began to slope towards the falls. He hoisted Patterson aboard and pushed off just as O'Toole's tiny gnarled

223

hands clutched at the baggy material of his jeans. The skateboard gained momentum down the platform and O'Toole fell behind, cursing and spitting.

Mich and Patterson reached the lip of the platform and flew straight off into the darkness. Behind them, Mich could hear his mother scream, he heard the sound of O'Toole's footsteps, and then he felt the icy-cold embrace of the shining skin as they burst through the barrier of The Gateway and fell to Earth.

PART TWO

RETURN OF THE TEENAGE ZOMBIES

CHAPTER 1

On August 3rd 1998, Harun Mamat, a forty-seven-year-old Malaysian man, climbed a tree in order to pick fruit. He was shot by hunters who said they had "mistaken him for a squirrel".

Associated Press, 5 August 1998

Mich crash-landed with a bone-jarring thump and immediately an almost overwhelming rush of sensations flooded in. The first was pain, lots of it and then more pain as Patterson fell on top of him in a whirl of elbows, knees and legs.

"OW!" Patterson winced as her back connected painfully with the upturned edge of Mich's board. She sat up and looked around, rubbing her back gingerly and was suddenly over-whelmed with a crushing realization of how fresh and new everything seemed. Up there, she now realized, her senses weren't operating at full throttle, they'd been muffled, dimmed.

Back on Earth, in the land of the living, everything was instantly cranked up to maximum volume, the throttle thrown open as sensation crowded in upon sensation.

Mich too savoured it all, greedily gulping great lungfuls of air, full and rich and cold. It tasted wonderful. It tasted like life.

He barked out an involuntary laugh and let his nostrils flare to suck in all the incredible, dizzyingly subtle odours, strands of diesel fumes, winter, wet grass, the asphalt they were sitting on, all blending in a rich heady brew. His fingers brushed the new snow which dusted the side of the road. Delicately crystalline on his fingertips – Mich had never before noticed quite how beautiful snow was. Strangely the snow lay intact on his fingertips, not melting. Then he realized why. He had no body heat to dissolve the white flakes. Patterson stuck out her tongue and some of the softly drifting flakes settled there. She giggled in delight.

Mich had to scrunch his eyes against the sheer volume of visual information streaming in, like someone emerging from a movie theatre into daylight. Every gleaming tailfeather on a large black bird staring at him from a nearby fence-post stood out in sharp, distinct detail.

He looked in wonder at the soft, almost infinitely varied, blue-grey tones of the clouds, the white snow, the glittering reds and dirty yellows and dusty greens of the cars. They

 228

sounded like rockets, louder and throatier than any Mich could ever remember hearing. Even the way he was hearing felt different too, like he could separate the different threads of noise into their component parts, the way a mixing desk divides up sound: the hiss of the tyres on wet concrete, the deep rumble of auto engines, the ambient background noise of birds and wind.

A huge semi roared past, no more than sixty centimetres away, its horn blaring. Mich yelped and instinctively rolled back, pulling Patterson with him. They tumbled down a slight incline and came to rest with their backs against a shallow snow bank, Patterson holding her ears and grinning.

They looked at each other and burst into laughter.

"This is *fantastic!*" shouted Patterson, and her voice boomed into Mich's ear canal, echoing off the walls and hollow bones of his inner ear.

"Stop shouting!" he said, then realized she hadn't as his own voice rang inside his head.

"Wow!" said Mich. "This is like, *too* much."

Patterson got to her feet and pulled Mich up. Her face was beaming and Mich wondered how intense the feeling must be for her. It was like an entirely new world to him and he'd been away from this for less than a week. Patterson hadn't experienced this for thirty years. He looked at her and they laughed again.

"You have snot on your face," Patterson pointed out when they had calmed a little.

Mich wiped his face with the back of his sleeve.

"Thanks."

They were standing in a snow-covered field alongside the freeway. Beyond the field, low hills covered in snow-dusted trees ran into the distance. A blue sign about ten metres away displayed the interstate number: I-91. Deep gouges of dark mud cut through the snow twisting towards a newly repaired fence. A twisted fender lay discarded in the shallow ditch, close to where a solitary cow was dispiritedly foraging at the margins of the field.

The cow glanced at them before resuming her meal. It was snowing softly, the sort of snow that can't decide if it's water or ice.

"This is where it happened," said Mich.

Patterson didn't have to ask what he meant. This was where Mich and his family had died, just a week ago. It felt like decades to him.

The two of them stood looking at the traffic.

"Er, what now?" Patterson said.

Mich scratched his nose.

"I don't know. I was so sure that getting here would be next to impossible that I hadn't thought much past this bit."

He looked around and put his hands in his pockets, his toe idly scraping some snow.

 230

"I guess we should try and find where they took Alaska."

Behind them there was a sudden movement as the cow bolted, a loud bray making Mich and Patterson turn and watch as it lurched, wide-eyed and panicky, across the field. Neither Mich nor Patterson had seen the shape that had fallen to the ground and spooked the cow.

It watched them, transparent and silent, and oozed into a ditch at the side of the field.

"What was that?" asked Patterson.

Mich shrugged and they turned back to the freeway.

Patterson suggested hitching.

"Which way?" said Mich.

She jerked a thumb north.

"If the wreck was on this side they most probably took Alaska in this direction. Anyway," she added, seeing Mich's sceptical face. "It's as good an idea as anything else. Unless you have a better suggestion, Einstein?"

Mich didn't.

They moved to the freeway and Patterson stuck out a hopeful thumb. For a while, they stood, freezing and ecstatic, as cars and trucks zoomed past in a spray of dirt and sleet. Then a battered tow truck pulled in just ahead of them. The tail-gate was plastered with bumper stickers. Mich read a couple of them. *The Truth Is Out There. Shoot 'Em All, Let God Sort 'Em Out.*

"Hop aboard, little lady! Plenty of room up front!" A man in a dirty orange hunter's jacket leaned out of the cab and shouted to Patterson. He eyed Mich and his smile wavered for a moment. "You too."

"What do you think?" said Patterson.

"He looks OK . . . I guess," said Mich. Then he smiled as a thought occurred to him. "But he should be the one who's worrying; he's just stopped to give a ride to a couple of zombies. . ."

Patterson laughed, bugged her eyes out zombie-style and they trotted forward to climb into the musty cab.

As Mich hoisted himself up behind Patterson, he got a good look at the driver. It didn't reassure him. He was a thin guy with bad skin, no chin and a pot belly. His collar-length hair needed a wash and from this distance he looked like he might smell bad. Patterson hesitated.

"Jest step on in, girly." He smiled, revealing crooked, yellowing teeth. He patted the seat beside him and Patterson gingerly sat down. Mich's instincts had been right; he did smell bad, a pungent, funky aroma of clothes left unwashed, cigarette smoke and greasy food.

His movements were furtive and reminded Mich of a pole-cat he'd once seen at Mason Dooley's house. Mich was about to climb inside when he stopped on the cab step. A movement out of the corner of his eye had caught his attention.

"Well, young feller?" said the driver. "You got a problem, or whut?"

Mich looked back towards the field and blinked.

There was a rustling sound and the air above the field seemed to part for a moment, like fabric being torn, and a small, yelling figure dropped to the ground and bounced into the snow about twenty metres behind the truck. He lay belly up for a moment, wriggling and spluttering like a beetle on its back, before managing to right himself.

"Jaysus Mary and Joseph! Sweet Mother of Christ! What in the name of. . .!"

Officer O'Toole sat up and tenderly rubbed his green beard. His cap was set at an odd angle and he adjusted it very carefully and deliberately. He looked around, spotted Mich and erupted into a fresh volcano of colourful Irish curses.

"Hoy! Stop right there!"

Mich jumped into the cab, slamming the door behind him.

"No problem at all," he said to the driver, leaning forward to get an angle on the wing mirror. O'Toole was up and racing after the truck as fast as his tiny legs could carry him.

Mich looked at the driver.

"What're you waiting for? Let's go!"

The driver gave Mich a thin look, and for a moment Mich thought he too had seen the leprechaun Controller, but he pressed the pedal and the truck peeled back into the traffic on

233

the freeway. Behind them Officer O'Toole fell away in the wing mirror, incandescent with fury. He stood in the dirty slush, shaking his fist at the truck and leaping up and down. He took off his hat and jumped on it.

Mich breathed out slowly. That had been close.

The driver was talking.

His name was Bobby. Bobby DuPont Sinclair. He told them he'd been on a hunting trip with a few of his buddies from the power plant up in North Morton but somehow he'd lost 'em all in the woods and here he was comin' back early. S'funny, said Sinclair, that kind of stuff was always happenin' around him: people losing him, he couldn't figure it out.

"Is there a hospital in North Morton?" asked Patterson.

"Why? You sick or sumpin'?" Bobby snorted. "You look just fine to me, girly."

"Sorta."

He gave Patterson an oily smile and patted her knee. Patterson squirmed like he'd placed a live toad there and Sinclair put it back on the steering wheel.

There were some empty beer cans rolling around on the floor of the cab. Bobby Sinclair's driving was erratic and Mich wondered about how dangerous he really was. Maybe they should try and get a different ride to the hospital. This guy could cause a crash. Then, with a jolt (it always surprised him), he remembered that he and Patterson were already dead

 234

and he smiled. Hell, he was a goddamn car crash veteran.

"Whut's so funny, young feller?" said Bobby Sinclair.

"Oh, nothing," said Mich. "How far's North Morton?"

" 'Bout thirty miles or such up the road."

Sinclair turned to Patterson and grimaced at her in what he imagined was a friendly smile. He looked like the winner in a village idiot contest.

"Plenty of time to get friendly."

He rubbed her knee again. Patterson picked up his hand and moved it back to the wheel.

At Patterson's touch, Bobby Sinclair recoiled, his oily grin gone in an instant.

"Damn! Whut is the matter with you, girly? Your hand's colder'n a Eskimo's icebox! Guess you bin standin' out there too long, huh?"

Patterson nodded.

"I jes' gotta make me a stop 'fore we gets to Morton. Kind of a refuelling and drainage stop if you get my drift." He winked at Mich.

"Fact, here's the place now."

Sinclair whipped the truck on to the exit ramp and headed towards a low-roofed building standing next to a gas station. A large red neon sign sat above it, standing out clear against the grey-blue winter sky. *Lou's Bowlerama and Lounge* it read. A line of cars stood nose up against the side of the

235

building like pigs nuzzling the sow.

"But. . ." said Mich. "What about getting to Morton?"

"No 'buts' kid," said Sinclair. "I gotta see a man about a dog, ya dig?"

CHAPTER 2

Art thief Peter Gruber was chased by a security guard at an art museum in Bonn, Germany. He was accidentally killed when he ran on to a sword which was part of a statue called "Blind Justice".

Guardian, 29 June 2000

Moorcroft had the shakes bad. The heater in the truck was cranked to maximum, turning the cab into a sweatbox, but Moorcroft couldn't stop shivering. It had taken almost all his energy just to get out of the motel and across the sleety parking lot to where he'd parked up. He'd made good and sure to park it a long way from his room out of habit; you never knew when the cops'd run a check and find the truck coming up as reported stolen. If that happened, Moorcroft didn't want it to be parked right outside his room. But now, cold and sick, the last thing he'd needed was that goddamned cross-country

237

hike in a winter storm. The icy sleet slanted across the lot, racing in off the Atlantic out of a slate-grey sky and knifing straight through Moorcroft's heavy coat as if it wasn't there.

He'd stopped halfway in the lee of a big semi and hawked up gobs of blood on to the slush covering the parking lot. Christ! He needed a doctor just as soon as he'd taken care of the problem up at North Morton Teaching.

Trembling, he started the engine, moved out of the motel lot and pointed the truck in the direction of the hospital. It was New Year's Eve and most people were staying inside, making plans for the holiday. Traffic was light. Five minutes down the road, Moorcroft pulled into a Walgreens drugstore and lurched inside.

The aisles were slanted at a thirty-degree angle to the walls. Just inside the door a thin, sly-looking girl stood behind a till. She was serving a teenage boy and when Moorcroft came in they looked at him. The boy said something to the girl and they laughed. Moorcroft believed (correctly) that they were laughing at him. Punks.

He wanted to do something about them, yell at them, stick that laugh right back down their weasely throats. Instead he banged into a display stack of plastic angels which had been reduced in price. The stack shook and a couple of the off-white angels fell to the floor. Passing them, Moorcroft briefly wondered about what kind of loser would shop for bargain

 238

Christmas trash a year in advance. Forgetting all about the punk kids at the till he moved down the aisles until he found what he was looking for amongst the packs of haemorrhoid cream and contact lens fluid. He pocketed the three packs of Tylenol and picked up a couple of cans of soda.

At the checkout he paid for the two cans of Coke. The Tylenols he didn't mention, hell they were $4.99 apiece and he was damned if he was gonna pay. The girl at the checkout looked at him funny, as if she knew what was in his pocket, but she didn't make any fuss. It was New Year's Eve and she could do without trouble.

Back in the truck he scarfed six of the tablets down, coughing as the soda hit the back of his throat. Whether it was mainly psychological or what, he didn't know, but he felt better, at least a little. He'd been feeling like death. The caffeine cleared his head and he leaned forward and started the motor.

He decided not to take the interstate to the hospital. If the truck broke down there he'd be stuck. On smaller roads he could always boost another car.

He looked at his watch. Plenty of time yet. There was no need to attract attention by turning up at the hospital too early. Maybe he'd just take a rest here, now the shivering had eased. He lay back and propped his feet up on the passenger seat.

He was in no rush.

CHAPTER 3

On September 17th 1998, environmentalist David Chain was killed by a falling tree while protesting against tree cutting in Grizzly Creek, California.

Rocky Mountain News, 18 September 1998

Phil Challenor had been driving for two days solid. Every year he faithfully made the trek from Montana to his mother's place in West Morton, New Hampshire for New Year's. This year's trip had been delayed thanks to the last-minute decision of Delia, Phil's wife, to stay in White Manor after all and look after the dogs. Now Phil was racing against the clock, cursing his wife; he'd have to be there before lunchtime or his name would be mud. His mother, the proud possessor of a tongue that could cut steel, would surely kick up a heap of fuss, although in his heart Phil knew things would run more smoothly without the usual Christmas friction between Delia and his mother.

There was something at the side of the road ahead of him. His eyes felt gritty after so long peering through the rain-lashed windscreen. He blinked. At first he didn't trust what he was seeing. He looked again and wiped the inside of the screen. Then he pinched the flesh on the bridge of his nose and squinted as if that would clear his vision.

No, he'd been right first time: he *had* seen . . . it, he just didn't believe what he was looking at. He flashed by, craning his neck and wondering what to do, if anything. It was a couple of miles before he saw the police cruiser in front of him and flashed his headlights.

"Lemme get this straight, sir," said Officer Flint in the big rain slicker, leaning in to Phil's window. "You want to report a *what*?"

Phil Challenor took a deep breath and adjusted his glasses. This wasn't going well. His face was bright red but now he'd started he had to go on.

"You heard me."

Flint smiled and spoke into his radio.

"Tony, you wanna come back here and hear this."

The door to the cruiser opened and the second patrolman walked wearily back to where Phil's car stood. He leaned in through the window. The name on his badge read *Officer Fortelli*.

Officer Flint nodded towards Fortelli and spoke to Phil Challenor over Fortelli's shoulder.

"Tell my partner here what you just told me."

Phil coughed.

"Well, like I was saying, erm, I was driving down the inter-state on my way to my mother's, when I saw a, that is, I saw a. . ." He tailed off.

"Yes?" said Fortelli, raising his eyebrows, his expression all innocence.

"Oh, all right then. I saw a leprechaun, OK?"

"A leprechaun?"

"Yes, that's right, a goddamn leprechaun! A leprechaun dressed like a policeman and riding a cow down the side of the interstate. And there's no need to look at me like that, I saw what I saw." Challenor sat back, scowling, red-faced, defiant.

"Can you describe the, er, leprechaun, sir?" said Flint. "I mean, was it a regular leprechaun with little green boots and a sweet little green hat? Or was it more of a modern-day leprechaun with—"

Challenor interrupted, irritated.

"I already said, it was dressed like a policeman!"

"So how did you know it was a leprechaun, sir?" Flint put his hand to his face, stifling a laugh. Fortelli was doubled up, one

 242

hand on the roof of Challenor's car, laughing like a drain.

"Because it had a green beard and big pointed ears! It just looked like a goddamn leprechaun, OK?"

Flint and Fortelli exploded into uncontrolled laughter. When they had recovered, with only minor tremors still erupting every few seconds, Flint leaned back in.

"Could you step out of the car, sir? I have reason to believe that you may have been drinking." He looked at Challenor. "On account of it being New Year and all."

O'Toole spotted the police car up ahead, its blue lights flickering through the white sleet.

He dug his heels into the sides of the big cow and urged it forward.

"C'mon yer big useless lump!" he shouted. "Move!"

The cow continued to plod along.

O'Toole was beginning to have doubts about using the cow. His leprechaun training back in cow-rich County Cork had enabled him to get the beast moving, but that was about it. O'Toole wasn't sure if he'd have been quicker running, but he was a martyr to his bunions and stayed on the cow. He'd seen the exit sign about half a mile back. His plan was to take that exit and find the nearest hospital. Officer Moorcroft had filled him in on what had happened to her son and O'Toole guessed that North Morton was where he'd find Alaska, not to mention all the other wee rapscallions and n'er-do-wells. But if he could make that police cruiser up ahead he could get whisked there in no time!

He urged the cow onwards.

Phil Challenor was protesting loudly as he was pulled from his warm car and stood up in the sleeting rain. Flint ambled back to the cruiser and started to speak into the radio.

"Hey! I'm gonna sue! What's your badge number?"

Fortelli ignored him.

"We need to get a few things sorted out back at the station," he said. "Sir. I'm arresting you on suspicion of DUI. You know what that means; DUI, right? Driving Under the Influence, OK? I'm arresting you on suspicion of DUI. You have the right to remain silent, you have the right to an attorney. If you do not have an attorney one will. . ."

He trailed off as he caught sight of Challenor's face looking back down the interstate over his shoulder.

Fortelli turned as Phil started doing a little dance of celebration.

"See!" he yelled at the policeman, prodding him with his finger. "Who's DUI now, eh? Eh?"

Officer O'Toole jumped down from the cow and slapped its rump, chasing it back into a field. It ran away gratefully.

"Am I ever glad to see yer, boyo!" said O'Toole to the stunned patrolman. Fortelli, his mouth open, stood looking down at the small figure. The patrolman rocked back and forth as Phil Challenor gleefully prodded him again and again.

"Now, are yer gonna jest stand oot here in the miserable pourin' rain all day like a great wet nelly, or are yer gonna get yer skates on an' let us all get a warm? It's colder'n a witch's heart oot here."

The patrolman shook himself and turned to face the police cruiser.

"AL!" he yelled. "I need some back-up out here!"

CHAPTER
4

Inside Lou's Bowlerama it was hot and noisy and smoky. Every lane was full and the roaring crash of bowling balls filled the space completely. Bobby Sinclair looked around and spotted whatever it was he was looking for.

"Jes' make yourselves comfortable, fellers," he said, oozing a yellow-toothed smile at Mich and Patterson. "I'll be back in two shakes of a duck's tail. Don' be goin' nowheres, y'hear?"

He winked and moved towards the restrooms.

Patterson shivered.

"What a creep!" she said and Mich nodded.

"Let's get another ride," said Mich. "There has to be someone heading towards Morton."

They hung around near the entrance hopefully for a few minutes but no one seemed to be going anywhere. Mich walked over to the counter behind which a large man sat on a high stool reading a newspaper. An enormous bowling trophy sat on the counter next to him.

"Hi," said Mich.

The man grunted and flicked an eyebrow at Mich.

"Do you know if anyone's heading towards Morton?" asked Mich. "We could do with a ride."

"Gonna hafta wait," said the man. "Ain't no one going anywhere till the competition's over."

He nodded his head in the direction of the bowling lanes. Now that Mich and Patterson looked they could see that each lane was occupied by a team, each team wearing silky shirts in matching colours. High fives were exchanged when a strike was made and friendly insults filled the air.

They wandered over to a booth and moodily watched the teams nearest to them.

"We could get a cab," suggested Mich.

Patterson said, "We don't have any money."

They sank into gloomy silence and waited for Sinclair.

From a nearby lane came the sound of a strike, the rattle of

247

pins and the chorus of cheers. A lanky, painfully thin guy raised his hand, palm up and walked back to his team, each of them smacking their palms against his.

"Way to go, man!"

"Nice action!"

"You the man!"

The thin man, wearing a lime green shirt with *Vincent's Tyre Emporium* picked out in white glanced over in Mich's direction and stopped dead, a surprised expression on his cadaverous features. He winked and cocked a finger, gunslinger style at Mich. There was something spookily familiar about him, something about his movements and a chill around the eyes, but Mich couldn't quite put his finger on exactly where he'd seen him before.

"Friend of yours?" said Patterson.

"I don't know," said Mich. "He reminds me of someone. . ."

Mich trailed off, his mouth falling open. He had remembered. He knew now who the man reminded him of; no, who the man *was*. As he watched, the man detached himself from the rest of the Vincent's Tyre team and ambled across to Mich and Patterson.

"Mr Moorcroft?" said the man. "What a pleasant surprise. I didn't expect to see you here. I presume you must have found a way through? Silly question; of course you have, otherwise how would you end up down here. . ."

 248

He shrugged and waved his arms around at the Bowlerama.

"Aren't you going to introduce me to your friend? I can see from your expression that you've recognized me."

Mich coughed and nodded towards Patterson.

"This is Patterson," he said. "Patterson, this is, erm. . ."

The man thrust a bony hand towards Patterson.

"The name's Reaper. You can call me Grim."

Patterson looked at Mich and raised her eyebrows.

"Oh yeah," said Mich, nodding. "The Man himself."

"Oh," said Patterson weakly. "Er, hi."

The Grim Reaper slid into the booth alongside Mich and rested his thin arms on the red formica.

"Please don't be alarmed, my dear," he said to Patterson. "I'm here purely for pleasure."

He glanced across at a red-faced fat guy smoking a cigarette and munching a double burger with cheese and all the trimmings in a booth behind lane four.

"Well, maybe a little business," he murmured.

"But. . ." started Mich.

"The bowling?" said the Grim Reaper. "We meet every third Thursday at Lou's. All started as a bit of a joke, but now we're completely hooked."

"We?" said Mich.

"Well, there's myself and Famine, Pestilence and War. Down here we're called Bob, Lee, Chuck and Kevin." He

249

pointed to the team name embroidered on his shirt pocket; *The Four Horsemen*.

"Neat, huh?"

He nodded over to the rest of the Four Horsemen and they all waved back. Mich and Patterson shivered.

"And you remember Mike, don't you? From our first meeting? He's the reserve; no real action to speak of but keen as a hound after a rabbit."

Mich looked over and, with another jolt, recognized Mictlantecuhtli, the Aztec Lord of the Underworld, taking a pull on a Diet Coke. He too was dressed in a lime green bowling shirt, although he had toned down his bloody skeleton appearance somewhat. No one in the bowling alley seemed to notice anything unusual about the odd-looking team. Mike winked and shouted over to Mich.

"Hey kid! You come back! You onna vacation, or what?" He cackled wildly. "Honestly, I cracka mysel' uppa sometime!"

Mich waved limply at Mike.

"So all the other teams," said Patterson. "Are they, er, you know. . .?"

"Harbingers of doom from the afterlife?" chuckled the Grim Reaper. "No, not all, my dear. Well, not unless you include Ossie's lot."

"Ossie?"

The Grim Reaper waved a hand over Mich's shoulder. A

 250

bunch of olive-complexioned men were looking with concentration at the overhead electronic scoreboard.

"Lane seven. Osiris, Lord of the Egyptian Underworld. He usually manages to get a team together as well. Lot of gods over there in the Egyptian afterlife. They're playing the guys from Mario's Pizzeria. Between ourselves this is a bit of a crunch match."

Before Mich could speak there was a commotion in one of the lanes. The fat smoker was lying on the wooden boards, his face now a strange blue colour.

"Must dash," said the Grim Reaper. "Looks like a spot of work for yours truly. Can't get a minute's peace down here; still, mustn't grumble, eh?"

He rose to leave and as he did so Bobby Sinclair appeared again. He was breathing heavily and carried a small brown paper bag.

The Grim Reaper stood and shook Sinclair's hand.

"Pleased to meet you," he said quietly. "Be sure and drop in on me soon, you hear?"

"Not in my lifetime, buddy," said Sinclair.

"Precisely," said the Grim Reaper smiling. He winked at Mich and Patterson and drifted across to the knot of people gathered round the gasping fat man.

"Let me through," Mich heard him say. "I'm an expert."

Sinclair watched him go.

251

"Loser," he sniffed.

He turned back to Mich and Patterson.

"OK, c'mon, I ain't got all day. You guys still wanna hitch a ride?"

He coughed and scratched his belly.

Patterson looked like she was about to be sick when Mich stepped forward.

"Sure, mister. Let's go."

"Well, OK!" said Sinclair. "Let's rock and roll!"

They left Lou's Bowlerama as an ambulance pulled into the parking lot. Two paramedics raced past them towards the fat man inside. Mich wondered if he'd pull through but didn't rate his chances highly. Not with the skinny member of *The Four Horsemen* in attendance.

Sinclair slid into the driver's seat followed by Patterson and Mich. He gunned the engine aggressively and the truck shot across the asphalt and back on to the interstate, only just missing a semi coming off the exit ramp. Sinclair flipped a finger in response to the semi's blast on the horn.

"Jumped-up grease jockey!" snarled Sinclair. "Think they own the road."

He turned to Patterson and smiled at her. A waft of stale onions made her cough. *I'm dead*, she thought, looking at Sinclair, *and you've got worse breath than me*.

"Hey honey," said Sinclair. "How 'bout slidin' a l'il' closer?

You look like you need warmin' up."

"I —" started Patterson. She turned towards Mich and grimaced.

"Think of something!" she hissed under her breath. "This guy is creeping me out!"

Mich nodded, bent forward and let loose a series of phlegmy coughs. His entire body shook as he rocked back and forth.

Sinclair looked at him in alarm.

Mich started shivering, wrapped his arms around himself and began to moan.

"Oooooooohhhhhhhhhhhhhh! Owwwwohhhhhowwwhhhh!"

"Hey!" said Sinclair. "Is he all right, or whut?"

"We're sick, mister," said Mich. "Real sick. Ohhhhhh!"

Sinclair's eyes were on stalks.

"You *are* kind of greeny-lookin' mothers come to mention it. You sure you OK to be out, you know, around folks?"

"I don't know!" said Mich theatrically. "Before we . . . got out, the doctors at the Secure Unit said we had to stay on quarantine."

"Doctors?" said Sinclair. "Secure Unit? What the hell is goin' on?"

"It's some kind of government mutant bug thing," moaned Mich. "They've been running experiments on us out in the woods and we escaped."

"Whut!" says Sinclair, bug-eyed. "Like in that *X-Files* on TV?"

"Sure," said Mich. He coughed once more.

"I knew it!" said Sinclair and slapped the steering wheel.

"So, is it con – contajes – I mean is it, can I *ketch* it?"

"Dunno," said Patterson. "Most everyone else jes' died! I'd get us to the hospital real quick."

Bobby Sinclair swallowed and tried to put as much space between himself and Patterson as possible. Mich stifled a laugh and turned it into a pitiful moan.

"Ohhhhhhhhhhhwohhhhhowhhhhh!"

"Maybe I should set you down right here," said Sinclair.

"Well, sure," said Mich. "I wouldn't blame you one bit. But say you *have* got it, and say maybe we already got the antidote you need to get fixed up? What would you do then?"

Sinclair's beer-fuddled mind struggled with this for a few seconds. Patterson and Mich could almost see his brain trying to calculate the odds. Then he floored the accelerator and the tow truck surged forward. Sinclair kept darting glances at them and then increasing his speed. He wound down the driver's window and stuck his head out. He insisted on driving this way, presumably in an effort to prevent becoming infected. Five minutes later they exited the interstate, the wheels of the truck sliding as Sinclair whipped round the exit ramp towards North Morton.

None of them noticed the translucent shape curled in the back of the truck, where it had been since Sinclair had picked them up.

CHAPTER 5

A Minneapolis man called Sherman Killsplenty was arrested in December 1996 for murder.

Fortean Times, March 1998

Officer O'Toole had never travelled in a dirtier police car. Then again, he usually sat up front with his partner. In the back, where he was now, things were much, much nastier. There was the wire separating him from the front seats which had bits of dried chewing gum wedged, rock-like and immovable, in dozens of places. The seats were sticky and grimy and looked a thousand years old. *Not far off my own age*, thought O'Toole. *Before I died, that is*.

As well as the filth, O'Toole had to put up with Phil Challenor. He hadn't stopped blustering and wailing since the patrol officers decided to bundle everyone up and get them back to the station. The plan was to sort out who was drunk, and who was or wasn't a leprechaun, back in the warm, dry police station.

Out of the dirty windows, O'Toole watched with interest as they drove through the outskirts of Morton and into town. Things had certainly changed amongst the Breathers since his last visit. *That must have been about 1776,* reflected O'Toole as they passed a seemingly endless procession of car dealerships, fast food places and furniture stores, office suppliers, lighting shops, gas stations, hospitals. . .

Hospital! Officer O'Toole sat upright as they sailed past North Morton Teaching Hospital. Like most hospitals, it was a vast modern structure, its concrete surface streaked with snow and rain. A tall chimney stood at the rear, its grey smoke whipped sideways by the wind. Dull, straggling trees had been planted in a vain effort to hide the place from view. A huge sign indicated what seemed like hundreds of different departments around the site. O'Toole sighed. He needed to get in there and get to the kids. They didn't know what they were doing and O'Toole was running out of time.

"Desperate times, desperate times," he murmured under his breath.

"What?" said Flint, shifting in his seat to eyeball the leprechaun.

"You say sump'n, little guy?"

257

"I was sayin' that desperate times call for desperate measures, big feller," replied O'Toole.

Flint raised his eyebrows.

"Whatever," he said and turned back to the road. They were almost at the precinct.

O'Toole pondered.

He had been a leprechaun for nearly a thousand years. For most of that time he'd contented himself with causing mischief in the lanes and hills of western Ireland, but for the past 243 years he'd been as dead as a Dublin dodo with a hell of a long time still up in Purgatory to go. The authorities never knew what to do with the likes of him, did they? Neither fish nor fowl, so to speak. Wasn't strictly good, now, so can't go to Heaven, yet not precisely what you'd call *bad*, is he, so that's the other place out, too. Which just left sittin' around up there with nothin' to do except twiddle your thumbs.

O'Toole hadn't joined the Controllers happily. With almost a millennium of mischief behind him, it didn't come naturally to swap sides. But after a while, O'Toole had started to like being poacher turned gamekeeper, and had become one of the Controllers' most committed officers. He'd bagged more than twelve thousand miscreants, deviants, crims, flim-flam artists and paper-hangers, and had never once used his considerable leprechaun powers to nab any of them.

This looked an altogether different brand of animal, though.

This looked like he might have to cause some mischief to get what he wanted. He hoped that She would look kindly upon it and see it as the necessary evil it was.

"Hey fellers," he said to the patrolmen. "Take a look at this."

Fortelli and Flint turned around and O'Toole wrinkled his nose.

The patrol officers laughed out loud and turned back.

"Whooh!" said Fortelli. "Was that some weird scary leprechaun voodoo or what?"

He laughed loud and long. O'Toole sat and waited patiently.

"I guess we were wrong about the little guy after all, Tony," said Flint.

He turned the cruiser into the precinct parking lot and pulled to a halt around the side of the building.

"OK," said Fortelli, opening the door.

Phil Challenor stepped out followed by the tiny figure of O'Toole. The two cops were still chuckling as the air filled with lilting Irish music.

"What the. . ." said Flint as his toes began to tap lightly.

"What the hell you doin', Al?" said Fortelli. Then he clasped his hands behind his back and, standing ramrod straight, began to dance an Irish jig, his legs flipping out and up, his heavy police issue shoes clicking and clacking on the asphalt. Fortelli's face filled with panic.

"I can't stop it, Al! I can't stop!"

259

Flint wasn't listening. He had his own problems. His legs too were rapping furiously as the music increased in tempo. The muscles in his arms stood out as he fought to stop them locking behind his back. But he was powerless, held in the leprechaun's grip and the lilt of the Irish pipes.

Phil Challenor was backing away in terror when his feet too began to tap to the rhythms.

"Noooo!" he wailed. "Not 'The Wild Rover'!"

O'Toole stepped out of the way as he wrinkled his little Irish face and pointed it towards the police precinct doors.

Fortelli, Flint and Challenor lined up, still dancing, backs straight, arms held stiffly at their sides, legs flailing away in unison as the pipes wailed. With faces locked in despair, they danced up the steps and into the station. O'Toole waited until he heard the howls of laughter from inside before jumping into the police cruiser.

"Humiliation," he murmured, stretching for the pedals. "Does the trick every toime!"

CHAPTER 6

In December 1998, a Cameroonian chicken thief, cornered by a mob, was forced to eat the entire bird as punishment. The thief had an allergic reaction to the chicken and died.

Reuters, 3 December 1998

Fear of dying of some freakin' bug mutant goddam government *X-Files* disease was not improving Bobby Sinclair's driving. He had insisted on driving all the way to North Morton Hospital with his head hung out of the side window. The rain bit into his face and, no matter how hard he screwed up his eyes, he could only see flashes of the road ahead. Water streamed down his unlovely features. Car horns blared as he slewed his truck across the road and up the ramp into the grounds of the hospital. Mich and Patterson hung on, laughing. Every now and then Patterson faked a fit for Bobby's benefit, clawing dramatically at her throat and rolling her eyes. Each time she did it, Bobby broke into a fresh bout of moaning and pushed the tow truck faster.

Finally, they slid to a halt in the *Ambulance Only* section right outside the hospital entrance, the tow truck slanted diagonally across the bay, its hoist swinging crazily before it settled. Sinclair jumped from the cab before it stopped moving and began screaming at a couple of nursing staff who were standing near the doors watching impassively.

"Help me! Help me! Get the stuff offa them freakin' mutants! C'mon! Ah'm *dyin'*!" he wailed. Mich and Patterson dropped down from the truck and watched as Sinclair did a fair impression of a headless chicken. One of the nurses, a large, square-built black guy, dropped his cigarette and ground the stub into the floor. He moved forward and took hold of Sinclair's arm.

Mich looked at the nurse and made a small circular motion with his index finger next to his head.

"Wacko, eh?" said the nurse.

"Completely nuts," Mich said. "He picked us up and then went freaky on us. He needs help."

"They's aliens, or sump'n, or experimentals! *Mutants!*" screamed Sinclair.

"You see?" said Mich, shaking his head sadly.

Patterson nodded and then added in a small voice:

 262

"Please don't let him hurt me again."

Bobby's eyes grew red and he lunged at Patterson.

"You lyin' trash! I'm gonna rip yer head off when I get loose!"

Flecks of spittle flew from his mouth as he twisted and wriggled in the big nurse's grip.

"Let go of me, ya big gorilla!" he yelled (unwisely as it turned out) at the nurse.

The nurse glared at Sinclair.

"Is that right, now?" he said softly, and tapped him on the top of his head with a fist that looked like it could bang in nails without the aid of a hammer. Bobby Sinclair dropped to the floor as if all his bones had turned to Jell-O.

"You wanna file a report about this guy?" said the nurse.

"Nah," said Mich. "We just want to get away from him."

"I hear that. You two scoot. Me and Hector here'll take care of this guy."

He turned, picked Sinclair up by his jacket, and carried him into the hospital. At the door he stopped and spoke to Mich and Patterson.

"You sure you don't need anything? You don't look too good. That's a nasty bruise you got." He gestured at Mich and touched his own forehead.

They shook their heads and the two nurses carried Sinclair inside.

263

"Bruise?" said Mich.

Patterson looked at him. High on the right hand side of Mich's head was a large ugly purple-green bruise.

"Maybe when you fell out of The Gateway," said Patterson.

"Yeah," Mich replied, although he couldn't remember being hit by anything. "That's probably it.'

He looked at Patterson.

"You know, you're looking a bit funny too," said Mich.

"Funny ha-ha, or funny peculiar?"

"Peculiar. Green."

They looked at each other. They did both look peculiar. As they examined one another they saw that their skin had slackened and appeared to have changed colour. It was now an unpleasant, flat, light blue-green flecked here and there with unsightly mottles and blotches, the most obvious being the one on Mich's head.

Patterson was the first to speak. "Remember what the Guardian of The Gateway said?"

"About the side-effects?"

"Yeah. Well I think they're happening quicker than expected, Mich. We may not have much time."

The hospital entrance was in front of them.

"In that case, what are we doing standing around here?"

CHAPTER 7

April 1993: Willie Murphy, a sixty-one-year-old worker at the Golden Peanut Company, Georgia, was killed when he was caught in a peanut avalanche.

USA Today, 5 April 1993

Moorcroft woke with a start and cracked his head painfully on the door pillar of the truck. He launched into a stream of cursing. Rubbing his head he looked out and saw the big red Walgreens logo filling the windscreen. He swore some more and punched the rim of the steering wheel with the flat of his hand.

He'd fallen asleep! He couldn't believe it. Musta been the pills. He looked at his watch; he'd been asleep a whole hour. He was lucky he'd given himself an early start, but he'd have to be careful not to slip again. Stupid, stupid, stupid. He cursed and pounded the steering wheel again, so hard he drew blood.

With his mouth feeling like something had recently died in it, he started the engine and drove away from the drugstore. Two minutes later he pulled into the huge parking lot of a nearby shopping mall. He dumped the stolen car and picked out another, an anonymous grey Taurus. He was driving towards the hospital within eight minutes of leaving Walgreens.

He was hot and feverish again, a prickly, slick sweat gleaming on his face and running in an uncomfortable trickle down the small of his back. Every couple of minutes he shivered uncontrollably and goosebumps started up all along his arms and legs. Then the fever bit and the sweats began again. He just wanted to get this done, snuff the kid and get out of North Morton for good. He was going to head back south, he'd decided, somewhere hot; it was too goddamn wet and cold up here. It had already got him with this bug.

He pressed the accelerator and pushed the Taurus a little faster towards North Morton Hospital and Alaska Moorcroft.

When he arrived, Moorcroft parked at a distance from the building and waited. You could find out plenty just by watching and waiting.

Despite falling asleep at the drugstore he was still early, and he planned on taking no more unnecessary risks. The kid might not have come out of the coma and blabbed about the guy with the tattoos who hadn't stopped at the crash scene,

 266

but Moorcroft didn't know that for certain. There'd been nothing on the TV news about a miracle recovery, but maybe the cops were sitting on it, baitin' the trap, sorta. It wouldn't take too much hunting for a nosy cop to find the outstanding warrants on Moorcroft. If that had happened, reasoned Moorcroft, as he sat out in the lot, then they'd be watching the hospital to see if he'd turn up.

From the car Moorcroft had a good view of the hospital's two main entrances. He sat and watched for an hour. He did see two cops in that time but he correctly guessed that they were there on ordinary business and he watched them depart soon enough.

A short time later Moorcroft had just about decided to make his move, when a battered tow truck weaved through the narrow entrance to the hospital. It bounced off the kerb, its hoist jiggling wildly as the truck drove fast and wild up to the ambulance entrance. Two nurses, one black, one Hispanic, were outside smoking in the shelter of the concrete canopy which jutted out over the ambulance bay. The truck slammed up, directly in front of them, and Moorcroft watched as a nutty-looking guy in an orange hunter's jacket jumped out and began shouting. Moorcroft was too far away to hear what was going on, but it was obvious the guy was upset about something. *Probably a hunting accident*, thought Moorcroft. Then two kids stepped out of the truck and Moorcroft sat up.

267

"I'll be damned," he murmured, leaning forward.

It was the kid. The kid from the car wreck.

Even from a distance Moorcroft recognized him. He was still wearing the same goddam T-shirt for cryin' out loud. He looked funny, somehow, though Moorcroft couldn't quite say how. The girl looked kind of screwy too, loud clothes, out-of-date, thought Moorcroft. He couldn't tell, though; these days kids wore clothes like that, the retro look or some such non-sense. But there was something off-kilter about the kids. They were too pale, bleached out like an over-exposed photograph. Moorcroft saw the scene play out, watched as the big nurse tapped the tow truck guy and carried him into the hospital. The two kids waited a couple of minutes and then followed them in.

Moorcroft took a few minutes to think about what he'd just seen.

That this was the kid he'd seen in the car wreck was some-thing he knew for certain. It also felt to Moorcroft like the kid hadn't talked to the cops yet, although he couldn't quite under-stand why. There was something off about the way the kids'd arrived with that wacko tow truck guy too. The kicker came as Moorcroft remembered the four graves he'd visited in Communion. How was that? With one kid in the hospital and one outside, there was something not adding up in this equation. Maybe it *was* a sting, after all and the kid had

 268

survived the wreck? But why arrive with all that hoop-la, if the cops wanted to keep quiet? And what about the girl? What did she know?

Moorcroft chewed his thumbnail.

He could go, now, just press the pedal and put some miles between him and here, forget all about the kid, the cops, the wreck.

Or he could kill them all and let God sort them out, just like that old bumper sticker said.

Those were the choices.

He stepped from the truck into the rain, shaking his head. Who was he kidding? There were too many loose ends, too many trails pointing in his direction.

There was only one choice; there was only ever going to be one choice for him.

He walked towards the hospital.

CHAPTER 8

Tom Gray, 86, a retired Glamorgan coal miner, was crushed to death by coal when the wall of his bunker collapsed in his back yard in August 1997.

Daily Mirror, 8 August 1997

Inside, the big hospital was a labryinth of corridors and confusing directional signs. Soothing elevator music played at a volume just this side of annoying. Instead of the rushing crowds that populated TV hospitals, North Morton was quiet; here and there Mich and Patterson passed a cleaner pulling a rotary waxer across the linoleum, a nurse or orderly walking past softly, unhurried.

They had already been there too long, blundering from corridor to corridor, and Mich was becoming edgy. They had another problem, too. Although Mich was too preoccupied to notice, Patterson had seen that the people they passed were looking at them strangely. They shot quick, wary glances at them before looking away furtively. They were the same gestures she remembered making herself when she saw somebody with a disfigurement: a snatched guilty peep from under hooded eyes, and then the sudden feigned interest in carpet, walls, whatever, when the look was detected.

"Mich," she said and then was brought up short, her breath catching as she looked at him.

The large bruise on his forehead had ripened and split, a ragged five-centimetre gash, rancid yellow and sour purple outlining a dull, wet red below the skin. His flesh had shrunk a little on his bones, even in the twenty minutes they'd been wandering the halls of North Morton. The fingers on his left hand, the ones burnt in the River of Lost Souls, were in particularly bad shape, the acid eating away at the skin. The side-effects they'd been warned about at The Gateway were arriving faster now.

"What?" Mich said, absently, his mind still fixed on locating Alaska.

Patterson looked away.

"Oh, nuthin'," she said.

A cold bolt of fear slid through the middle of her at the sight of Mich. It was fear tinged with self-pity; if he looked like that then she too must look as bad. She bit back tears, cursing

271

herself for being a stupid girl.

You're dead, *for cryin' out loud*, she told herself, *it's a bit late to be worrying about your looks*. Besides, she was *in* this thing now, right at the centre of it, and it would have to be played out to the end, there was no going back. She straightened her back and increased the pace slightly.

They came to a busier part of the hospital where there were rows of potted plants, and lines of lime-green and burnt-orange seats, dotted about with people waiting, talking, reading. It was the main reception area. Oddly, for such a clean hospital, there was a small, scruffy-looking dog sitting next to a large ficus tree. It was playing with a ball of wool and seemed, to Patterson, to be watching them. She shook her head and looked around. She noticed the double-take reaction of one or two of the people in there as they caught sight of the strange children. She turned to warn Mich but it was too late; he was already walking up to the reception desk.

"Yes?" said the thin woman behind it, not glancing up from her computer screen. "Can I help you?"

"I need to find my brother. His name is Moorcroft, Alaska Moorcroft. I think he's been brought here. Is he here?"

"Let me see." She punched Alaska's name into the computer. She had still not looked at Mich.

"Ah, here we are." She smiled and only then glanced up, her

272

face involuntarily morphing into an expression of shock and revulsion.

"Oh Sweet Jesus, Mary and Joseph!" she muttered looking first at Mich and then at Patterson. She made the sign of the cross and then stopped.

"Sorry," she said, recovering slightly and pressing a hand across her heart. "But you two *do* look in bad shape. What happened?"

Mich looked blank. All this was taking up valuable time. It was Patterson who spoke.

"We just got out of another hospital. We were in the car wreck with his, our, brother. Alaska. I know we look kind of bad but we wanted to see him and we need to find out where he is so if you could please just tell us we can find him and get back to getting better ourselves."

She stopped suddenly, aware she was babbling, and forced herself to stay quiet while the thin woman thought about what to do.

"I don't know," she said, slowly. "I think we should get someone to take a look at you two, you don't look so good – Hey!"

She shouted as Mich leaned across the desk and twisted the monitor around.

"Room E12a," he read and turned to Patterson. "C'mon!"

They turned away from the woman at the desk and ran, Mich checking the signs hanging above the doors.

Rooms A-E said one, and Mich plunged through a set of double doors into another corridor.

"Hey!" shouted the woman again. "Hey!"

A security guard came through the doors. He started after them but Patterson could see he was quite an old man, almost fifty, and out of shape, with a big fat rear end. He took a few steps and then flipped an out-turned palm at them dismissively.

"I seen you!" he shouted down the hallway. "I seen you!"

They rounded the corner and ran towards Room E12a.

Full darkness crept in on the back of the heavy afternoon rains, and by five it was as black as midnight outside. In Room E12a Alaska Moorcroft lay somewhere between living and dying. The rain beat a steady tattoo against the window but Alaska didn't hear it. He didn't hear the soft electronic hum and pings of the equipment, and he didn't hear the latch of the door click as it swung open.

CHAPTER 9

A twenty-eight-year-old life insurance agent laughed so much after seeing a stand-up comedian that he choked to death. Mark Anthony had been to see comedian Lee Hurst in London.

South London Press, 27 August 1997

Moorcroft ran into problems at the security office. He wanted to fix that camera feed in E12a before he set foot in there, and now, instead of the regular shift change-over, there was a small party going on. It was some idiot's birthday and Moorcroft swore violently as the sound of laughing voices came from behind the half-open office door. He sat down on a bench and waited. It was ten minutes before the four security staff came out, two in street clothes, the night shift already in their brown hospital security uniforms.

When the security guy had turned the corner, Moorcroft

waited ten beats and walked purposefully towards the office. He checked both directions up and down the corridor before opening his heavy jacket and reaching into his toolkit. He put on a pair of surgical latex gloves and produced two short lengths of stiff wire. Inside thirty seconds the office door was open and Moorcroft looked around once more before stepping through. He wiped his brow and took several deep breaths.

The small, stale office was empty apart from the remnants of birthday cake and a couple of empty beer cans on the table in the centre of the room. Along one wall was a desk with eight monitors mounted above it. They showed views from eighty cameras dotted around the hospital. Every ten seconds the camera angles switched. The feed from Alaska's room was on a rotation with four other cameras located in the intensive care wing. Moorcroft waited until Room E12a flipped on to the monitor to confirm what he knew already. He opened a control panel with a small screwdriver and disconnected the line from E12a. The monitor that had showed Alaska's room now showed just four views instead of five. Moorcroft guessed that the security staff wouldn't notice the change until next year, if ever.

He opened a large pocket on his toolkit and shook out a white orderly's jacket. He put this on and opened a pale green laundry bag from another pocket on his toolkit. Moorcroft crammed his own heavy jacket down into the laundry bag and moved to the door. This was all taking longer than expected. His fingers shook as his body trembled with fever. He kept having to stop and cough. His bones felt old and weary, and muscle cramps shot through his legs. Dammit!

With an effort he completed his tasks and moved to the door. He carefully opened it a crack, checked the corridor was empty and slipped out. He smiled to himself; the corridor where the security office was was one of the few places in the hospital that wasn't covered by the CCTV system. Dumb suckers.

He moved along the corridor, just another hospital orderly carrying a laundry bag, and headed for Room E12a. It wouldn't take him long to get there.

He'd been there before.

This place is certain confusin' and no mistake, thought O'Toole as he tried to make sense of the hospital layout. Like Mich and Patterson, O'Toole was attracting his fair share of attention. His green beard, pointed ears and blue Controller's uniform marked him out, as did his habit of blurting out "sweet bejaysus!" and "Mudder of Christ!" whenever he turned into yet another endless corridor. *If I'd known it was this far I'd have taken the train*, he thought, his little leprechaun legs working hard. *Still, no time to waste.* He pressed forward.

* * *

There it was.

Room E12a. And about freakin' time. Moorcroft badly wanted to lie down and sleep for ever, but despite feeling as bad as he'd felt in his entire life he forced himself forward and pushed open the door.

Moorcroft glanced at the camera mounted in the corner as he went in. The dull black eye of the lens confirmed what he'd done in the security office. No one could see him. He walked across to the boy and put down the laundry bag on a chair and checked his watch. The two kids he'd seen coming in on that tow truck must be heading this way. Moorcroft would take care of one little problem right now and wait for the other two to come to him. He picked up a pillow from a stack sitting on a bench over by the window and leaned over the boy. There was an oxygen mask over the kid's face and Moorcroft lifted it off and placed it over his own mouth and nose. He sucked down the oxygen greedily before a coughing fit made him rip it away. The room swayed and Moorcroft had to steady himself against the wall. A film of cold sweat stood out in beads on Moorcroft's grey skin and the mother of all headaches settled behind his eyes.

"C'mon, man," he whispered to himself. "Let's get this thing done."

He placed the pillow over the boy's face and pressed down. Deep inside Alaska's coma, instinct took over. Nerve-endings

 278

registered the sudden decrease in oygen and the brain instructed the body to fight back. Alaska thrashed uselessly under the suffocating pillow, searching for air. His heart rate leaped and Moorcroft suddenly became aware of the heart monitor beeping faster and faster as Alaska's body asked it to supply more blood. It was something he hadn't thought of. If it stopped, Moorcroft realized, it would trigger an alarm somewhere in the nursing station and a wotchamacallit, recovery team would be in real quick. He'd be long gone, but that would still leave the other two brats. He'd have to switch the order, wait for them to arrive, do them and then do the kid in the coma.

He swore softly and lifted the pillow. Man, but this was becoming one complicated deal! Alaska sucked in air, the ping of the heart monitor slowing gradually.

Moorcroft sat down to wait.

CHAPTER 10

Delhi, India: To settle an argument, two brothers were told by community elders to hold a contest to see who could hold their breath underwater the longest. Both drowned.

Daily Mail, 22 October 1997

No one had seen the shape that had been following Mich slip down from the truck. Nobody saw it as it slipped along the hospital corridors, hungry and malevolent, blending easily into the walls, moving like the faintest of mists. It followed the friends and watched. They were close, the shape could sense it. It watched their exchange with the desk clerk and followed them towards Room E12a. It could almost taste its prey now; it wouldn't be long. It had known this moment would come from the first time it had found Michigan Moorcroft outside Purgatory High and brushed through and past him, reading him like a reference book, then watching and waiting and following, until here they were, in this place. It had known that Mich would lead it to where it needed to be. The girl was important too, but it was the boy who would lead it to its destiny.

As they moved nearer to E12a and its victim, the shape forgot its cloak and began to take form, the mist growing more solid for an instant as it thought about the satisfaction it craved, so near, so close. It wanted to feed its anger, to hurt someone, someone specific, *someone in this hospital*.

A nurse stepped out of a door and dropped her tray of equipment as she glimpsed something forming in the shadows. The malevolence calmed, realizing its mistake, and grew invisible once more. The nurse shook her head. Had she seen something? The shape brushed against her, cold and unwelcoming, and she gasped and moved quickly away down the corridor, frightened.

The shape hurried, flowing along the walls of the hospital, and caught up with the two children as they stood outside Room E12a. They slipped inside and closed the door. The shape drifted under the door after them. It would happen now.

Mich and Patterson were inside. It was strange being in the room he'd seen so many times on the TV up in Purgatory. Alaska lay on his bed in one corner, a pool of soft light coming from the angled lamp above the bed. An orderly, a man in a white jacket, had his back to them and appeared to be checking something on Alaska's monitors. He hadn't seemed to notice them come in. Mich looked at Patterson and she shrugged. Mich coughed.

"Excuse me," he said.

The orderly turned, the dim green light from the monitors bathing his thick features in an unearthly glow. Mich looked at him with a shuddering jolt of recognition. It was him, the man, Moorcroft. The man in the red truck.

Patterson gasped.

"About freakin' time," said Moorcroft. He produced the bone-handled knife from his belt and waved it at them.

"Now sit down, you little punks."

He pointed the knife towards two plastic chairs lined against a wall. Mich and Patterson hesitated then walked across and sat down. Moorcroft coughed again, his lungs rattling and his face blotching red and purple. He steadied himself against a rack which held a bag of saline drip. It shook and clanked as he hung on, wheezing and spluttering. Gradually the coughing slowed, then stopped. Moorcroft spat into a sink.

"Goddammit!" he hissed, wiping his face with the cuff of his sleeve.

"You wanna get that fixed," said Mich. "You don't look too good."

 282

He didn't know why he was talking, he just wanted the guy to forget about Alaska.

"Shut yer yap," said Moorcroft.

He leaned in closer to Mich and Patterson. "Besides, you two don't look so hot yourselves." He pressed the tip of the knife against Mich's neck and the tip sank in just a fraction. Moorcroft looked at it, puzzled that there was no blood. He shook his head and turned back to Mich.

"So let's have it. What's goin' on? Did you talk to the cops about me?"

Mich couldn't speak. His mind was blank. All he could think about was the knife.

"Don't matter anyhow," said Moorcroft. "I'm gonna kill y'all anyway."

Mich looked at Patterson and smiled. She looked at him as if he was mad and then it sank in and she started laughing too.

"What the. . ." Moorcroft stood back and waved the knife angrily. "You don't think I'd do it? Is that it?"

Mich smiled again.

"No, it's just you said something funny."

"Funny? I'm goin' to kill you, you dumb punk, what's so funny about that?"

Mich stood. He wasn't scared any more. Just angry.

"What's funny? I'll tell you what's 'funny', *Moorcroft*. It is Moorcroft, isn't it? Mitchell Freestone Moorcroft?"

Mich put out his left arm, the one that had been burnt by the grip of a hand in the River of Lost Souls. The flesh was almost gone where the hand had grabbed him. As Mich turned the wrist this way and that, the white of his bone glinted in the light. It was hideously painful but Mich didn't seem to notice. He reached up and, in one fluid motion, pulled the dead flesh away in a long green strip so that almost all his forearm was exposed. Moorcroft screamed.

"What's so funny is this: you can't kill us, Moorcroft," said Mich. "You can't kill us because we're already dead, you see."

Moorcroft was staring at Mich's wrist in disbelief.

"Oh sweet Jesus!" whispered Moorcroft. He backed away from Mich and Patterson and was stuck in the corner, his eyes flicking back from one to the other.

"Boo," said Patterson.

Moorcroft flinched and gave a small squeal of animal fear.

Patterson laughed and Mich walked forward. He figured that scaring Moorcroft was the only way to stop him killing Alaska.

He had miscalculated.

Moorcroft was scared, terrified even, but as Mich approached he saw that Moorcroft was straightening, recovering, and coming to some kind of decision. Now Moorcroft began to smile and it was Mich's turn to be scared.

"Dead, eh?" said Moorcroft. "What are you two freaks? Some kinda zombie thing?"

 284

He laughed and pushed Mich in the chest. Mich staggered back.

"You got some kind of freaky dead kid voodoo thing you're gonna work? No? So what are you gonna do, punk? You gonna fight? You gonna haunt me or stuff? Get some skanky-ass ole sheets and rattle some chain and scare li'l' me?"

He pushed Mich again and Patterson came forward and hit Moorcroft. Her fist bounced harmlessly away. Moorcroft laughed and slapped Mich open-handed. Mich's head spun to the left and something bounced across the floor.

"Jesus!" said Moorcroft, laughing and coughing, a crazy tilt in his eyes. "Your nose! Your goddamn nose came off, man!"

Mich looked and saw his nose lying up against a trashcan. Patterson was looking at him in horror. Mich clamped his hand over his face and turned away.

"That's what I call a nose job, punk!" Moorcroft laughed. "Guess your little girlfriend preferred the 'before' picture this time! Now, let's quit foolin' and I'll take a shot at knocking your goddamned zombie head clean off your goddamned zombie neck. Then I can get on with gettin' rid of your little brother over there."

He drew back his fist and Mich closed his eyes waiting for the blow. Nothing happened and he risked opening an eye. Moorcroft was staring over Mich's shoulder, his mouth a rictus of terror.

Mich turned and looked.

In the middle of the room white mist was bubbling and boiling. A shape began to emerge from the white-green whirl. It was the shape of a man, a small man. Details began to stand out; the figure was wearing dungarees, an old work shirt and boots, and had a long, drooping moustache. Mich could see clear through the figure, yet every detail was etched with sharp precision. The air inside the room dropped to arctic levels in an instant. The mists swirled and the figure, shining as if lit from within, hung a few centimetres from the floor. A feeling of barely contained energy filled the hospital room.

Moorcroft looked at the apparition, open-mouthed.

The figure spoke quietly, yet its voice boomed and echoed around the little room.

"Don't you recognize me, Moorcroft?" it said, opening its arms.

Moorcroft shook his head furiously. His eyes were bugged out, red-rimmed, wild with fear.

"No?" said the figure. "Let me remind you."

It drew itself up and held itself straight and dignified.

"My name is Jesus Hernandez Victor De La Cruz, the son of Luis and Maria De La Cruz. I come from Truth or Consequences, New Mexico. I drove a red Dodge truck with 80,000 on the clock. I was forty-three years old when you killed me like a dog and dumped my body near Roebuck,

Louisiana on December 21st 2002. Now do you remember me? Because I remember you, Mitchell Freestone Moorcroft. I remember everything about you and I have travelled a long way to find you. Now you are mine."

"What are you?" whispered Moorcroft. "Are you a ghost?"

"No, Moorcroft," the apparition replied. "I am your destiny, and I have come to claim you on behalf of myself and the others you have killed."

He pointed to Mich.

"People like him. Now it is your turn."

Moorcroft looked wildly about the room, his breath shallow and ragged, his eyes wide and filled with animal fear. Bubbles of saliva formed at the corners of his mouth. He backed into the corner, his hands scrabbling in vain for something, anything, to help him. There was nothing.

Patterson and Mich backed towards Alaska's bed.

The door to the room opened and a tall thin figure clad from head to toe in black came in. The figure was carrying a scythe in one hand and a bowling trophy in the other. Mich caught glimpses of a green silk bowling shirt underneath the ragged shroud.

"Am I too late?" said the Grim Reaper. He caught sight of Moorcroft.

"Ah, just in time I see. Sorry," he said to the apparition. "Don't mind me, just carry on."

287

The Grim Reaper turned to Mich and held the bowling trophy up.

"We won!" he whispered.

Moorcroft watched everything in total disbelief.

The ghost figure of Jesus Hernandez Victor De La Cruz threw back his head, opened his mouth and howled. The edges of the room warped, then blurred and distorted as a pulsing wave of pure energy poured out of the screaming mouth. The fabric of everything around them shimmered and bent with the force streaming from the pale figure. De La Cruz raised a finger and pointed it at Moorcroft. He was lifted off his feet and drawn forward into the centre of the room. When Moorcroft was about a metre away, De La Cruz held up a palm and Moorcroft hung helplessly in mid-air. He screamed but the sound was lost in the howl of fury coming from the ghostly figure of De La Cruz. Moorcroft's eyes bulged and the flesh on his face rippled as he took the full blast, as if he were standing in front of a jet engine. His hands were clasped together, pleading with De La Cruz so that from Mich's angle, Moorcroft appeared as if he was in an attitude of prayer.

Room E12a began to vibrate and then break up as if caught in the mother of all hurricanes. Walls crumbled and were blown away into dust. The Grim Reaper waited motionless, the ragged ends of his cloak blowing in the wind. He cast admiring glances at the bowling trophy. Furniture in the room

 288

crashed and banged before being sucked away into infinity.

Moorcroft, his face bending and twisting like an astronaut in a centrifuge, clamped his hands over his ears.

The sound was astonishing.

Mich looked up as the ceiling dissolved and was stripped down to its metal skeleton, and then that too was splintered into limitless fragments and sent whirling into space. The rest of the hospital was revealed and then it too appeared to soften and bend, then explode outwards as an enormous shock wave simply vaporized everything. Mich and Patterson clung to one another and hugged the edge of Alaska's bed, which was the only stationary thing left in the universe. They watched as everything was stripped away, buildings, people, cars, land, trees, until all that was left were themselves, the Grim Reaper, Alaska, the ghostly white figure of Jesus Hernandez Victor De La Cruz and Moorcroft; all of them floating in a bottomless black void.

Then, as suddenly as he had begun, De La Cruz closed his mouth and everything fell deathly silent. Moorcroft took his hands from his ears and looked up at the white figure fearfully. There was a long moment as the white figure regarded Moorcroft. Then he reached out and touched Moorcroft on the arm. His arm softened and melted, the particles breaking down and being sucked into the whirling energy spinning around the room. Moorcroft watched them dissolve into nothing, then he looked down at where his arm had been and moaned. His face collapsed into tears and mucus ran from his nose.

"Mommy!" called Moorcroft.

Jesus Hernadez Victor De La Cruz reached forward and plunged his hand deep into the centre of Moorcroft's belly. Moorcroft screamed, looked down and then seemed to deflate like a balloon with a slow leak. His body was sucked into the vortex, organ by organ, bone by bone, atom by atom, his screaming mouth and staring eyes the last things to disappear. When he had gone completely the room once more fell silent.

The ghostly figure still hung in the air. It turned and looked at Mich and Patterson. And then it too was gone.

"Phew!" said the Reaper hoisting his scythe on to his shoulder. "Quite a show, eh?"

He waved a bony hand towards them, picked up his bowling trophy and he too began to dissolve.

"It looks like you may have had a point after all, Mr Moorcroft," said the Reaper. "I'll make sure that She gets a full report."

Only his face remained.

"Take care, Mr Moorcroft," he shouted, and then was gone.

In a fraction of an instant, the hospital reappeared around them, exactly as it had been. They were back in Room E12a with the winter rain beating against the window. Mich and

Patterson both let out long breaths as they clung to each other. Mich looked at Patterson and his heart sank. She looked terrible, like something from a cheap zombie flick. Her hair had fallen out in clumps and her skin was puckered and wrinkled, shrinking back against the bone. Mich could almost see it happening in front of him, like some kind of speeded-up trick photography. He knew he wouldn't win any beauty contests at the moment either.

Mich opened his mouth to speak and several of his teeth fell out of his loosened gums and bounced on to the floor.

"I'm shorry," he said. "I should have shtopped you coming wish me, Pash."

Patterson shook her head, tears leaking out of her eyes.

"Stop me?" she said. "This is the best fun I've had since I fainted at a David Cassidy gig in 1974. Now let's see if we can help your brother."

They turned to the bed and both of them realized something at the same time.

Alaska was dead.

CHAPTER 11

In Treviso, Italy in 1991, a twenty-year-old woman died merely from smelling milk. She had a severe allergy to milk which was triggered when she delivered census forms to a dairy.

Observer, 10 November 1991

Mich slumped across Alaska's bed and wept. To have come this far and gone through everything they'd gone through, all for nothing.

It sucked.

Alaska lay cold and peaceful under the sheets, his heart monitor silent. Patterson hovered awkwardly, tears rolling down her cheeks. This was terrible.

"We have to go, Mich," she said softly. "The doctors will be in here any minute."

Mich let himself be led across the room and the two of them

stepped out of Room E12a. A recovery team was bustling down the corridor towards them. None of the team appeared to have noticed Mich and Patterson as they passed but a young doctor bringing up the rear glanced at them and then came to a complete halt, her mouth open in disbelief. Before she said anything one of the nurses shouted back from the door to E12a.

"Doctor! Now!"

The doctor gave them a last horrified look and raced off.

Mich was about to speak when someone shouted.

"Oi! Stop!"

They turned and saw O'Toole running down the corridor towards them as fast as his little legs would carry him. Mich's shoulders sagged. He shrugged at Patterson.

"Whatsh he goin' to do, arrest us?" Mich said. "He'll be lucky if there's anything left."

The leprechaun arrived puffing and wheezing. He grabbed hold of Mich's arm and it came off in his hand.

"Oops, sorry about that." He put the arm down gently on the floor. "Well, you probably won't be needing that any more, eh son?" said O'Toole.

Patterson loomed over him.

"You nasty little man! Leave us alone!"

"Oh, I'm afraid I can't do that, miss," said O'Toole, producing a notebook from his jacket. "And let you wander

293

around frightenin' folk all over the place until you crumble into dust? Oh no, that won't do at all."

"So, what are you going to do?" she replied, exasperated.

"Do? I'm a-goin' to arrest you, of course, on account of you contravenin' the code of The Organization as set down in Rule 34563777/B2."

"You've just made that up!" said Patterson.

"No I haven't!" Officer O'Toole puffed his chest out and looked up at Patterson. "Not completely, anyway. It doesn't matter, I'm arrestin' youse, youse is definitely contravenin' somethin'!"

He lifted a flap on his jacket and flipped out a tiny green radio.

"Officer requesting assistance, come in. Officer requesting assistance, come in please."

There was silence.

Mich and Patterson looked at O'Toole.

"S'funny," he said tapping the mike. "Officer requesting assistance, come in! Officer requesting as—"

"That'll do, O'Toole," said a voice. "I'll take over from here."

All three of them turned towards the voice. The little dog Patterson had seen in the hospital reception area was standing next to them.

"What?" said O'Toole. "Did you say something?"

The dog tilted its head and spoke very clearly.

 294

"Yes, O'Toole, I said that I'll take care of things as of now. Is that clear?"

"Er, yes, I suppose," said O'Toole, scratching his head. "Hold on! Wait jest a moment! Who gave you the authority to be tellin' me what to do? Yer jest a dog!"

"Oh," said the dog. "I forgot."

There was a crackle of static and the dog morphed into the familiar shape of the old lady Mich had first met in his living room.

O'Toole snapped to attention.

"Stand easy, Officer," said God.

"Of course, ma'am," said O'Toole frantically tugging his forelock. "And forgive the impertinence back there if you'd be so kind, only with you bein' in the form of a wee dog an' all, I was forgettin' me manners."

"Of course, O'Toole. I had forgotten what I looked like for a moment. Sometimes I find it quite relaxing to have four legs for a while, but I realize it makes giving orders a little difficult. Now, let's get this mess cleaned up, shall we?"

As She spoke an orderly pushing a cart came past. As he drew level with the odd-looking group his mouth fell open. He started to back away and God gently bowed her head. The orderly relaxed, an expression of complete happiness on his face. God waved Her fingers along the corridor and the orderly moved off, enveloped in a pink cloud of bliss.

295

"I suggest we take this discussion somewhere less noticeable," She said and clicked her fingers. Before Mich or Patterson could say a word, all four of them vanished, leaving the barest scrap of mist floating behind them.

"Oops," said a voice. The little old lady's hand shot out of the mist, scooped up Mich's arm where it lay on the floor, and then vanished once again.

CHAPTER

12

A sixty-eight-year-old man collapsed with a heart attack in Bonn, Germany in 1996. He might have survived if it hadn't been for his pet rottweiler, Otto, preventing paramedics getting to his fallen master.

Guardian, 11 December 1996

Alaska bounced down the stairs and out of the front door into the bright sunshine. He spotted Mich's skateboard lying on the drive and jumped on it, zigzagging down the incline towards the street. He was about halfway down when Mich tackled him from one side, bringing him crashing on to the lawn.

"I told you; keep off the board, freak!" said Mich pushing Alaska's face into the grass.

"Get off, loser!" replied Alaska, his voice muffled and

indistinct. He pushed himself free and rolled on to his back propping himself on his elbows.

"Boys, don't make me come over there," said Mrs Moorcroft glancing up from her work out on a punchbag hanging from the roof of the garage. The door was rolled back and Mrs Moorcroft was sweating lightly in the perfect late spring weather. Her official Controller physical was next week and she wanted to be in tip-top condition.

"Leave him alone, Mich," said Patterson lazily from the sun-lounger, but Alaska had already jumped on top of Mich and the brothers rolled around the lawn, wrestling and laughing.

It was a hot Saturday in June, or maybe it wasn't, or maybe it just felt like that. Who knew and, more importantly, who cared? Whatever day it was, this was the day of the Moorcroft celebration barbecue. Everyone was there.

Dakota, lying next to Patterson, lifted her shades and looked across at Mich and Alaska.

"Boys," she said and bit into her burger. She wasn't really annoyed. Nothing really annoyed her these days, mainly because Dakota was dating. Her choice of date was causing a fair amount of friction in the Moorcroft household at the moment.

Dakota's new boyfriend sat next to her on the lawn, looking slightly out of place in his dark business suit and jet-black shades. He was busy talking into a tiny telephone which

 298

curled around his enormous head on a metallic stalk.

"We're talking big numbers boss, real big; triple digits," said Baz into the phone. "I'm negotiating a corporate rate for the entire plane-load, apart from a couple of Hindus, a sprinkling of Muslims and one loser who claims he's some sort of atheist."

There was a pause and then Baz spoke again.

"Uh-huh. Um. Yeah. Right, yeah that's what I said. Anyways, I'm real close to clinching all of them on one contract. Cuts down on paperwork, keeps me on target for that sales quota this month! Hey! Thought ya'd like that one, big feller! Maybe it's time we started talking 'bout that new pay ri – Boss? Boss?"

Baz tapped the phone and turned to Dakota, a puzzled expression on his face.

"S'funny, we musta got cut off or something."

Dakota smiled at him and blew him a kiss. Once she'd got used to his breath, Baz wasn't such a bad devil, even if he was a moron. Besides he drove that nifty little red convertible and had promised Dakota one to match "as soon as he made the nut on that sales quota, baby".

From the lawn Mich frowned as he watched them. No matter how he tried he just couldn't get used to the idea of his sister going out with Satan. Jeez, if they ended up getting married that'd make Baz his brother-in-law! Part of Mich thought that was pretty cool actually, having Beelzebub as a close relative; imagine what the rest of the guys back at Communion High would make of that. . .

"He's not Satan," Dakota had said indignantly when asked about her new friendship with Baz. "He's the Chief Regional South-West Division Vice-President in charge of Sweetwater Canyons Sales, actually."

"OK, he's 'Satan's Little Helper' then," Mich had said. "I still don't trust the guy."

"That's your trouble," Dakota replied. "You've gone all high and mighty since your little trip."

Mich wondered if that was true. It was certainly true that things had improved dramatically since their teenage mutant zombie adventure. It had been about six weeks since they'd been in that hospital room, or at least Mich guessed it was about six weeks; you tended to lose track of time in Paradise (if that was where they were; Mich was still a little sketchy on the details). When they first arrived back from the trip through The Gateway it hadn't seemed like Paradise at all. They'd failed; they hadn't saved Alaska.

It was the little old lady who'd put them right about one or two things.

"You know, he wouldn't have been very happy if he had lived."

It was the first thing she'd said when they had all reappeared outside Mich's house. There were no tricks, no magic. One second they'd been standing in North Morton Hospital with chunks of them falling off, the next they were all back in Purgatory standing on the sidewalk, complete, all body parts intact and looking pretty good (all things considered).

Except, somehow, it kind of wasn't Purgatory, which was where Patterson and Mich got more than a little confused. It certainly *looked* like Purgatory, but God assured them that they were no longer in Purgatory. They were in Paradise, she had said in an authoritative voice.

"But it looks exactly the same as before we left!" Mich said. "The same as Communion, the same as Purgatory. I always thought there'd be, you know, clouds and harps and . . . stuff."

God wouldn't be drawn into too many details (She had an annoying habit of telling them that their minds were too small to comprehend the vast majesty of the cosmos and Her grand design for all of creation), but lying here in the sun Patterson thought that maybe she'd figured some of it out at least. She made a mental list:

1. The Nature of Paradise.

Paradise wasn't any particular place; Paradise was anything you wanted it to be. Everyone, said God, carried around with them their own personal Paradise. The trick was to be able to recognize it when you saw it. Some people did in fact prefer a traditional route, and you sometimes saw them drifting along

301

on little white clouds strumming golden harps. They seemed happy enough, although they did always seem to be complaining about the untidiness of the rest of Paradise. Patterson herself thought that the cloud/harp option looked pretty boring.

2. Belief.

"What happens to people who don't believe in you, in all this?" Patterson asked God.

"Whatever they believe happens, happens, at least some of the time," said God. "That's what it's all about; believing. The mistake a lot of them make is insisting on their belief being the only belief. Causes no end of trouble, I can tell you. That's the problem with all you lot, humans, I mean; a right bunch of know-it-alls. The dolphins never give Me any difficulties."

3. Eternal Happiness.

She felt happiest just hanging out with Mich. She was happier than she'd been at any time since she'd died. That was why she was here too, it felt *right*. Maybe when her parents eventually made it up here she'd move somewhere else, but for the time being, simply lying out on the lawn while the Moorcrofts flipped burgers, or worked out, or worked on their tans, or wrestled, or just goofed around, felt pretty close to Paradise.

4. Retribution, or, What goes around comes around.

Here she was sitting out in the sun eating barbecue; from

what she'd seen of the River of Lost Souls she was pretty sure that Mitchell Freestone Moorcroft was far more likely to be *getting* barbecued than anything else at the end of his journey.

5. Judgement.

She had wondered about how she'd ended up spending thirty years in Purgatory. It wasn't like she had been so bad or anything, compared to all the really horrible people there were, but maybe that wasn't the point. Maybe The Organization wasn't judging you, not completely. Maybe it was waiting to see which choices you made, to see if you were ready for eternal bliss. It was only recently that Patterson had come to realize that Purgatory and Paradise were one and the same thing; the only thing that changed was your approach.

6. The Beauty of Uncertainty.

Patterson didn't know what lay ahead. It wasn't at all like the things she'd been told about Paradise while she was alive, this was infinitely richer, more exciting, more full of delicious uncertainties and doubts. You lived and then you died and began to live all over again. Everything else was so much hot air.

That just about covered it, she thought, rolling the sleeves of her T-shirt a little higher. Time to get down to the serious business of catching a few rays. *Do dead people still tan?* Patterson wasn't really sure. It wasn't something she'd given a great deal

303

of thought to, but she was going to give it her best shot.

Mich was taking a little while longer to recover. Even when they'd arrived back in Purgatory, complete and looking human once more, Mich had fallen into a black mood which had lasted several weeks. He was convinced they'd failed; that if only they'd done this, or that, then they could have saved Alaska.

This mood might have lasted longer had Alaska seemed in any way worried about being dead. He'd taken the news of his death pretty well, considering.

He *had* freaked when he found out he had to go to school, but Mich guessed that if Alaska was honest, he'd much rather be dead and back with all his family (school and all), than alive and living out at Gamma's house. Alaska himself figured that spending eternity as a ten-year-old wasn't half bad. Just imagine, he could have been old and wrinkly when he copped it, maybe thirty or even forty, think how bad it must be for them, poor old things. At least he could skate and run and swim and goof off, and all the other million and one things that made being ten years old so fantastic.

But the feeling still persisted in Michigan that he could have saved his brother. He was talking about it now.

"Saved him for what?" said Patterson. "A lifetime of growing up without the rest of his family? A lifetime at Gamma Slubb's?"

God, sitting on an adjacent sunlounger under the shade of a

 304

tree, was much more direct. She waved her half-eaten burger at him to emphasize her points.

"You never had anything to say on the matter, Michigan," She said. "Do you think that you control anything? Your role in this wasn't to 'save' Alaska; you were simply part of the mechanism to correct a clerical error."

"Error? What error?"

"Moorcroft, of course. The mistake wasn't that he was alive instead of you. The mistake was that he was alive at all. You were always going to die in that car wreck, if it had happened. If it hadn't happened, then you would have been alive. Human life balances on billions of tiny accumulated connections and coincidences, not all of which are controlled by Us. In this case, in this precise set of circumstances, you were always going to die. The problem was that Moorcroft was supposed to die too. He just got away somehow."

She broke off and eyed Officer O'Toole carefully. He was here at Mrs Moorcroft's invitation and was wearing his off-duty clothes: a ghastly brown polyester shirt and cream leisure slacks. The colours clashed horribly with his pale skin and green beard.

"Beggin' yer pardon, ma'am," he said, blushing. "It won't happen again."

"Hmm," She said, shrugging.

She wolfed down the rest of her burger and took a swallow

of Irn Bru, an obscure Scottish soft drink She was extremely fond of. She held her burger up to inspect it.

"I forgot just what a good job I'd done on these things."

She broke off as Mr Moorcroft came buzzing across the lawn. He was wearing a cook's apron with the words *Don't Ask Me, I Just Work Here!* printed on it in cartoon lettering. He'd put a little weight on and it suited him. His progress across the lawn was erratic as he was wearing his new ankle wings, part of his new role at The Ministry: he'd become a Winged Messenger.

"These things are taking some getting used to," he said as he barged into God. "Sorry, Your Holiness."

"I keep telling you, Mike," said God, adjusting her glasses. "Call Me Ethel."

Mr Moorcroft nodded but, like all his family, he had great difficulty calling God "Ethel". It just didn't seem right some-how, kind of disrespectful. Besides, he didn't want to take any chances of offending Her, not when he'd just got this new job. These wings were nifty, difficult or not, and he was enjoying getting to grips with what they could do. The uniform looked pretty good too, even if the tight-fitting neoprene did show a little more of his new paunch than he'd have liked. Still, Urma seemed to like him in it and everyone at the WM training centre said he'd soon lose that weight once they began the stamina exercises.

"Pat?" said Mr Moorcroft holding out a plate and wobbling a little a few centimetres above the ground.

Patterson shook her head and lay back contentedly.

"I couldn't eat another thing, Mr M," she said. She folded her arms behind her head and looked skywards. A large flock of white swans flew slowly across her view and Patterson watched them until they disappeared from view. She listened to the music coming from over by the grill. It was an old song, one that was old before Patterson had died, but she liked it anyway; it was one of her mother's favourites and was called "Love Me Tender". When the song finished she rolled over and shouted, "Hey, King, play that one again, would you?"

Elvis put down his guitar.

"Sure thing, l'il' darlin'," he murmured. "Just lemme grab one a those burgers, y'hear?"

He wandered over to the grill and grabbed a plate which he piled high with burgers, all the trimmings. Mr Moorcroft had struck up a friendship with the singing garbage man over the last few months. They played golf a couple of times a week (Mr Moorcroft had discovered that contrary to Baz Rheingold's pitch, there were plenty of golf courses here. The only down-side was that they shared the facilities with Hell. To some people, playing permanent golf was punishment for crimes on Earth) and Elvis had become a frequent guest at the Moorcrofts'. Occasionally (like now) he treated them to a song. The only weird thing about the King was that he was often accompanied by a small green alien being who looked a little like a miniature version of the President of the United States and seemed permanently irritable. Elvis referred to him as "General" and they seemed to spend a lot of time looking at maps of the world.

Mich had once asked Elvis why he was a garbage man in the afterlife.

"Ah get plenty of time off to play golf," he'd replied and winked. Mich had scratched his head but left it at that.

Back on the lawn Mich continued to question God.

"What about De La Cruz?" said Mich. "How did he fit into the scheme of things? Shouldn't the Admissions Officer take care of people like him?"

God looked a little peeved and for a moment Mich thought She might be tempted to throw a minor thunderbolt his way.

"The Admissions Officer is a very busy individual, Michigan. Besides, he is present (or someone very like him) in a purely observational capacity. He can't actually 'take' anyone unless something happens to them. That's where apparitions like Mr De La Cruz come in; nothing like a good dose of old-fashioned vengeance sometimes. Back in the old days We used to appreciate a good bit of revenge. An eye for an eye and all that. . ."

She tailed off for a moment, lost in happy memories before

 308

picking up where She'd left off. "There are plenty of De La Cruzes, Michigan. He wasn't unique. Every time someone takes a life it is an affront to My Organization. We just don't like it; so unforgivably impolite. Plus it creates havoc with Our book-keeping. Normally these people are taken care of in due course and punished appropriately. However, in a few cases," She paused and eyed Mich. "A *very* few cases, the system misses people like Moorcroft and that's when We end up with the likes of Mr De La Cruz."

She waved to the small Mexican-looking guy talking to Elvis near to the porch. He waved back (a little nervously, it must be said) and gave his moustache a reassuring stroke.

"You see?" God continued. "Quite a pleasant chap once he'd got all that unpleasantness out of his system. Keen gardener. Hope you didn't mind Me bringing him along; doesn't know too many people here just yet."

Mich murmured approval.

"But I can't stand here all day gassing. I have a board meeting at three. Cosmic engineering problems, no doubt. Thank your mother and father for the invitation, please, Michigan."

She stifled a belch (the effects of the Irn Bru) and gathered up Her bag. She shot a withering glance in the direction of Dakota and Baz (even Dakota had the grace to blush) and moved off. Instead of simply vaporizing in a cloud of golden smoke as they expected, Mich and Patterson watched as She walked about fifty metres down the street and stood at a nearby bus stop. She sat on the bench and took out her knitting.

O'Toole coughed.

'Well, I reckon I was too soft with the pair of youse this toime," he wagged his finger at them. "But don't let me catch either of yers messin' about with no Gateway nonsense again, or I'll be all over yer loike a bad rash, roight?"

They nodded in agreement, and O'Toole looked about to say something more when his beeper went off. Mich heard his mother's beeper at the same time. O'Toole's uniform morphed instantly into place as Mrs Moorcroft ran across, her uniform forming around her as she ran. O'Toole jabbered into his microphone and a police cruiser zoomed up immediately, sirens blazing. Dakota dragged Baz out from behind a sunlounger.

"Sorry, hon," he said, nodding at the cruiser. "Just instinct."

O'Toole hopped into the passenger seat.

"You drive," he said to Mrs Moorcroft. "It's a 720 in Tokyo 13."

She jumped behind the wheel and leaned out of the window.

"Bye, sweetie!" she said to Mich, blowing him a kiss. "Make sure your dad shuts down the barbecue!" she yelled and revved the engine.

 310

O'Toole lifted his head out of his window (*Must be sitting on a cushion*, thought Mich).

"To be honest youse both did foine, yer little tinkers," he said. "But I meant what I said; no more funny business, roight?" His head shot back into the car and they screeched off only to pull up next to the bus stop. O'Toole stuck his head out of the cruiser once more and shouted to God, "Will yer be wantin' a lift anywhere, ma'am?"

God shook Her head.

"I'll take the bus, O'Toole, if you don't mind. Gives me a chance to catch up on My knitting."

"Aye aye, ma'am," he said and saluted as Mrs Moorcroft gunned the cruiser and raced off down the street.

Mich leaned over Patterson. Bits of grass were stuck at odd angles in his hair from his tussle with Alaska.

"Well, that just about wraps everything up, doesn't it, seventies throwback?" he said, smiling. "Wanna shoot some hoops?"

"Maybe later, sport," replied Patterson, lazily. "We've got plenty of time."

Mich leaned back against her sunlounger and scarfed down another burger. He watched his sister dancing with the devil. He picked up his headphones and the familiar sounds of Alien Death Factory filled his head. Mich smiled.

"DIE!DIE!DIE!DIE!DIE!

GONNA DIE!DIE!DIE!DIE!DIE!DIE!DIE!DIE!DIE!DIE!
DIE!DIE!DIE!DIE!DIIIIEEEEEEEE!
GONNA GO TO HELL!
BABY I THINK YOU SMELL!
I DON'T FEEL WELL!"

It doesn't get any better than this, he thought, and closed his eyes against the clean blue perfect sky.

CHAPTER

13

A circus performer in northern Thailand died when he trampolined into a yawning hippopotamus's mouth. The hippo gagged automatically and swallowed the performer, who was a person of restricted growth. Members of the audience did not react as they believed it was part of the act.

Melbourne Herald Sun, 16 July 1999

The Guardian of The Gateway was having a quiet night. He checked the folded newspaper that lay across his lap. Fourteen across: This country has a watery blockage for ever, 7,9. The Guardian took a long pull on his coffee and wrinkled his brow. "Watery blockage for ever"? He racked his brains. First word begins with "e", the second with "d".

It was the last clue in the crossword and The Guardian was struggling with this one. He stretched and yawned. The familiar sound of the falls faded into the background. The Guardian had worked at The Gateway for so long that he no longer heard the noise unless something extraordinary happened.

As he doodled on the margins of the crossword, he heard a noise rising above the din of the river. A scream rose, cutting through the water like a laser. It was a scream of pure anguish, fear and hatred. There was a separate strand of noise inside the scream; another level of pure, unrefined evil.

The Guardian sat up and listened as the scream fell away, its owner dropping down the falls and into the River of Lost Souls the way they all did. Although it wasn't common, from time to time The Guardian did hear unusually loud screams rising from the river. It happened, he guessed, when particularly nasty characters realized what was happening, that they were on their way to . . . of course!

The Guardian smiled and picked up his crossword. The owner of the scream had given him the answer. It was the scream of a man who realized he was on his way to one place, and one place only.

The Guardian murmured, "Watery blockage for ever" and carefully printed in the crossword spaces: E-T-E-R-N-A-L D-A-M-N-A-T-I-O-N. *Very clever*, thought The Guardian. *Eternal Damnation. Of course.*

* * *

Three hundred metres below the falls, the poison river bubbled. A nightmare figure erupted from its green-black oily surface, thrashing furiously as if it could escape its fate by simple fury. As he screamed, dozens of wet hands reached out of the river to claw at his legs and chest, dragging him back down. His head rocked from side to side in agony and his arms grasped in vain for something, anything, to cling to. It was useless and the figure's head sank beneath the water. As his hands clenched, the tattoos on his knuckles glowed as the river acid bit into the ink beneath the skin. The words *LIFE SUCKS* shimmered in the milky darkness for a brief moment before Moorcroft sank down, down into the River of Lost Souls, lost for ever in the endless torment of the damned.

Bummer.